A.W.O.L.
LAST BOY STANDING

BOOKS BY ANDREW LANE

AWOL: Agent Without Licence
AWOL 2: Last Safe Moment
AWOL 3: Last Boy Standing

Young Sherlock Holmes
Death Cloud
Red Leech
Black Ice
Fire Storm
Snake Bite
Knife Edge
Stone Cold
Night Break

Lost Worlds
Lost Worlds
Shadow Creatures

Crusoe
Dawn of Spies
Day of Ice
Night of Terror

A·W·O·L

LAST BOY STANDING

ANDREW LANE

Piccadilly
PRESS

First published in Great Britain in 2019 by
PICCADILLY PRESS
80–81 Wimpole St, London W1G 9RE
www.piccadillypress.co.uk

A CIP catalogue record for this book is available from the British Library.

ISBN: 978-1-84812-667-1
also available as an ebook

1

This book is typeset using Atomik ePublisher
Printed and bound in Great Britain by Clays Ltd, Elcograf S.p.A.

Piccadilly Press is an imprint of Bonnier Zaffre Ltd,
part of Bonnier Books UK
www.bonnierbooks.co.uk

Dedicated to Mike Nicolson, Richard Cooper, Soo Cox, Mark Lawson, Ali Smith, Jerry Foulkes, Anissa Suliman, Mark Brookes, Nigel Douglas, Peter Bradshaw and the forty other teenage winners of the 1980 Barclays Bank Essay Competition, with whom I spent an incredible two weeks travelling around Europe, ending up in Venice. Thirty-seven years later, I get to write about what it was like to be a teenager in the world's most romantic city. And to Caroline Vass, who I thought was going to make it onto the trip but never did.

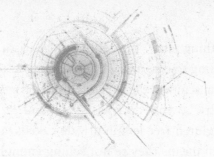

CHAPTER ONE

'What's your name?' the red-haired girl asked, smiling at Kieron.

'K-Kieron,' he stammered. 'What's yours?'

She sighed and tapped the name badge pinned to her shirt. 'Beth. And I just needed your name so we can call you when your coffee's ready.' She ostentatiously wrote *Keiron* on a Post-it note and stuck it on the side of a cup with a Sharpie. 'Like, when it's ready, you know?'

'Oh. OK.' He wondered whether to mention that she'd spelled it wrong, but decided to keep quiet. Everybody got his name wrong. Either they spelled it the way the girl had, or they put an 'a' instead of the 'o' at the end. He'd got used to it. Once he'd asked his mum why she and his dad had given him the most unusual spelling of his name they could manage. 'Oh,' she'd said vaguely, 'did we? I think it was the name of one of your dad's friends. He might have been at the wedding.' She'd frowned. 'Or am I thinking about Keely? No, she was the one he ran off with.' And then she'd reached for the bottle of rosé wine on the kitchen counter.

1

'Anything else?' the red-haired barista asked brightly. 'Something to eat, maybe?'

Kieron scanned the shelves of the refrigerated area to his right. 'Er . . . what do you recommend?'

'The gluten-free lemon drizzle cake is very nice.'

Which means they're not selling enough of it and want to shift some more slices, he thought cynically.

'Just the coffee, please,' he said.

He handed over a five-pound note, grimly surprised at how little change he got, then moved to the end of the counter where the coffee would magically appear with his name on it. Spelled wrong. Well, as long as they *pronounced* it correctly, he didn't really care.

He glanced around. The cafe was new, in a side street close to the shopping mall he usually went to. Bex had taken him there a couple of weeks ago, when they'd got back from America. This was where the more unusual shops lurked – the ones selling black or purple women's clothing with a lot of lace or embroidery on it, or men's clothes that seemed far too tight and probably required you to have a hipster beard before you even tried them on. Oh, and there was a comics and gaming shop. Someone he knew from school worked there. Sometimes Kieron managed to score a staff discount, if the manager wasn't watching.

'Kieron?'

'Yes?' He glanced around.

It was Beth. 'Your coffee is ready.'

'Thanks.'

He'd put his stuff on a small two-person table, just to

secure it. His bag was there, with his laptop inside. And his schoolbooks.

He stared at the schoolbooks, feeling a wave of despair wash through him. He'd started the new school year just after getting back from America, but it hadn't worked out well. Within three days the shouts of 'emo!', 'greeb!' and 'loser!' had begun, along with 'Why don't you get a proper haircut?' Someone had even painted his locker matte-black while nobody was looking – which he would have quite liked, except that the paint had dripped down onto the lockers below and the floor, and it had taken him a solid hour to convince the principal that it hadn't been him that had done it. 'Look for someone with black paint on their clothes!' he'd protested, to which the principal had just looked at Kieron's black trousers, black jacket, black boots and black T-shirt.

He'd stood it for a week, but the next Monday he'd been unable to get out of bed. He just lay there, curled into a ball, trying to force himself to go back to sleep for the rest of the day. His mum had found him there. To her credit she took the morning off work to talk with him, and by the next day she'd negotiated with the principal that they would email his work through and he'd do it at home. Sam, of course, had been furious. 'Why can't they do that for me?' he'd asked. The obvious answer was *Because when people call* you *names you hit them and they stop*, and Kieron had told him that. Sam had seemed to be caught between wanting to say, *Then why don't* you *hit them then?* and, *If I do hit them, will I get excluded?*

3

but the strain of trying to say two things at the same time just made him splutter.

Studying at home had seemed like the perfect way out, but the flat was empty with his mum working, and he felt uneasy there. He'd tried to cover the uneasiness with loud screamo music, but the neighbours banged on the walls, so he'd got into the habit of heading out to a coffee shop mid-morning. It was costing him a fortune, despite the fact that he could make a macchiato last for an hour, if he really tried.

So, back to attempting to prove the derivation of the magnetic field of a solenoid from a current loop. It involved integrals. He hated integrals.

As he sat down, his gaze slipped to his rucksack. In there, in a hard case, were the ARCC glasses that he'd found, months ago now, on a table in the food court of the shopping mall. Those glasses had opened up a world of adventure, excitement and danger for him. They'd also introduced him to Bex and Bradley – the two MI6 agents (well, freelance contractors, Bex would always point out) who had changed his life. Given him confidence. Trusted him with their lives. And those ARCC glasses could access any computer anywhere in the world – not just the obvious ones, like the Internet, but secure databases as well. Secret ones.

So why did he have to painstakingly prove a mathematical equation when the sum of all human knowledge was right there, in his bag? Why did *anybody* have to learn how to do *anything* when they could just ask about it and get an answer in a few seconds?

He sighed. He knew why – kind of. Because intelligence came from knowing these things and being able to apply them and extend them, or at least that's what his teachers would have said. What if he was on a desert island or, God forbid, the Internet had failed because of a zombie apocalypse? How would he be able to survive then?

Still, if his survival during a zombie apocalypse depended on his being able to prove the derivation of a magnetic field of a solenoid from a current loop, then he was in serious trouble.

He opened up his laptop, sighed, leaned back in his chair and took a sip of his coffee. Just a few weeks ago he'd been flying through the air with what could only be called a high-tech military jet pack, risking his life in order to stop an insane billionaire from selling biologically engineered viruses that could target particular *types* of person based on their DNA. A few weeks before *that* he'd been helping Bex prevent the detonation of a series of neutron bombs around the world. And now, here he was, sitting in a cafe that smelled of burnt coffee beans trying not to look at the cute red-haired barista.

Life sucked. And he couldn't tell anyone apart from Sam *why* it sucked. It wasn't the bullying per se. It wasn't the fact that he felt like a loner, an outsider – he was quite proud of that. No, it was the huge gulf between the life that he'd *experienced* over those weeks and the life that, for want of a better word, *life* seemed to want to push him back towards.

Helping Bex and Bradley wasn't sustainable. He knew

that. He was a temporary solution, a last resort while Bradley was medically unable to use the ARCC kit. Bradley was meant to support Bex while she was on missions by passing her useful information, like blueprints of buildings or identities of people she was looking at. Once Bradley had recovered sufficiently to work again, and once he and Bex had discovered who in their MI6 parent organisation was working with the fascist group Blood and Soil, then they wouldn't need him any longer. *That* was why he didn't want to go into school any more. *That* was why he was depressed. It was like being in a car on a motorway and seeing the exit ramp you wanted to take, *needed* to take, passing by, and knowing that the road you were stuck on just kept on going into the distance, monotonously, forever.

'A horse goes into a bar,' a voice said from behind him, 'and the barman says, "Why the long face?"'

He recognised Sam's voice instantly. Without turning around, he reached out with a foot and pushed the other chair away from the table so his friend could sit down.

'So, *why* the long face?' Sam asked, sitting. 'It's long even from behind.'

Kieron shrugged.

'A white horse walks into a bar,' Sam went on. 'The barman says, "We've got a whisky here named after you!" and the horse says, "What – *Brian*?"'

'Shouldn't you be in school?' Kieron asked.

Sam shrugged. 'You know what – I probably should.' He sniffed. 'They've burned the coffee beans. You can tell. My mum's into all that. She's been watching videos on

YouTube on how to make the perfect cup of coffee, from selecting the right bean from the right country all the way up to choosing the absolutely optimal steam pressure on the machine. And she's got one of those fancy machines as well. Dad bought it for her for Christmas last year.' He nodded his head at the counter. 'Like the one they've got. Well, I say *bought*, but it might have come out of the back of some van in a pub car park. You can never tell with my dad.'

'That joke, by the way,' Kieron pointed out, 'only works if you know that there's a brand of whisky called White Horse.'

'I thought everyone knew that.'

'In your world, maybe.'

Sam shrugged. 'It's all my Uncle Bill drinks. He gets a bottle for Christmas from everyone in the family – I mean, a bottle from each person, not just one bottle from everyone. Same on his birthday. That pretty much sets him up for the year.' He paused. 'OK, a horse walks into a bar and says, "Pour me a pint of beer, will you?" The barman rubs his eyes in disbelief and says, "Did . . . did you just talk?" The horse says, "Yes, why?" and the barman goes, "It's amazing! I've never seen a talking horse! You know, you should really go talk to the local circus – they would *love* to have someone with your skills!" The horse replies, "Why? Are they short of plumbers?"'

This time Kieron sniggered. 'Yeah, OK, that's good. I like that.'

'I'm thinking of setting up a website – all the best "horse walks into a bar" jokes in the world.'

'How many have you got?'

Sam winced. 'You've heard them.'

'Just three?'

'I could expand the website to other animals. "A bear goes into a bar –"'

'Don't,' Kieron interrupted. 'Just . . . don't.'

'Just let me do this one. A bear goes into a bar, right, and says, "I'd like a pint of . . . beer," and the barman goes, "Why the big paws?"' He stared at Kieron. '*Big paws*. Like, bears have got big paws. And he *paused* before finishing the sentence.'

'Yes, it was funny when you told it and it was funny when you explained it.' Kieron looked properly at Sam for the first time, and sat up straighter in his chair. 'What's wrong?'

'Nothing's wrong.'

'Yes, there is.'

'No, really. Nothing's wrong.'

'I can tell. I know you, and I know the way your face goes when there's something wrong, and it's gone there now. It's gone there so much it might just as well pitch a tent and stay there for the night. So, come on – what's wrong?'

Sam sighed. 'Get me an iced latte and I'll tell you.'

On his way up to the counter Kieron surreptitiously counted the change in his pocket and checked the price on the board fastened to the wall. He just about had enough.

'What's your name?' the barista – Beth – asked him brightly.

'Still Kieron,' he said. Her smile faltered slightly.

8

After a lot of faffing about with a blender, ice cubes and a double shot of coffee, Kieron took the drink and returned to the table. 'So?' he asked, putting it down in front of his friend.

'So . . .' Sam sighed. 'You know my dad, right?'

'Yeah. You described him to Bex once as, "a lifelong drifter who can't hold down a job for more than a week". I think those were your exact words.'

'Yeah, that sounds about right. I counted up once: he's had just under a hundred different jobs, some of them overlapping. Longest he's ever stayed at one is three months; shortest is three days.' Sam stared out of the front door of the cafe at the bright street outside. 'Thing is, he's actually found himself a real job now. A proper job.'

'That's good, isn't it?'

'It's in Southampton. Loading stuff onto the cruise ships before they leave – food and drink and stuff. Still, at least that means we'll be OK for lobster and champagne at Christmas.'

'Oh.' Kieron frowned, trying to work out where this was going. 'How does your mum feel about that? I mean, I know she gets irritated at him – I've heard the arguments from halfway down the street when I go round to your place – but I don't think she'd want him to go away for weeks on end.'

'She doesn't – mainly because she doesn't trust him not to find a girlfriend down there and spend all his money in the pub.' Sam hesitated. 'That's why she's talking about all of us moving down there with him. "Make a new start," she says; "All of us, together. It'll be wonderful." But the thing is – it won't.'

'*All* of you? Including Courtney?'

Sam shook his head. 'No, not Courtney. She's sorted. She's got a good job and her own flat. And a boyfriend, although Mum doesn't know about Bradley yet. But Caitlin and Amber still live at home, so they'd go down to Southampton. And so would I.'

Kieron suddenly felt as if he was standing in the middle of a minefield. Whichever way he stepped, something might explode. 'How do *you* feel about that?' he asked carefully.

'I think it's stupid.' Sam took a gulp of his iced coffee. 'I mean, yes, it's a new place, and if anyone could do with a new start, it's us, but –' he shook his head – 'I don't *want* a new start. I may not love Newcastle, but I'm used to it. I know where everything is. And –'

He stopped, but Kieron thought he knew what Sam had been going to say. *And you're here*.

He felt a lump in his throat, and he had to blink quickly to get rid of the prickle in his eyes.

That feeling he'd had earlier, of life being like sitting in a car going nowhere forever? That landscape the car was driving into was looking bleaker and bleaker now. Just dry earth and the occasional cactus. He only had one real friend in the world – Sam. Bex and Bradley felt like friends, but they were older and he knew in his heart of hearts they were temporary. In a few weeks, or months at the most, they'd be gone. But Sam – he'd assumed he and Sam would go on and on, to the end of their schooldays and beyond.

'Maybe,' he said carefully, 'your mum would let you

come and stay at my flat. I mean, changing school at this late stage is bound to affect your grades. There's space on my floor, and I'm sure my mum won't mind.'

'Do you think that's an actual possibility?' Sam asked plaintively.

'Yeah, course. Do you want me to ask her?'

'Please.' Kieron noticed that Sam's throat was working, as if he needed to swallow. He handed his friend his glass of water and Sam took a grateful gulp.

'Just bear in mind,' Sam said, 'I'm not going into school and leaving you studying at home.'

'Don't worry – we'll find a way around that.'

'When school's over,' Sam asked suddenly, 'what do you want to do?'

'I dunno. Just hang out.' Kieron suddenly caught up with the conversation. 'Oh, you mean, after we *leave* school!'

'Yeah.' Sam shrugged casually. 'You ever thought about going to college?'

'Kinda. Difficult to think of any subject I'd want to do though. I wondered about film studies. Or maybe psychology.'

'Psychology – good idea. Try to explain our dark teenage thought-processes.'

'Why are you asking?'

'I've been thinking . . .' Sam sounded unusually hesitant, '. . . maybe we could, like, set up a company together. Do something that'll make us some money.'

'Secret agents?' Kieron laughed. 'Or maybe private detectives.'

11

Sam scowled. 'I was thinking more like website design, or repairing computers and tablets and mobile phones, but if you're just going to laugh –'

'No.' Kieron forced himself to sound serious. 'Actually, that's not a bad idea. We could get ourselves a little unit on an industrial estate maybe.' A vision of how all this might work started unfolding in his mind. 'We'd need to learn to drive, at least on a moped, so we could pick up the broken stuff and bring it back for repair. No, scratch that – we'd definitely need a car. We might just get a small PC CPU on the back of a moped, but definitely not any of the high-end gaming machines. We'd need some money, to set up and buy circuit boards and tools and stuff. Maybe we could apply for a loan. I'll ask my mum about that.'

'Actually,' Sam said, '*my* mum's got all the information. You can get things called Enterprise Loans.'

Kieron nodded. 'Sorted. We'll get one of those.'

'Sorted,' Sam said, and extended a fist. Kieron bumped his own fist against it.

They chatted for a while, reminding each other of things that had happened to them over the past few months and marvelling at how their lives had changed so much while apparently, to anybody else, having stayed the same. Eventually Kieron's macchiato was as cold as Sam's iced latte and he couldn't in all conscience keep sipping at it, so they left.

'You want to come back with me?' Kieron asked. 'We can get some lunch. There should be something in the fridge.'

'Might as well,' Sam replied. 'It's not as if there's any pressing need to save the world today, as far as I know.'

Kieron punched him on the arm. Hard.

The walk took them three-quarters of an hour. It would have been quicker, but they had to divert twice to avoid gangs of chavvy teenagers standing outside the off-licences. They both knew from harsh experience that they'd get called names, shoved and spat on if they went too close. Bitterly, Kieron thought the kids ought to have signs around their necks, like in a zoo: *Please do not provoke the chavs – they are liable to bite without warning.*

'We're nearly grown-up,' Sam pointed out darkly as they headed down a side street on one of their detours. 'We shouldn't have to be scared of them!'

'You adopt the moral and logical high ground,' Kieron replied, glancing back over his shoulder to see if they were being followed. 'I'll visit you in hospital and bring you grapes.'

'Why do people always bring you grapes when you're in hospital?' Sam frowned. 'When I broke my arm, I had so many bags of grapes by the side of my bed there wasn't room for anything else. What I wanted more than anything else was a Chinese takeaway, but nobody thought to bring one. Just grapes.'

'Something to do with the European Union,' Kieron said vaguely. 'I think there's, like, some kind of rule about fruit and hospitals – only grapes are allowed. And maybe tangerines.'

When they got to Kieron's flat, he noticed that his mum's

car was outside. 'That's unusual – she should be at work.' He checked his watch. 'She's not due back for another couple of hours.'

Sam shifted uneasily. 'If you want me to go . . .'

'No, come in. It's probably fine.'

He slid his key into the lock and pushed the door open. 'Mum – I'm home!' he called. 'I've got Sam with me.'

'I'm in the living room,' his mum called. It sounded like there was something wrong with her voice, as if she was choking on something.

'You go to my room,' Kieron said to Sam. 'I'll check on Mum.'

'All right if I get a can of drink from your mini-fridge?'

'Yeah – just make sure there's one in there for me.'

As Sam headed along the corridor to Kieron's room, Kieron stared at the doorway into the living room. He felt suddenly sick. Something had changed, and not, he thought, for the better. It was as if his life had suddenly lurched sideways, unbalancing him, but he didn't know how or why. An emotional earthquake with no obvious cause.

He took a deep breath and headed into the living room.

His mum was sitting on the sofa, staring at the TV screen. Well, not so much *sitting* as *slumping*. The TV was off, but she was staring at the screen anyway. Two bottles sat on the table beside her, next to a half-full glass, but they weren't the usual prosecco or red wine. One of them was a bottle of gin; the other a bottle of tonic water.

Well, at least she's not drinking the gin neat, he thought.

'Hi, Mum.'

'I thought you were supposed to be doing your schoolwork today?' she said, staring at him and frowning.

'I went to the library,' he said automatically. It was a lie, but if he told her he'd gone to a coffee shop to work she would have asked why, and the explanation would have taken far too long. Better just to avoid the truth entirely.

'The library?' she repeated. 'Can't you find out whatever information you need on the Internet?'

Fine time for her to become technologically literate! he thought.

'The Internet's great for superficial stuff, like names and dates and equations, but if you want to get into a subject in-depth you need books.'

'Oh. OK. Good to know that libraries are still useful for something.' She reached out for her glass and seemed surprised to discover that it was empty.

'Mum – what's wrong?'

'Nothing. Nothing at all.'

She wriggled around on the sofa so she could reach out for the gin bottle and poured a substantial amount into her glass. Then, putting the bottle back, she picked up the glass and took a gulp without bothering to dilute it with any tonic water.

'There is something wrong. Please – will you tell me what it is?'

She sighed. 'OK. Sit down.'

He sat in the armchair facing her. Suddenly he didn't want her to say anything. He didn't what to know what was wrong. If he didn't *know*, then nothing was wrong. It wasn't logical, but that was how he felt. Knowing would make it real.

'Sam's here,' he said. 'He's gone to my room.'

'Sam? Sam Rosenfelt?'

'Yeah.'

'I saw a post from his mum on social media. She said they might be moving to Southampton. Is that right? Southampton?'

He nodded, wincing inside. 'It's . . . a possibility. I want to talk to you about that, but –' he took a deep breath – 'first you need to tell me what's happened. It's something bad, isn't it?' A sudden thought grabbed him by the heart and squeezed. 'Is it Dad? Is he . . . is he dead?'

'Not as far as I know.' She took another gulp of straight gin. 'Although I wouldn't put it past him to die without telling us.' She shook her head. 'Sorry – that was uncalled for. No, as far as I know he's fine.' She seemed to realise that there was something wrong with her drink, and reached for the tonic bottle. 'It's work,' she said, topping her glass up until it was in danger of overflowing.

It's called a meniscus, Kieron thought, staring at the way the gin and tonic mixture clung to the rim of the glass all the way round the edge but rose up slightly towards the middle. It's to do with surface tension. I learned that last year. At school.

'I've been – made redundant,' his mum said, not looking at him. 'Laid off. Fired. I am officially "surplus to requirements".' Her face seemed to be twisting more

16

and more with each phrase. 'I have been "downsized". Dismissed. Sacked. Given the boot.'

Kieron felt like he'd suddenly been hollowed out. 'What happened?'

'I can't remember if I told you at the time, but we merged with another company a few months back. We were given all kinds of assurances that nothing would change and that our jobs were secure, but it was all hot air. They've decided to let the human resources department in the other company handle all the HR issues, and they're fully staffed. So – they've had to "let me go".'

'Do you get some kind of payoff?'

She nodded. '"Some kind" is about right.'

'Can you get your union on the case?' Kieron wasn't entirely clear what unions were for, but he vaguely recalled that they were good things to have in this kind of situation.

'I never joined. The company I *was* with was a good place to work. The bosses really cared about us. I always meant to join a union, but in a way it would've seemed like I was being disloyal.'

'But you can find another job, can't you?'

'I hope so. The marketplace is really difficult at the moment though, and there's a lot of qualified HR people younger than me out there, looking for jobs.' She laughed bitterly. 'All the times I had to counsel people who had been fired, for whatever reason. All the things I used to say. They all seem meaningless now. Just . . . reassuring platitudes. Ways of getting them up on their feet long enough to get them out of my office.' She gulped from the over-full glass.

Trickles of clear liquid splashed onto her blouse. 'And to add insult to injury, they're sending me on a course to help me "acclimatise" to the new situation, work out my strengths, construct an impressive CV and find a new job. It's like someone's stolen your TV and then the burglar sends you a leaflet telling you where the best bargains are so you can buy a new one.' She sighed. 'I'm sorry, but I'm not going to be around for a few days. It's a residential course, somewhere down in the Midlands. I'll do an online supermarket order tonight so you've got stuff to eat. If there's a problem, call me and I'll come straight back. I mean, it's not like I actually want to *do* this stupid course. You'll be all right, won't you? I mean, I know what you kids are like these days. You quite like being alone, don't you?'

I'm supposed to help. The thought made Kieron feel cold. I'm the man of the house. It's my responsibility.

'I'll get a job,' he said. 'An apprenticeship maybe. Or I'll stack shelves in a supermarket.'

His mum smiled and leaned her head back against the sofa. 'You're a good son, Kieron. I don't tell you that often enough. We'll be all right. I've got some savings, and there'll be other jobs out there. It's just – a blow to my self-confidence, you know? Suddenly not being wanted – it's just like . . . just like when your dad left. You think you're loved, but it turns out you aren't. Not at all.' She closed her eyes. 'You go and play with Sam. I'll be fine.'

Kieron watched her for a few moments, but she stayed that way – eyes closed and head back. Eventually he got up, moved across to her and took the glass from her fingers.

She didn't even seem to notice. He put it on the table beside her, then picked up the bottle of gin and took it out into the kitchen. After a moment's thought he put it in the fridge. It wasn't exactly hiding it, but then again it wasn't in plain sight either.

Sighing, he went down the corridor to his room.

Sam was playing on Kieron's PC. He glanced up when Kieron entered. 'Everything all right?'

'Mum's lost her job.'

Sam shrugged. 'Like I said: my dad's lost loads of jobs. It got to the stage where he'd come in the house and say, "I've lost my job," and we'd say, "Have you looked behind the fridge?" like it was a ritual or something.' He paused. 'Things'll work out. Don't worry.'

Kieron shook his head. 'She's been in this job for years – not days, like your dad. This has never happened to her before. I've never seen her like this.'

'Maybe this is life telling her that it's time for a change.'

Kieron held up his hand. 'Maybe this is me telling you to shut up before I slap you.'

'Fair point. Grab a spare controller and join me on this thing – I'll put it on two-player mode.'

Kieron was about to pull up a chair and join Sam when his mobile beeped. He pulled it from his pocket and glanced at the screen. 'Message from Bex,' he said. 'Give me a minute.'

'I haven't seen her for a while. How's Bradley?'

'I'll find out. Hang on.' He checked the message.

Kieron – can we meet up? We need to have a serious talk. That cafe in Hooley Street, 4 this afternoon?

The cafe he'd been in just a few hours ago. Funny, the way life seemed to loop back around on itself sometimes.

'Everything OK?' Sam asked, eyes still fixed on the screen.

'I don't know,' Kieron said carefully. 'I think I'm about to be dumped.'

CHAPTER TWO

'OK,' Bex Wilson said, 'I've sent it.' She gazed out of the window of the flat she and Bradley Marshall had rented a month ago, and which had quickly become their home and their base. She felt sick. This was the right thing to do, but she knew the effect it would have on Kieron. He would be devastated, and she didn't want to hurt him. The trouble was, she *had* to hurt him so that he didn't get hurt worse, later.

Bradley watched her from the sofa. 'It had to be done,' he said gently. 'We can't ask the boys to risk their lives any more than they already have. It's time for me to get back to supporting you on our missions. It's time for me to start using the ARCC glasses again.'

'Are you sure you're up to it?' She turned away from the window and stared at him, trying to evaluate from the way he was sitting how he might be feeling. It wasn't that long ago that he'd been knocked out, kidnapped, beaten up and tortured right here in Newcastle while working on a mission with her. Any normal person would have been traumatised by all that, but she knew how strong Bradley was. He didn't look it, with his hipster beard and his friendly smile, but she knew he had an inner core of pure steel.

He nodded. He was sitting up straighter than he had been a few days before, she noticed, and he didn't have that look of a person perpetually wincing slightly at the world. 'Yeah – the headaches have pretty much gone away now, and so have the visual disturbances. I can even stand up and go for a long walk without keeling over. The private doctor you called in has given me a clean bill of health. She's pretty sure it was concussion, but it's gone now.' He smiled gently. 'She kept saying that I should get checked out in hospital, have an MRI scan and an X-ray, but I told her I had a phobia about technology.'

'And what did she say?' Bex asked.

'She looked at the LCD screen and the Blu-ray player, shrugged and went back to checking my blood pressure and pulse. Whatever you were paying her, it kept her from asking too many difficult questions.'

'What I was paying her was partly to *stop* her asking questions.' As Bradley nodded, Bex went on: 'Now for the one-trillion-dollar question: what about the ARCC glasses? Can you really use them properly, for sixteen hours a day if necessary?'

'Yes,' he said firmly. 'I can.'

Bex wasn't convinced. The glasses were her link to him when they were both on a mission for their employers in the UK's spy agency: MI6. Undercover anywhere in the world, Bex wore a pair with hidden cameras, hidden speakers and a hidden microphone, all transmitting real-time information via encrypted satellite link back to Bradley, who sat somewhere that was supposed to be safe – probably with a coffee and a pastry in front of him. The set *he* wore showed him what Bex was seeing and allowed him to hear what she was hearing and saying. But that wasn't nearly the end of their technological wizardry – they also acted as virtual-reality goggles, enabling him to call up any information or image he wanted from the Internet, the dark web or classified government databases so only he could see them. That way he could provide instant facts and guidance to Bex without anyone knowing. He had to be aware of what was going on around him, but also be sensitive to Bex's requirements – which could be life-threatening and depend on him to respond with the right information. The problem was, looking through Bradley's ARCC glasses meant he was seeing the real world and Bex's world at the same time, one overlaid on the other. He had perpetual double-vision while wearing them. Long-term, that could lead to distraction, confusion and possibly even hallucinations if Bradley wasn't careful – and that was when he was in perfect health. Now . . . now she wasn't sure.

'Have you tried them out?' she asked.

'You told me not to,' he said virtuously, 'in case they caused a relapse.'

She stared at him for a few seconds without saying anything, then repeated: 'Have you tried them out?'

He did his best to meet her questioning stare with an innocent one of his own, but she knew him too well. Eventually he crumbled. 'Yes,' he said, blinking. 'Kieron brought them over a couple of times, and I've had a go on

23

them. The first time was just for a few seconds, then for a few minutes, then for a few hours. No bad effects – no headaches, and no passing out. Look, I'm fit for duty. Honest.'

Bex sighed, feeling relieved. It had been stressful while Bradley had been incapacitated – more so than she had admitted to herself. At the back of her mind there had always been the question: would he ever recover? Would he ever be able to work again?

'Has any work come in from MI6 since the Goldfinch mission in Albuquerque and Tel Aviv?' he asked.

'I would have told you if it had. We've only just finished that job – they're probably letting us have a few days to recover before they send us something else.'

He sighed. 'Sorry. Sometimes I worry that you might have been keeping stuff from me while I was sick.'

'I wouldn't do that. We're a team. Total honesty – right?'

He nodded. 'Right.' After a slight pause, he added, 'In that spirit, I suppose we need to talk about MI6.'

She winced. 'You mean about how one of our MI6 bosses is a traitor, working for an extremist right-wing organisation of fascists and racists? *That* talk?'

'No – I was going to ask where this year's Christmas party is taking place.'

Bex laughed, and the sudden relief of being *able* to laugh took her by surprise.

'It's good to hear you laugh again,' Bradley said. 'But yes, we need to talk about that whole "traitor" business.'

Bex sat down before replying. She'd been thinking this over obsessively, and she hadn't come up with any answers.

For a start, they didn't know very much. In the first few days after Bradley had been kidnapped by the Blood and Soil organisation, and Bex had met Kieron and Sam, it had become obvious that someone in MI6 was passing information to a neo-fascist organisation – and had passed them Bradley's information when he'd been sent to Newcastle to help Bex track them down. A sympathiser, if not an active collaborator. The problem was, apart from being able to identify the traitor as a woman, they didn't know very much more. Yes, they could report their suspicions to MI6, but half of their bosses in the SIS-TERR department were female. What if they reported their suspicions to the actual traitor? They'd be exposing themselves to risk. As it was, they were living off the grid, under assumed identities and in untraceable accommodation, accepting missions from anonymised and encrypted email accounts. Being untraceable was hard work.

Bradley knew all that of course, so she didn't bother rehearsing it again. Instead she sighed and said, 'We can't let it ride. We have to do something.'

'Agreed,' he said. 'We could go up the chain, I suppose. Go right to the Director; tell her.'

'*Her*,' Bex pointed out. 'That's the problem. It might *be* her, for all we know.'

'So is there *anyone* we could report it to?' Bradley asked. 'I mean, MI6 operate overseas – it's MI5 who operate within the UK. We could tell them. Or the police.'

Bex shook her head firmly. 'The problem is, we don't know how far up the tree the rot goes. What if MI5 are compromised as well? What if the police have been infiltrated by Blood and Soil? No – reporting it isn't enough.'

'So we need to do something more active. We need to use our own particular skill sets to investigate, and identify the traitor.'

It felt like she should reject this as being too risky, but Bex found herself reluctantly nodding. 'It feels wrong, investigating our own bosses – even if we are freelancers rather than registered agents – but I can't see any alternative. We're going to have to use the ARCC kit against MI6, if only to flush out the traitor.' She sighed. 'And that means it's even more imperative that we get Kieron and Sam off the books. God knows we've exposed them to enough risks already. We can't let them get involved in something *this* dangerous, and this close to home.'

Bradley nodded. 'It's the right thing to do. Kieron in particular has been brilliant – not just at providing support, but also at going undercover. He's got natural ability, but we mustn't encourage him – or Sam. We'd better relocate to a different town as well. If we don't, we'll keep finding the two of them on our doorstep. They've become addicted to this lifestyle, I think.' He seemed to be about to say something else, but closed his mouth and deliberately looked away.

'What?'

'What what?'

'You were going to say something.'

'I was not.'

'You were.' She laughed suddenly. 'You know what – we're sounding like *them*.'

26

Bradley nodded slowly. 'That's part of the problem. We're all growing together into some strange, dysfunctional family, the four of us. I know Kieron's started thinking about you as the big sister he never had – I can see it in his eyes. I don't know what he and Sam think about me – a big brother maybe –'

'Or that uncle who thinks he's really down with the kids but he's really not,' Bex murmured.

'– but they're definitely fixating on us, the way little baby ducks fixate on the first thing they see and assume it's their mother.'

'Those two kids,' Bex said carefully, 'are not ducklings. Not in any sense at all. They've already proved themselves in action better than some agents I could name.'

'Agreed, but we've warped their lives enough. We need to back away gracefully, disengage and let them live the way they were supposed to.'

Bex stared at him for a long moment. 'Do you know what their lives are like? *Were* like, before they got involved with us?'

'Do you know what *my* life was like before I met you?' he countered.

Bex shook her head. Bradley had always been close-mouthed about his family, his childhood, his history.

'I didn't have the greatest start in life,' he said, avoiding her eyes and staring towards the window. 'Bad things happened. I got over them.' He looked back at her, and his face was serious. 'We've given those boys the tools they need to make something of themselves. We've given them confidence in themselves. It's up to them now.'

In the silence that followed, Bex found herself quietly saying, 'And what about you? You and Courtney?'

He sighed. 'If Sam is off-limits to us, then his sister is off-limits to me. The relationship has to finish. I'll tell her tonight.'

'Seems hard on you,' she said gently.

He shrugged, trying to appear casual, but she could see the sudden tension in his shoulders, and the way he was sitting. 'It won't be the first relationship that I've had to end because of the job, and I doubt it'll be the last.'

'And I'll tell Kieron that it's all come to an end,' Bex said, rising from her chair. 'I'll be firm, but fair. I'll let him down gently.'

'Make sure you emphasise how important secrecy is. I know he and Sam don't have that many friends –'

'They don't have *any* other friends, as far as I can make out.'

'– but I'd hate to find out they were boasting about how they'd been helping out secret agents on undercover missions, in an attempt to impress some girls at a party. That would be a *bad* thing.'

'Yes – I know.'

'Tell him what "Top Secret" actually means – that people might die if that information gets out. And by "people", I mean you and me.'

'I'm sure he understands all that, but yes – I'll remind him.'

'And I'll get to work finding a new town for us to live in, and a flat there. I've always fancied Leamington Spa, just from the sound of it. What do you think? Ever been there? Any family there?'

'No – you?'

'No – so it's perfect. We have no previous connection. Whoever is the traitor in MI6, they'll have trouble tracking us down.'

Bex glanced at her watch. 'I'd better go. I've probably put Kieron on edge already. If he has to wait for me to turn up then he'll just get twitchy.'

'Treat him gently,' Bradley said. 'Remember – it's probably his first break-up.'

'I'm not his girlfriend, remember,' Bex protested. 'I'm his big sister. You said so yourself. And all little brothers secretly want their big sister out of their life so they can grow up.'

'And so they don't get covered in make-up and have their hair done by their sister and her friends.' Bradley grinned. 'Yes, I had a big sister. Two of them in fact.' He waved towards the door. 'Go on then. Start cutting our ties. Just bring a takeaway back. Indonesian, please.'

Bex left Bradley in the apartment and headed down towards the outside world. She'd left her car parked in a different street, just a short walk away. It was a security measure, one of many small habits she unconsciously went through every day to protect herself and Bradley. It was theoretically possible that someone connected with a job they were on, or maybe even someone connected to Blood and Soil, might see her in the street or the supermarket and recognise her. It was also possible, she supposed, that they might tail her to her car and discover what make and model it was, and its registration. She always took care when she was out in public to check every couple of minutes for faces that seemed to be hanging around and staying behind her, but crowds made it difficult, and there were ways that followers could change their appearance – put a hood up or take it down; turn a reversible jacket inside out; take a scarf out of a pocket and wind it around their neck. She couldn't rule out the fact that she and her car might have been connected, and that her car might be traced. If she parked outside the apartment then the followers – if there were any – would quickly find out where she and Bradley were living. Parking a street or two away was just another level of security. One of many.

It was cold outside, and she zipped her coat up as she walked. She felt her fingers tingling and stuck them into her pockets to keep warm. The sun was low in the sky, casting a reddish light on the roofs of the buildings she passed.

When she got to her car she reached into her pocket for the keys. As she bought them out she made a show of fumbling them, and dropping them to the ground with a jingle of metal on concrete. Cursing, she bent to pick them up. As her hand closed around them she glanced under the car. If anyone was going to place a bomb on the vehicle, the easiest thing was to attach it to the underside with magnets. She quickly scanned it from front to back. Nothing. No suspicious lumps or bumps.

Before she opened the door, she glanced at the bonnet. She always left a leaf underneath, trapped between the bonnet and the body of the car with its stem just poking out. The second-most-likely place to put a bomb would be in the engine compartment. If anyone tried they would disturb the leaf, which would fall away. Again, it was a simple countermeasure, but could potentially be a useful one.

The leaf was still there. As it always was. But she still kept on checking, every time.

She opened the car door and slipped inside. Despite all the precautions, all the countermeasures, as she turned the key in the ignition she felt herself tense slightly. Just in case.

Three years ago, a friend of hers, someone she had gone through training with, had got into his car and turned the key in the ignition, just like he'd done every day. A device nestling right beside the engine had exploded, killing him instantly and sending shards of metal and glass flying for hundreds of metres, propelled on a wave of burning gases. And every time Bex started up a car, she remembered that. If they wanted to get you, if they *really* wanted to get you, then they would find a way.

Not a comfortable thought.

Before she could pull away from the kerb, her phone *ping*ed. She checked the number. If it was one she recognised then she would answer it. More often than not, it was just cold calls wanting to know if she'd had any accidents recently that weren't her fault, and claiming she could be entitled to millions in compensation. Sometimes – just sometimes – she was tempted to actually tell them about the 'accidents' she'd had during the course of her covert missions abroad, just to see what their reaction would be. Crashing a light aircraft on top of a lorry carrying guns in Mozambique, for instance, or having a scorpion deliberately thrown in through her car window while she was going at over a hundred miles per hour on a German *autobahn*. But . . . best to keep those things to herself.

The *ping* was from Kieron. *Pls phone*, he'd texted.

Bex would be seeing him in less than half an hour, but she'd better call him back. Maybe he was delayed.

'Kieron?'

'Hi. Thanks for getting back to me.'

'I'll be with you soon. Everything all right?'

He didn't sound panicked, or stressed. 'Kind of, except that I've got some stuff to tell you. Like, personal stuff. But the reason I'm calling is, I put the ARCC glasses on, just before leaving, and saw there was a message for you on there.'

'Why are you using the glasses?' she asked calmly but firmly. 'You know you're not supposed to wear them unless you're helping me out on a mission – and you're not.'

'If I don't put them on every now and then,' he said reasonably, 'how would you know if you'd got any messages?'

Bex sighed. The best solution would have been for him to leave the glasses at the apartment with her and Bradley, but on the couple of occasions she'd politely asked for them back he'd 'forgotten' to put them in his bag. She knew perfectly well what was happening. He'd become addicted to them. So had Sam. The two of them loved the way the glasses gave them access to information they shouldn't have, and they didn't want to give that up.

Too bad. That was part of the conversation she and Kieron were about to have.

'OK,' she said, not willing to have an argument about it, 'what's the message?'

'There's an attachment that needs a code word to decrypt it, but the subject line is: *Immediate Threat Assessment – Falcon Team*, and it's from someone or something called the Threat Cell.'

A shiver ran through her. *Immediate Threat Assessment* was a trigger phrase. It meant what it said – there was an immediate threat to the recipient that needed to be acted on. The Threat Cell was the team of people within MI6 whose job it was to track threats – of whatever form, in whatever context – and alert the target.

Someone was after her. Or Bradley. Or both of them.

'Right,' she said in a tone of voice that suggested, *Nothing to worry about here*, which was not what she was feeling. Not at all. 'Good work. Not to panic. I'll respond to the message as soon as I get to you.'

'OK.' He didn't sound convinced. Smart boy. 'Am I safe here?'

She closed her eyes and took a deep breath. She'd have to give him something. 'You remember you told me about that time when you'd set up a folding ladder so you could cut your mum's hedge, back at the house where you used to live, and you were balancing on the rungs of the ladder, and your foot went between two rungs and you fell backwards, and you thought your leg was going to break but you managed to pull it out from between the rungs just in time? Do you remember that?'

'Ye-es,' he said uncertainly.

'You're as safe there as you were back then. Do you understand?'

'Ye-es.' A long pause. 'Should I stay here?'

'Are you at the cafe?'

'Yes.'

'Then stay there.'

She cut the connection, feeling guilty. This was exactly the kind of thing she wanted to avoid involving him in. Invisible, intangible threats.

The drive from the apartment to Newcastle city centre took twenty minutes, but to her finely honed nervous system it seemed like an hour. Bex left the car across and down the street from the cafe, but chose a spot where she would still be able to see it. As she crossed, she felt as though she was moving through treacle. Her gaze moved across all of the faces she saw – old and young, male and female. Any of them might be a threat. *All* of them might be a threat. Her gaze moved upwards, to the rooftops above the shops: an irregular line of chimneys, gables and slanted tiles. Plenty of places to hide up there. Plenty of places someone with a rifle could take cover while they lined up a shot.

No. She had to pull herself together. She'd been in situations like this before. Threats had been made on her life before. And besides, it was probably something simple, like her photo had been found on a jihadist website, or her name mentioned in an email from someone in the Russian secret service. She wasn't naive enough to believe that she'd conducted her undercover operations without ever being noticed. Just because someone had flagged her up somewhere in the world didn't mean there was an immediate threat now.

She felt her heart rate slow down. Her breaths came more easily now.

As she pushed open the door of the cafe she scanned the crowd inside for Kieron. He was sitting over by the far wall, by the entrance to the toilets. He smiled when he saw her, but it was a tentative smile, a nervous smile.

'I got you a black Americano,' he said. 'And a doughnut. I couldn't afford it, so they've put it on a tab at the counter. I hope that's all right.'

'Thanks,' she said, sitting down. She stared at his drink, with its conical topping of whipped cream and marshmallows. 'Is there a hot chocolate under there somewhere, or is it all just empty calories?'

'I'm a growing lad,' he protested. 'My mum says I need to keep my energy up.'

'You and Sam are like hummingbirds,' she observed, noticing the way his face had clouded over when he'd mentioned his mum. 'You subsist on a constant diet of sugar.'

'What do you think of my choice of seat?' he asked.

'Away from the windows, and next to a corridor that leads to a fire door,' she said. 'And in a corner, which means we can both sit with a view of the room. Very good. Very *tactical*.'

'I thought you'd like it.'

He was trying to impress her. He knew why they were there.

'Kieron –'

35

'My mum's lost her job,' he said, taking a spoonful of the whipped cream and staring at it for a moment before slipping it into his mouth.

'I'm sorry to hear that.'

'She says we've got savings and we can last for a while, but I don't believe her. She also says it'll be easy to find a new job with her qualifications, but I don't believe *that* either.'

'Things will work out,' Bex said, knowing as she uttered the words how lame they sounded. And also knowing that there was no way to get from that conversation to the one she wanted to have without there being a jarring disconnect, which was probably why Kieron had jumped in with it. 'Look, Kieron, we need to talk.'

'I know what you're going to say,' he said morosely. 'Bradley's much better now, so he can use the ARCC glasses again. You don't need me any more, and you're worried about my safety, so you and he are moving to a different town.'

'Then you've worked it out, and there's nothing else I can add.'

'Can you send me an anonymous message on social media every now and then, just so I know you're OK? Cos I'll worry about you.'

'Better than that,' she said brightly, but feeling her insides knotting up, 'I'll make surprise visits. You'll look around somewhere, maybe in a cafe like this, or at a gig or something, and you'll see me. You'll smile, and I'll smile, and then we'll both know the other is all right. Or I'll turn up in the crowd at a school sports day. You'll be crossing the finish line, and you'll look up and see me waving and cheering.'

'Please don't come to a school sports day,' he said, wincing. 'I don't want you to see me crawling on all fours for the last few yards.'

'OK. Sports days are out. Everything else is fair game though.'

'Date nights are out too – if I ever get any. I don't want to be with a girl watching a film and turn around and see you behind me.'

'All right, date nights are out too.'

Kieron's head turned, and his gaze flickered towards the counter, where a red-haired girl was serving coffee. Just as he turned away, the red-haired barista glanced across at him, smiling slightly. Something going on there, maybe? Bex hoped so. Kieron deserved to meet someone nice.

She caught herself. She wasn't his mum, and she wasn't his big sister. She couldn't get involved.

She sighed. 'You're going to have to give me access to some kind of online calendar, so I know when it's safe to see you.' She took a breath, trying to push down the hard knot of emotion that seemed to want to block her throat. 'Did you bring the glasses with you, like I asked?'

'Yeah, I did.' He shrugged. 'Forgot them the first time, and had to go back for them.'

'Pass them over, and then we can talk about other stuff.'

'Until we say goodbye,' he said bleakly.

'Until we say goodbye.'

Bex wasn't sure what it was that attracted her attention. Maybe nothing. Maybe it was that strange sixth sense that experienced agents have that alerts them when something is about to happen, a big, terrible event echoing back in time a few seconds, in contravention of every known law of physics. Whatever – the hairs on the back of her neck suddenly rose, and she felt herself tense.

Kieron felt it too – she saw his knuckles suddenly go white as he clenched his fingers.

'Wha – ?' he started to say.

Bex had turned her head to scan the cafe for threats, the queue at the counter, the seated customers with their lattes and macchiatos and flat whites. She looked out of the window to the street, to where her car was parked. Until it wasn't. A sudden flash of light obscured it, and then it was just an expanding cloud of dust and debris and flame that filled the road. The window bowed in, bending under the force of the explosion before it fractured into a crazy cobweb of millions of small fragments of glass all held together by some plastic film that incredibly didn't tear or rip but just sagged.

And then the noise. A sound like a skip full of rubble falling off a lorry onto concrete, a rushing noise, screams, the *whoomph* of the expanding window compressing the air in the cafe.

All that in one second. Less than a second.

Bex grabbed Kieron's shoulder and pulled him off his seat with one hand while her other hand pushed their table over, sending their drinks flying. In her mind the only thought, apart from that of protecting Kieron and herself, was, *I should have paid more attention to that threat assessment . . .*

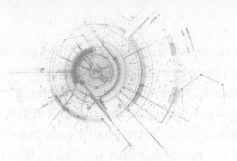

CHAPTER THREE

Kieron's head felt like a bell that had been violently struck with a hammer. Not only was there a high-pitched ringing in his ears, drowning out any other sound, but his skull seemed to be *vibrating*. His stomach kept lurching, and despite all of the devastation and chaos around him he found himself obsessively churning over the same trivial thought in his mind: *That whipped cream and those marshmallows were a mistake . . .*

He peeked over the top of the table in shock. The cafe, which just seconds ago had been a comfortable, warm, safe place to be, now looked like a war zone. Dust was settling over everything, and smoke filled the air. He could smell burning, and his mouth tasted like metal: hot and coppery. Maybe it was blood. Perhaps he'd bitten his own tongue.

The wide window at the front of the cafe now looked like a billion spiders had covered it with their webs, but the webs were actually shards of broken glass, mercifully held together by a plastic film that had previously had the name of the place, its logo and a series of enticing extracts from the menu printed on it. *Thank heaven for advertising,*

Kieron thought – another trivial thought that made him want to giggle hysterically.

No flames. At least that was something. No flames, so nothing was burning, so they weren't at risk from fire.

He noticed that his thoughts were moving in discrete chunks – *a* meant *b* which implied *c*. Was that an effect of shock? Or was he more badly injured than just a bitten tongue? He quickly ran a hand across his face, but there were no bits of wreckage sticking out of wounds: just a lot of dust.

The table shifted, and Bex's head appeared. Her eyes were wide, pupils dilated, but Kieron thought that was probably tension rather than, say, concussion. At least, he hoped it was.

'We need to get out of here,' she said. Her voice sounded flat and muted against the ringing in his ears.

'We have to help!' he replied.

'That was my car! Someone's trying to kill me! Which means I am a danger to everybody here. We need to get away!'

'We're covered in dust, so nobody out there looking for you will recognise you,' he pointed out, 'at least, not right away. And if we run, we'll automatically look suspicious. If we stay and help, even if only for a few minutes, we'll blend in.'

She nodded. 'You're right. If people can walk and aren't obviously seriously injured, let's get them outside. Someone will already have called the emergency services.' She glanced upwards. 'I'm not sure about the structural stability of this place. That ceiling might come down any minute. You look after people here – I'll check the toilets in case there's anyone trapped inside.'

As Bex moved away, Kieron moved towards the table that was between him and the counter. Two men in their twenties were picking themselves up and dusting themselves off.

'What the hell was that?' one of them shouted.

'Gas main?' the other one replied.

The first one shook his head. 'Terrorist bomb.'

'In Newcastle?'

Kieron gently steered them towards the door. 'Get to safety,' he said. 'Take anyone with you who looks like they can be moved.'

They nodded. Under other circumstances maybe they would have argued, asked him who he thought he was, but they meekly went along with his orders. Maybe that's how people reacted in situations like this, Kieron thought. Maybe they just wanted to be told what to do.

As the men helped a mother and her two children at the next table along, Kieron moved towards the counter. It still stood, but the explosion had rocked it back, tearing it loose from its connections with the floor. Steam from a pierced pipe on the ornate coffee machine drifted across, but he saw the red-haired barista sheltering beneath the flat surface where the coffees were placed to be picked up. She had curled herself into a ball, with her arms around her head. He knelt down and gently held her shoulders as he looked her over for any signs of injury.

'It's OK,' he said reassuringly. 'I don't think you're injured. Can you stand up?'

'What happened?' she asked shakily as she uncurled.

'I don't know,' he replied.

'I never did trust that machine,' she said. 'I told the manager, "Don't buy second-hand – it's a false economy." But would he listen?'

'I don't think it was the coffee machine, although frankly I wouldn't use it any more if I were you. I think it's had its day.' As he spoke he was leading her towards the door. She was hunched over and limping.

Bex had checked the toilets out and was moving parallel to him and the barista, half-supporting an old man with a cane. She glanced at Kieron and nodded.

Paramedics were already arriving on the scene. Maybe they'd already been nearby. They were setting up a triage area outside, where people could quickly be evaluated for any necessary treatment. Several police officers were running along the street towards the cafe.

Bex grabbed Kieron's shoulder and tugged. 'Time to go,' she muttered.

He turned back towards the red-haired barista. 'You'll be all right,' he said firmly. 'Go over there and get checked out.'

'Kieron,' she said, wonderingly. 'You were in here earlier. Two lattes. And this time it was a hot chocolate with all the trimmings.'

'And your name is Beth.' He smiled. 'Maybe I'll see you some time – in a different coffee shop.'

'Maybe.' She smiled hesitantly.

Bex pulled him away. 'Time for teenage hormones later,' she growled. 'We need to get out of here *now*.'

The street was chaotic, with walking wounded, first responders and confused onlookers. Kieron looked back over his shoulder as Bex pushed her way through the throng. Her car – the epicentre of the explosion – wasn't a car any more. It pretty much wasn't anything, except for a twisted abstract metal sculpture sitting on four melted piles of rubber that had been tyres.

'Is that – *was* that something to do with the threat assessment email I told you about?' he asked breathlessly as he tried to keep up with Bex. Somewhere in the distance he could hear sirens. Lots of sirens. 'Was it a *bomb*, or was it just, like, bad maintenance?'

'It seems like too much of a coincidence to be a coincidence,' she shouted over her shoulder. 'I need to read the message, see what it says. And no, cars don't just explode because you haven't been maintaining them properly. They explode because someone has done something to them.'

'Where are we going?'

'To the apartment. If whoever it was that planted the bomb in my car knows where the apartment is, they might try to do something to Bradley. I need to warn him.'

'Mobile?' Kieron asked.

Bex held up her hand. She was holding her phone. 'Funnily enough, I did think of that. I've been trying to get through to him, but the network is down. I can't get a signal.'

'The network is *down*? Like it's been jammed?' Kieron couldn't believe what he was hearing. This was *serious*.

Bex shook her head. 'More likely so many people are

trying to make calls that the network can't cope. It's flooded. It'll just be a temporary thing, but it means we're stuck with no comms for now. The same thing happens whenever a bomb goes off in a crowded city centre – the network is optimised for the average number of calls for that time of day, plus a margin. It's not set up for everyone being on the phone at the same time.'

'It happens on New Year's Eve too,' Kieron said. 'Or rather just after midnight, on New Year's Day. I've been at parties and tried to call Mum to wish her "Happy New Year", but it's taken me twenty minutes to actually get through.'

'You've been to New Year's Eve parties?'

'Hey – I get invited to parties. Sometimes.'

Bex held the mobile up to her ear again, then took it away, cursing under her breath. 'Still nothing. I'm worried.'

'I hate to tell you this,' Kieron said, 'but the apartment's probably half an hour's walk away. Or twenty minutes if you run. We're better off getting a taxi.'

'Chances are we'll be waiting longer than twenty minutes for it to arrive.'

'Have you got a better idea?' Kieron challenged.

'I have, as it happens.' Suddenly she diverted down a side street. Kieron skidded to a halt and followed her.

'That's not a short cut!' Kieron called.

Bex stopped by a parked car, looked around to see if anyone was watching, then turned her back on it and abruptly jerked her elbow backwards. The driver's side window shattered. Kieron braced himself, waiting for an alarm to blare out, but nothing happened. Reaching in, Bex unlocked the door.

'We only need it for a few minutes,' she said half-apologetically, as she opened the door and climbed in, brushing as much glass off the seat as she could manage. She raised her voice so Kieron could still hear her as, reluctantly, he went around to the passenger side. 'We'll abandon it near the apartment and I'll leave some cash in the glove box, OK?' She reached across and unlocked the door for him.

'I suppose,' he said, getting inside. 'Aren't we supposed to be the good guys?'

'We *are* the good guys,' she said. 'I'm not going to debate relative morality with you now, but borrowing a car is a lesser sin than letting a friend die, OK?'

'OK.'

Reaching beneath the dashboard, Bex pulled two wires sharply down from beneath the slot where the key would normally go.

'Why *do* they call it a glove box?' Kieron asked. 'I mean, who keeps gloves in there? Normally it's a pack of tissues, some coins, a couple of CDs and maybe, if you're lucky, some sweets that you forgot about.'

Bex brought the wires close together. A blue spark suddenly spat across between the bare metal ends and the motor sprang into life with a gruff roar.

'Tip for stealing cars,' she said, letting go of the wires. 'The modern ones have got engine-management systems, alarms and wireless key fobs, which mean the engine won't start if the key fob isn't inside the car. So always steal older cars. Much, much simpler.'

'I've been in stolen cars before,' he muttered. 'I know how it's done.'

Bex guided the car away from the kerb. 'And yet I'll bet you can't decline a single Latin verb. I worry about the youth of today.'

'Declining Latin verbs won't save my life,' Kieron pointed out. 'Or get me and Sam home from a New Year's Eve party when the buses have stopped running.'

'Fair point.'

She sped surely through the streets of Newcastle, not fast enough to trigger any speed cameras, but varying her speed so that traffic lights that were red up ahead of them turned green just as they got to the junction. Two police cars, an ambulance and a fire engine passed them by, heading in the opposite direction, blue lights flashing and sirens blaring. Probably heading for the cafe, and the wreckage of Bex's car.

Bex turned the wheel and the stolen car suddenly slewed across the road and neatly into a parking space barely larger than it was.

'Come on,' she said, getting out.

'You said you'd leave money in the glove box!'

'We need to get Bradley out first – and we might still need the car!'

Bex raced ahead, and Kieron followed as best he could, aware that his general lack of coordination, which had served him so badly on school sports days and in cross-country runs, was really holding him back. He so needed to get into shape.

At the corner, Bex paused. It looked like she was scanning

46

the street for threats or observers. 'Can't see anything,' she said as Kieron caught up.

He stared up at the apartment block in which Bex and Bradley lived – at least for the moment. He counted up and along, window by window, until he found the actual apartment. 'Me neither,' he said cautiously.

Bex had her mobile phone clamped to her ear. 'Still no signal,' she groaned. Her gaze followed his. 'We'll have to risk going –'

It seemed to Kieron that a dark shadow swept across the building. Before he could even wonder what it was, the window they were staring at suddenly smashed outwards with a *whoomph*! Orange and yellow flames flickered out like eager tongues, leaving black soot marks on the brickwork. As the falling glass fragments hit the pavement like frozen raindrops, Bex whispered, 'Oh no!' from beside him. Her face gleamed in the light of the fire.

Something screamed in the night – a cat maybe, or someone inside the building – but it didn't sound like any cat Kieron had ever heard. It didn't sound like anything *alive*.

He thought he heard a *hiss* from inside the apartment. The flames vanished, replaced by a mass of smoke that erupted from the glassless window.

'At least the sprinkler system kicked in,' she muttered. 'That's something, at least, but if Bradley was caught in the blast –'

'I wasn't,' a voice said from behind them.

They both whirled around. Bradley stood there, by the kerb. Sam was with him. They both looked pale and shocked.

'Why weren't you in the apartment?' Bex asked. She sounded almost *angry*.

'Was I supposed to be?'

'I thought you *were*!' she yelled.

Bradley looked up at the smoking remains of their apartment. 'Good thing I wasn't.'

'I asked Bradley if I could come over,' Sam said plaintively. 'I was at Kieron's place, and I didn't want to go home.' He looked at Kieron. 'Your mum was getting – well, she was talking to herself, and slurring her words, so I thought it was time to leave. I get enough of that at home.'

'When he got here,' Bradley interrupted, 'he asked if I had anything to eat or drink. Apparently the stuff in the fridge isn't palatable for teens, so we went to the corner shop to get some chicken nuggets and a bottle of something sweet and fizzy.' He waved a hand at the apartment block. 'And then we came back to *this*.'

'Did you leave the gas on?' Sam asked.

'That was no gas explosion,' Bex said. 'My car was blown up, just a few minutes ago.'

Bradley winced and nodded. 'I heard the sirens,' he said. 'You know what it's like – you hear sirens and the first thing you think is, I hope that's nobody I know. But in this case it was.' He glanced back over at the apartment block. People were spilling out of the front door and onto the street, looking shocked. 'At least with the sprinkler system the flames didn't spread. I'm hoping that nobody got hurt. Are *you* all right?'

'I was in the cafe with Kieron. There was a lot of damage, but I don't think anyone was killed or even badly injured.

Just cuts and bruises, and probably a lot of people in shock.'

Bradley stared at Bex. 'Someone out to get us?'

'I think lots of people are out to get us. The question is, how did they *find* us?' She closed her eyes for a moment and took a deep breath. 'Right – we're all OK. We're all safe. We need to get out of here – sit down somewhere and compare notes. And then work out what we do next.'

'There's a burger place about ten minutes' walk away,' Kieron offered. 'We could go there.'

They walked in silence, each one in their own little bubble of thoughts. For the second time that evening Kieron heard sirens behind him.

The 'burger place' was quite upmarket, closer to a restaurant. They sat down and perused the menus.

'Do you think –' Kieron started to say, but Bex held up a warning hand.

'Not until we've ordered,' she said. 'I don't want someone overhearing us.'

'I'm not sure I'm even hungry,' Kieron said quietly. 'Not after . . .' He shrugged.

Bradley patted him on the shoulder. 'First rule of this kind of work,' he said, 'always say yes to food. Sometimes you don't know where or when you'll be able to eat again. It's important to keep your strength up.'

'I'm not sure what to have,' Sam muttered. 'Do I even *like* blue cheese?'

'Take it from me, you don't,' Kieron said. 'Go for the pulled-pork burger with Jack Daniel's sauce. Mum bought it for me once. It's great.'

After they'd given their orders to the server, and after their drinks had arrived, Bex leaned forward and glanced at each of them in turn. 'I hate to be obvious about it,' she said, 'but someone is trying to kill us. At least, they're trying to kill Bradley and me. I think you two are safe.'

A sudden chill gripped Kieron's heart. It hadn't even *occurred* to him that he or Sam might be targets. Bex and Bradley had probably carried out a whole load of missions which might have made them enemies, and they were trying to expose a traitor in MI6 – which would expose *them* to a high level of risk – but he and Sam had worked with them twice. Maybe they *were* on the target list. And that meant –

He pulled his mobile out of his pocket at the same time Sam did his. They both accessed their contact numbers and dialled their mothers, staring across the table into each other's eyes. Kieron saw the panic in Sam's face, and guessed his own face had the same expression.

Kieron's mum's number rang and rang. He could feel his heart thudding hard in his chest, like a caged animal beating itself against the bars, trying to get out. 'Come *on*, come *on*,' he muttered.

From across the table he heard Sam say: 'Yeah, it's me . . . No, nothing's wrong. I just wanted to check you were OK . . . What, can't I get worried about you if I want to . . . ?'

Kieron's mum's phone was still ringing. Any second now it would switch to voicemail, and that would freak him out. In his head he saw their living room consumed by fire: curtains burning, plaster peeling from the walls, plastic picture frames melting and dripping down the walls.

'Look, I'm going,' Sam said. 'No, nothing's wrong. Bye . . . Yeah, bye.'

'H-hello?' Kieron's mum's voice. Thank God.

'Mum, it's me.'

'Kieron?'

'Yes, Mum.' He recognised the careful tone in her voice, the way she very precisely articulated her words. Too much wine. 'I just wanted to let you know there's been some kind of incident in town, but I'm all right.'

'That's . . . that's nice of you to let me know,' she said. 'Thank you. You're very thoughtful. You're the most thoughtful person I know.'

'OK, Mum. I've got to go.'

'Not like your father. He was the least thoughtful person I ever met.'

'Love you, Mum.'

'I've ordered that food online for you – and dishwasher tablets, and toilet paper. You won't run out of anything while I'm gone. And I got you a Blu-ray that's just come out as well. It's a horror-film thing. You like horror, don't you? I'm pretty sure you said you liked horror films.'

'Mum –'

'And I'm going to bring you a cup of tea in the morning, just before I leave, just so I can say goodbye.'

'Mum. I've got to go. Bye.'

He hung up before she could say anything else. He had a sudden vision of her still talking into a dead mobile, not realising he wasn't there any more. The pain that rose in his throat to choke him wasn't the same pain as the one when

51

he'd thought she might have been caught in an explosion meant for him. No, this was an older pain. A more familiar pain.

'She's all right,' he said, looking at Bex apologetically. 'Sorry, but I had to check. Do you think she's safe in the flat?'

Bex nodded. 'I think the attacks were meant to be simultaneous, or as near as they could get. If nothing's happened to her or to Sam's parents by now, it probably won't.'

'They're OK?' Bradley asked Sam.

'I wouldn't go that far,' Sam said, frowning, 'but nothing unexpected has happened.'

Bex opened her mouth to say something, but Bradley interrupted her: 'You said your car exploded?'

She nodded.

'But I know how careful you are. You always check for suspicious devices.'

'That's right,' Bex said. 'So how did they – whoever *they* are – manage to get one past me? And, while I think about it, why didn't it explode when I started the car? The usual thing would be to put a trembler switch in there so that the vibration of the engine would trigger the bomb, but that wasn't the case here.'

'A timer maybe?' Bradley suggested.

'Possible, but how would they know when to set it for? I'd only decided a few minutes before to drive to the cafe to meet Kieron. I suppose they could have set the timer to go off while the car was parked near the apartment, but what would be the point?'

Kieron watched the two of them bat facts and theories back and forth, like a cat watching a table-tennis match.

'The bomb could have been placed while you were parked outside the cafe,' Bradley observed. 'Maybe it went off by accident while they were placing it. Self-inflicted casualty.'

Bex shook her head. 'Too busy – they would have been seen. And besides –' she winced – 'I quickly scanned for any human remains around the car while we were there. I didn't see anything.'

'And then there's the apartment,' Bradley went on.

'Yes. How did they find it? We took care to cover our tracks perfectly.'

'And how on earth did they get inside, past all of our security, to place a bomb?'

'It's not possible.'

'So,' Bradley said heavily, 'we've got two impossible things – a car that couldn't have been booby-trapped, and an apartment that couldn't have been found or infiltrated. Where do we go from here?'

'The threat assessment?' Kieron offered.

Bex nodded. 'Good point.'

Bradley frowned. 'Threat assessment? Do I know about this? *Should* I know about this?'

Kieron opened his mouth to answer but Bex beat him to it. 'Kieron told me about it earlier, just before we met up. Apparently we've got an email through from the Threat Cell. I thought it was probably just a standard "Be careful out there, people – it's a dangerous world" thing, but I'm starting to reconsider now.'

Bradley held out his hand. 'Could I have the glasses please, Kieron? You did bring them, didn't you?'

Reluctantly Kieron delved into his rucksack. Pulling the ARCC glasses out, he handed them across.

Bradley slipped them on, his fingers lingering on the on button on the side. His hands began making precise little motions in the air in front of him, like a man conducting along to some piece of classical music only he could hear. 'Right – classified email inbox . . . quite a few general emails going to all agents . . . oh, Mrs Gibbons in Admin is retiring – they're organising a collection . . . no new missions for us . . . ah, there it is, right at the top: *Immediate Threat Assessment – Falcon Team*, from the Threat Cell . . .' A long pause, then: 'Oh. Oh, that's not good. In fact, that's bad.'

'Meaning?' Bex asked darkly.

'Bad, as in: the Threat Cell have intercepted some email traffic going through a server on the dark web. None of the criminals or terrorists who use that email server *know* it's been hacked – not yet anyway – but MI6 can see everything that goes through it. They've seen a message that mentions our names, so have alerted us.'

'Very considerate of them. A message from who, to who?'

'Difficult to tell. The sender and recipient are using code names, obviously. The "from" is someone claiming to be called Taskmaster –'

'Sounds like a supervillain in a comic,' Sam muttered.

'– and the "to" is called Asrael.'

'Those names mean nothing to me,' Bex said, shaking her head.

'Me neither.' Bradley's fingers kept moving. 'I'm looking up Taskmaster, but I can't see any other references. OK, let me try Asrael . . . Oh. That's *really* not good.'

'Bradley, you're killing me here!' Bex exclaimed.

'Bad choice of words,' Sam pointed out quietly.

Bex winced. 'Sorry.'

Bradley slipped the glasses off and put them on the table in front of him. His expression was as serious as Kieron had ever seen it. 'There are various references to Asrael. He – or she – is an assassin. Very new on the scene, apparently. Claims to be able to kill any target anywhere in the world, no matter how much protection they have.'

'That's quite a bold claim to make.'

'It is, which is worrying. This Asrael must be very confident. It's the kind of thing that comes back to bite you, the first time you fail.' He frowned. 'Which means that, now they *have* failed, they might try to correct their mistake.'

Bex drummed her fingers on the table. 'OK then – our working hypothesis is that this new assassin has been hired to kill us. There are three things we need to do: neutralise Asrael in any way we can; discover how Asrael managed to bomb the apartment and the car despite our stringent security precautions, and find out who hired Asrael so we can go after them.'

'I'd recommend two more things,' Bradley said seriously.

'Go on.'

'Firstly, and most importantly, we have to survive.'

Bex's lips twitched in a half-smile. 'I was kind of taking that as read.'

'And secondly, we have to tell someone in MI6 that Asrael has already found us.' He held up a hand to forestall Bex's reflexive protest. 'We know there's a traitor in the organisation, and obviously it might actually be that traitor who hired Asrael, but we can't act suspiciously. We have to do what we would do if we *didn't* know about the traitor, which in this case means notifying our employers. Also, we haven't got the time or the resources to do any forensic investigation of your car or the apartment. MI6 have.' He smiled. 'Ironically, the traitor in MI6 will have to do exactly what we're doing – pretend that nothing is wrong. So they'll be sending a forensic team down here straight away.'

'By which time we need to be gone,' Bex said. She thought for a moment. 'Anything else on Asrael? Anything at all that might help us track them down?'

'There is some email traffic suggesting that Asrael is arranging a demonstration for anyone who might want to take advantage of their services. In Venice apparently.'

'I hope your passport wasn't in the apartment.'

Bradley shook his head. 'No. Well, not all of them.'

Kieron felt as if a void had opened up in front of him. He'd known that Bex and Bradley would be leaving, but he'd hoped to have a few more days with them. Some time to hang out, even if he wasn't allowed to work with them any more. Now it looked like they were packing up and going within the next few hours.

'Asrael will know what we look like,' Bradley pointed out. 'They must do, in order to have tracked us down and tried to kill us. Surely they'll recognise us if we try and infiltrate this demonstration.'

Bex thought for a moment. 'We can both dye our hair, and make some small changes to our appearance with make-up. They won't be expecting us, and there must be tens of thousands of people who look enough like us that we won't be spotted.'

'We need to come with you,' Kieron blurted, surprising himself.

'You can't.' Bex's voice was firm.

'We must.' His thoughts were racing, but he managed to grab a couple of relevant conclusions as they whizzed past. 'Maybe Sam and I aren't targets for this Asrael, but we're a link to you. If the traitor in MI6 hired Asrael to kill you, and if you disappear, then one or both of them are going to come after us, on the assumption that we'll know where you've gone. We might be tortured. We'll only be safe if we go with you.'

Bex looked over at Bradley. He shrugged. 'Can't fault the logic,' he said.

Sighing, Bex nodded. 'OK then. It looks like the team is on the road. We're all going to Venice!'

After a slight pause Sam put up his hand. 'Where exactly *is* Venice?'

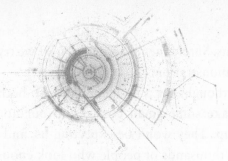

CHAPTER FOUR

'Venice is a city in Italy,' Bradley said. 'Very historical; very famous. For many hundreds of years it was a major trading port on the Mediterranean Sea, largely because of its advantageous geographical position. It was perfectly placed between the political powers of Western Europe and the various empires of the East. Huge amounts of trade flowed through it, and for over five hundred years it was an important financial centre. These days, of course, it's more of a historical curiosity and a holiday destination for arts students and romantic couples because it's so beautiful and contains so many works of art. Although it's a city, it's actually built over one hundred and eighteen separate small islands, linked together by four hundred bridges. Incredible architecture.'

'Thank you, Bradleypedia,' Bex murmured.

He gazed at the startled faces around the table. 'What?' He tapped the ARCC glasses. 'You think I always have to use these things in order to get information? I do actually *know* stuff, you know.'

'Have you ever been there?' Bex asked. 'Local knowledge is useful.'

'A few years back.' He smiled, obviously remembering happy times. 'It was before I went to college, long before I met you. I'd entered an essay competition for school kids run by one of the big banks, where the authors of the top fifty essays won a two-week coach tour around Europe, accompanied and completely paid for. Believe it or not, I was one of those fifty winners. I got to see Paris, Munich, Brussels, Geneva, Lake Lucerne and Venice in the company of forty-nine other teenagers. We stayed in the best hotels, we discovered French wine and German beer, we fell in love, and we all had the time of our lives. Incredible.' He shook his head. 'What were they thinking, sending fifty hormonal teenagers around Europe? Madness!'

'Sounds like a nightmare,' Kieron said, glancing at Sam. 'Unless all the other kids were emos and greebs of course. Then it might be fun.'

'Yeah, except that we'd all stay in our hotel rooms, so there'd be no point in taking us round Europe,' Sam pointed out. He glanced at Bradley. 'What was your essay on?' he asked curiously.

Bradley frowned. 'As far as I remember, it was about how worldwide computer connectivity would erase all secrets and give everyone access to all information all the time.' He shook his head, a half-smile on his face. 'How naive I was back then.'

'Right,' Bex said firmly, slapping her hand on the table, 'fun though this is, we have things to do. Bradley, you're in charge of making the hotel and travel arrangements, given you have prior knowledge of the location.' A thought struck her and she frowned. 'Kieron and Sam – we're going to have to come up with a cover story for the two of you to tell your families, and it's going to have to be convincing. I don't think they're going to believe that you've won a competition to travel to Venice on an all-expenses-paid and fully accompanied cultural holiday – not after Albuquerque. That kind of thing only works once.'

'Actually,' Kieron said, 'I don't think we need to, this time.' He glanced around, looking uncomfortable. 'My mum's away on some course for the next few days, so I'm going to be in the flat by myself anyway. All we have to do is ask Sam's mum and dad if he can come and stay with me to keep me company. As far as they're both concerned, we'll spend all our time in my bedroom, gaming.'

'That's brilliant!' Sam said. 'Hey, I know – if we take one of the posters off your wall, we can stick it up in the hotel, so if we make a video call to them they'll see it behind us and assume we're in your room!'

'Good thinking,' Bex said, impressed. Then she noticed that rather than the excitement she would have anticipated at the prospect of another secret mission, Kieron's face had settled into a scowl.

Bradley had obviously noticed as well. 'Kieron, is everything all right?' he asked.

'Yeah, fine,' he said, shrugging. He didn't look at her.

'His mum's been fired,' Sam said baldly. 'He found out earlier. That's what the course is for – it's helping her to find another job.'

'Cheers, mate,' Kieron muttered, staring at the table. 'Way to tell everyone.'

Bradley reached out and put a hand on Kieron's arm. 'I'm really sorry, Kieron. I had no idea.'

He shrugged as if it was no big deal, but he didn't pull his arm away. 'I'm sure she'll be all right,' he said. 'She's got, you know, skills. There'll be another job out there for her. That's what she said anyway. And it's a hard life, and nobody does you any favours. She said that as well.'

'I'll take a look around the Internet, using these,' Bradley slid the ARCC glasses back on. 'I can access a lot of member-only recruitment sites, and I can also look for any jobs locally that haven't been advertised yet but are lurking on company websites waiting to be released. I'll let you know if I find anything.' A thought obviously struck him, and he added, 'If she's got a CV and you can get it to me, I can submit it directly for her. That would be a surprise, if she got a job offer without even realising she'd applied for it.'

'Yeah,' Kieron said, 'she'll just think she sent the CV in while she was drunk.' He sighed and ran a hand through his long black hair. 'Sorry – it's been a difficult day, what with finding out she'd lost her job, getting bombed in a cafe and thinking –' he glanced briefly at Bex – 'well, you know.'

She nodded. 'That's a conversation for another time, I think. Events have moved on.'

'Are you guys going to be OK to pay for this Venice trip?' Sam asked.

Bex flashed him a quick smile to silently thank him for changing the subject.

'We've been paid for the Mumbai mission *and* Albuquerque,' Bradley said. 'Bonuses as well, for the unexpected danger level. We're actually quite flush at the moment, so don't worry about that.' Bex noticed that while he was talking he seemed to be staring off into the depths of the restaurant and his fingers were moving, making small gestures in the air. He was using the ARCC glasses. 'Right – when do you want to go? If you trust me to choose a decent hotel I'll go for the Danieli – it's right in the centre, virtually on St Mark's Square, and right next to where the waterbuses dock so it's a good base for getting around the city. The building is over five hundred years old. Harrison Ford and Steven Spielberg have both stayed there, among other famous people.' His lips quirked in a half-smile. 'Actually, it's where *we* stayed when we were on the tour of Europe. I remember we broke one of their antique tables while we were playing around in the lobby. Happy days.'

'Go back,' Sam said. 'Waterbuses?'

Bradley nodded. 'Yeah – apart from walking, it's the main way of getting around Venice. I mentioned the islands – well, basically, between them are a whole series of canals, some of them narrow, some pretty wide. There are virtually no roads at all. Most of the buildings look out onto a canal, and the locals use waterbuses to get around. They're called *vaporetti*.' His eyes focused back onto the here-and-now, rather than the rarefied virtual data spaces he'd been looking at. 'You guys really should make the most of this trip,' he said, glancing from Kieron to Sam. 'After all, within your lifetimes Venice might cease to exist.'

Bex knew what he was talking about, but his casual statement came as a bit of a bombshell to the boys, judging by the expressions on their faces. 'Why?' Kieron asked uncertainly. 'What's going to happen to it?'

'The city is gradually sinking,' Bradley explained. 'The actual ground underneath the buildings is mainly sand and mud saturated with water, and the buildings are constructed on closely spaced wooden piles set into the mud – mostly buried tree trunks. The weight of the buildings is gradually pushing the piles downwards, and rising sea levels caused by global warming aren't helping.' He smiled reassuringly. 'It's all right – Venice isn't actually going to sink while we're there.'

Sam and Kieron exchanged disbelieving glances.

'What's our cover?' Bradley continued. 'In Albuquerque Kieron was a teenage tech wizard, as I recall, and you were his personal assistant. Is that still going to work, or shall we try something else? We can't go under our own names, obviously.'

'Maybe,' Bex said, thinking as she spoke, 'we should go as a family – but we'd need to create fake identities and get passports and suchlike created.'

'A family?' Bradley glanced at the boys, then at Bex. 'If they're our sons, then we'd have been about ten when they were born. That's just creepy.'

Bex nodded. He had a point. 'Maybe we're fostering. Or maybe we're their older brother and sister – our parents are dead, and we're responsible for them. There – that's a good cover story. You can get the documentation pretty quickly, can't you?'

63

He nodded. 'By tomorrow. I've already got photographs of these two from the Albuquerque paperwork. I'll use the same details to make the travel arrangements as well. Are you happy that I go ahead?'

Bex nodded. 'Go for it.'

Sam put his hand up eagerly. 'Ooh – ooh! Do I get to choose my own name? Can I be, like, something from a game? Dutch, or Rocky, or something like that? Something that sounds like a computer-game hero.'

'No,' Bex said before Bradley could respond, 'absolutely not. We're meant to be undercover. No names that draw attention to ourselves, OK? We need basic, generic, absolutely *ordinary* names. Names that don't attract any attention. Do we understand each other?'

'I suppose.' Sam subsided back into his chair. 'Just, not Dwayne, OK? Or Brian.' He thought for a moment. 'Or Kevin. Or –'

'Yeah, we get the picture. Bradley – choose names that these two sensitive snowflakes will actually be able to say out loud without blushing, OK?'

'Understood. Leave it with me.' He gave a little half-shrug, looking strangely embarrassed. 'My middle name is Bernard. It's a family thing. I understand how names are important.'

'And you two –' Bex said firmly to Kieron and Sam – 'don't start thinking this is going to be some kind of undercover adventure. You're just coming along so we can keep you safe. You're not taking any part in our mission, OK. You're just going to stay on the sidelines this time. Do you understand me?'

Kieron and Sam both stared right at her. Their heads were

so still, so rigid, that she had the feeling they desperately wanted to look at each other but didn't dare.

'Stay on the sidelines,' Kieron parroted, 'while you track down an international assassin demonstrating their skills in front of an audience of potential clients? We can do that. Can't we, Sam?'

'We can certainly do that.' Sam nodded vigorously.

'Right,' Bex said, checking her watch, 'it's getting late, and we've got arrangements to make. Kieron – is your mum heading off first thing tomorrow for her course?'

'As far as I know.'

'Then pack after she's gone and we'll pick you up at lunchtime. Sam – can you clear things with your mum and dad and get to Kieron's by tomorrow lunchtime?'

'Yeah, no problem.'

'Right – pack light, but assume it's going to be cold and wet. We'll bring passports and tickets and stuff.' She stared hard at both of them, one after the other. 'Pack toothbrushes and spare underwear. I know what you kids are like. Now – off you go. I need to talk to Bradley.'

After the two boys had gone, chatting excitedly, Bex shook her head and sighed. 'This is all going to go so wrong. Do you ever get the feeling that your life is on rails, and you're just speeding along them, unable to change direction? That you're fated to end up in the same place no matter what choices you try to make?'

Bradley smiled. 'No,' he said. 'I've always felt the opposite – that I'm sitting on the edge of things, watching them happen to other people.' He reached across the table to touch her arm, the same way that he'd touched Kieron's arm in reassurance earlier. 'They'll be all right. They know the score. We'll keep them out of harm's way, we'll track down this Asrael person and we'll remove the threat to all our lives. And then the kids will go one way and we'll go another.'

'Ye-es,' she said, feeling herself wincing internally. 'That bit about "removing the threat to all our lives" once we've tracked Asrael down – we haven't really thought that bit through properly, have we? That could be the tricky part.'

'Well, considering the fact that half an hour ago we'd never heard of Asrael and had no intention of going to Venice tomorrow, I'd say we've come up with a large chunk of the plan pretty quickly. We can fill in the details later.' He took the ARCC glasses off and slipped them into a pocket. 'Now, I need to get to work on those passports, and book all of our travel, and you need to find an all-night supermarket and get us both several changes of clothes, as well as toiletries and stuff. As we can't use the apartment, I'd suggest we find a nearby hotel for the night and use that as a base. Are you up for that?'

'I am.' She leaned back in her chair and let out a slow breath. 'But maybe, just maybe, we could get some dessert first.'

They booked two rooms in a hotel that catered to business clients, in the city for one or two nights. After making all the necessary purchases, Bex had a shower to relax herself before getting into bed. As she washed her hair, she found little flecks of glass and metal in it, remnants of the explosions.

The water sluicing down to the drain was dirtier than she'd expected, and it took a few moments before she realised that it was the residue of dust and smoke from the explosions. She felt her stomach twinge and a shudder run through her as her brain processed the fact that she'd been just metres away from possible death twice today, and that she'd put Kieron at risk.

She suppressed the feeling ruthlessly. She was getting good at that.

Once in bed, she checked the news on her tablet. Both explosions were being reported, but nobody seemed to be sure whether they were terrorist incidents or accidents. Fortunately nobody had been killed, or even badly hurt. That at least made her feel better, and she managed to get to sleep quickly.

The next day passed in a blur. She and Bradley got together for breakfast and compared notes, each checking that the other hadn't had second thoughts about the mission. Neither of them had, so they spent a few hours restyling and dyeing their hair and making some subtle changes to the shapes of their faces with make-up and with rubber inserts that went between their cheeks and their teeth. Once Bex was happy with the way they looked, she hired a car to get them from Newcastle to Manchester, stopping at Kieron's house to pick him and Sam up. The boys were virtually twitching with excitement, and Bex had to stop herself from catching Bradley's eye, in case they both burst out laughing.

Each boy had a small rucksack with their clothes in, and Bex and Bradley had carry-on bags only. That meant they could avoid having to wait for their luggage to appear on the conveyor belt after the flight. It saved time, and Bex was a big fan of taking only what was absolutely necessary and buying whatever else you needed at your destination.

Bex drove the car, while Bradley handed each boy his passport.

'Kieron – you're Ryan Drewe, OK? Memorise that name. Keep repeating it in your head until you're completely comfortable with it. Sam, you're Craig – Craig Drewe. Do the same as Kieron. Make sure you call each other by your fake names from now on, even if you think no one's listening.'

'What about you two?' Kieron asked. 'What do we call you?' He frowned. 'You look different, by the way. I mean, I know it's you, but it's *not* you, if you know what I mean.'

'Thank you. I'm not going to confuse things by telling you that now – I don't want you to have too many names floating around in your heads. I'll let you know later.'

'What are our names?' Bex whispered as the boys in the back of the car practised calling each other by their new names.

'I'm Tom and you're Chloe.'

'Chloe and Tom Drewe. Check.'

During the hour or so they spent in the departure lounge, Bradley handed each of the boys a black-and-white map of Venice he'd printed off. 'Study them,' he said sternly. 'Any good agent familiarises himself – or herself – with the place they're going. Memorise the general shape of Venice, and the main canals, bridges and walks. I've marked our hotel, so you can orientate yourselves.'

'That was good,' Bex said quietly as he turned back to her. 'Do you have coloured pencils to give them as well, so they can colour them in?'

'Don't be sarcastic,' he replied. 'I've got a map for you too.'

The flight took off on time, mid-afternoon, and it seemed as if they were barely airborne before they were coming into land at Brussels Airport, where they had to change flights. The change-over was tight, but they made it with a few minutes to spare. Again, there was little time to do anything before they were landing at Venice's Marco Polo Airport.

'Are we actually in Venice now?' Kieron asked, looking around as they left the arrivals area and emerged into the late-afternoon Italian sunlight. The weather was cloudy and warm, but not uncomfortable, and the landscape beyond the airport building looked unremarkable, not that different from what you'd see outside any medium-sized airport: roads, car parks, taxis arriving and leaving.

'We're about five miles from the city,' Bradley said, looking around. 'We could get a bus, but we're not going to.'

'Taxi,' Kieron said knowingly to Sam.

'Did I mention that Venice is built on a hundred and eighteen islands separated by canals?' Bradley asked. 'There are no roads. No roads means we can't get a taxi there. If we took the bus then we'd have to get off at the bus station and get a water taxi to St Mark's Square. Fortunately, there's a better and much more scenic way to get there. Follow me.'

He led the way along a covered concrete walkway, past a number of frazzled-looking tourists with suitcases and shoulder bags. After a few minutes they arrived in an open area that looked like a small artificial harbour. Several boats bobbed on the grey water, taking on or letting off passengers. They were broad, with flat roofs and black hulls, and a kind-of conservatory-like structure taking up the back half of the deck, inside which were rows of seats. Wide windows provided a perfect view for everyone. The front third of the deck was open, with a canopy over it, allowing even better views.

'We'll take a *vaporetto*,' Bradley announced.

Sam frowned. 'I thought you said they were called *vaporetti*.'

'Nice to see you were listening. *Vaporetto* is the singular; *vaporetti* is the plural. It's Italian.'

'Oh. OK.'

They managed to get four seats on the front deck, out in the open. The boys stood up and pushed themselves right into the sharp part of the boat's bow. By the time the boat left the dock it was full.

The boat chugged steadily out of the harbour and into the choppier open lagoon, as it presumably had thousands of times before and would thousands more times. The almost-bored attitude of the crew was a perfect counterpoint to the eager excitement of the tourists. They took a direct line across the lagoon towards the dark mass of low buildings that sat on the horizon ahead of them, linked to the Italian mainland by a long causeway. As they got closer, and as Bex felt her own excitement rise, she could see that what had seemed to be a huge block was actually pierced at intervals by openings, into and out of which many boats were making their way. These, she thought, must be the openings of the fabled canals.

The *vaporetto* they were on headed for the widest of the openings. One moment they were on a wide lagoon, and the next they had plunged into the city itself. Bex stared around her in childish wonder, amazed at the way the buildings just *emerged* from the water, waves lapping against their ancient walls or right up to the footpaths that ran along their sides. No two buildings were quite the same, although they all followed the same general plan: they were *old*, three or four storeys tall, had high windows with wooden shutters and most of them had balconies where the occupants could sit and enjoy a glass of prosecco while the sun went down. Every few hundred metres smaller canals split off the main one, heading left or right, with footbridges curving over the water.

No cars. No mopeds. No bicycles. It was strangely magical, like a fantasy land where different rules applied.

But there *were* gondolas – long black boats with high bows, propelled by men standing at the back with long oars which they waved back and forth through the water, effectively *pushing* the gondolas along. 'Sculling', it was called – she remembered it from her Cambridge days. Each gondola contained a couple of camera-toting tourists, who were presumably paying extortionate amounts for the privilege of using this historical means of travel and looked vaguely embarrassed.

More tourists thronged the footpaths and the bridges.

Bex could tell they were tourists because they were looking around with the same sense of wonder she felt, and because some of them held cameras while others, more technologically literate perhaps, recorded their entire perambulation on tablet computers held up in front of them so that the lenses could capture everything the people would have seen if they hadn't been holding their tablets in front of their faces. The locals – much fewer in number – moved through and around the tourists like predatory fish through a shoal of prey: not attacking, but perhaps marking out their next meal.

'It's . . . *incredible*,' Kieron said. He glanced over at her. 'Thanks for bringing us.'

'Hey, it was your idea. Just remember that we're here on business.'

'It's really *bae*!'

'Bae?'

He smiled boyishly. 'Beyond all else.'

The *vaporetto* wound its way along the length of the main canal, with the boys tracing its S-shaped route on the maps with their fingers, until it emerged into open water again. Ahead of them, in the distance, Bex saw several low-lying islands unconnected to the main bulk of Venice, but these seemed to be more like natural islands and had fewer buildings. Instead of heading towards any of the islands, the *vaporetto*'s path curved around until it was heading back towards the city. Within a few minutes it had docked at one of many short piers extending out from a long, straight stretch of quayside which bordered a huge square lined with colonnades and outdoor eating areas with tables and chairs. This was the famed St Mark's Square.

'The hotel is over there,' Bradley said, pointing. 'Just a short walk.'

Local men jostled at the quayside, offering to take the bags of the tourists disembarking via the short gangplank that had been placed between the *vaporetto* and dry land. If you could call it 'dry land'. Bradley waved them away casually but firmly, and led the way across the flagstones towards a particularly ornate building. Uniformed doormen opened the glass doors so they could enter a cool and impressively large lobby tiled in marble and panelled with wood.

Bradley turned to them. 'Remember your names,' he murmured. He looked at Kieron. 'You are . . . ?'

'Ryan. Ryan Drewe.'

'And you?'

'I'm Craig.'

'And we are . . . ?'

'Tom and Chloe.'

'Well done. Now – let's get our rooms.'

Although Kieron and Sam had gone through the experience of booking into a modern American hotel when the three of them had been in Albuquerque a few weeks before, Bex realised that the boys had never been in an old, impressive European hotel like *this* before. They were obviously cowed slightly by the grandeur, the uniforms and the formality. When they got to their rooms they were equally stunned.

'This furniture,' Sam asked, looking around, 'is it, like, antique?'

'Probably not,' Bex replied. 'Most likely it's mass-produced to look antique. But enjoy the experience anyway, and don't break anything.' She stared meaningfully at Bradley. 'Especially tables.'

'We could probably all do with a shower,' Bradley said. 'I know I could – air travel always makes me feel dirty. And I'm sure we all need some dinner, so let's meet down in the lobby in an hour and we'll discuss our next steps over some decent Italian food.'

Long experience had taught Bex the value of moving as little out of her luggage and into the room's various drawers and shelves as possible, just in case she had to make a quick exit, so she just put her toiletries bag in the bathroom, had a quick wash and changed her blouse to something less creased. She then sat on the bed and went through all the channels on the TV. It was one of her guilty pleasures – flicking through foreign TV stations, checking them out and getting a feel for the rhythms of the local language and the body language people used when they talked with each other. Italians, she knew from previous visits to the country, always looked as if whatever they were saying was the most important thing in the world. A discussion about whether or not to get a coffee somewhere could give the impression a knife fight was about to break out. She arrived in the lobby just as the boys got there. Bradley was already in the entrance of one of the three restaurants, getting them a table.

'Right,' she said in a low voice, as the waiter left with their order, 'let's recap. Somewhere in this complicated mess of a city, a new assassin code-named Asrael is setting up a demonstration of his or her talents. We've already been warned that we're on their target list, and so we need to get to them, find out who hired them and dissuade them from fulfilling the contract.'

'Simple,' Bradley said. He checked his watch. 'If we can clear that by tomorrow lunchtime we can spend the next few days being tourists.'

'Can I have a beer?' Sam asked.

'No. You can't even speak, or offer any suggestions, because this is Bradley and me carrying out this mission, not you. You're observers, and you should be grateful we're letting you sit at the same table as us while we're discussing what to do.'

'Understood.' Sam hesitated. 'Maybe just a small glass of wine?'

'Also no.'

'Actually,' Kieron said seriously, 'I have been thinking about this. Can I say something? Please?'

Bex sighed. 'All right then. Go ahead.'

'There's basically four ways you can find this Asrael person,' he said, nervously stretching and rucking up the white damask tablecloth with his fingers. 'The first is just to search for them, but you don't know what they look like so that's not going to work very well. The second is to search for where this demonstration is going to take place, but Venice is a complicated city so that's probably not going to work either. The third is to pretend to be potential customers looking for an assassin and somehow get yourselves invited to the demonstration. That's more *likely* to work, but you'd have to somehow present yourselves as the kind of people who might hire an assassin and then find out how the invitation process works. Possible, but difficult.' He paused, collecting his thoughts. 'The fourth way is that you don't search for Asrael – you search for Asrael's potential customers who are here in Venice and you follow *them* until you find out where the demonstration is taking place.'

Bradley nodded approvingly. 'That's actually very clever.'

'He got it from a video game,' Sam said dismissively. 'It's called Alphamind. He sucks at it though.'

'Doesn't matter.' Bradley held a fist up. Kieron, grinning, 'bumped' it. 'Whatever works.'

Bex smiled, enjoying the easy banter between them all. To anyone watching them from another table they would look like a real family, joking and talking, enjoying their holiday. The smile slipped from her face as she remembered why they were *actually* there. Because she and Bradley needed to save their own lives.

She let her gaze wander around the restaurant as Bradley and Kieron worked out the details of how Kieron's plan might work, with Sam throwing in the occasional sarcastic interjection. There were probably a hundred people, spread across forty tables. Given that this was one of the four best hotels in Venice, someone in the restaurant was in all likelihood a customer of Asrael's, looking to check out the new assassin's skills. The trouble was, try as she might, she couldn't spot who it might be. Everyone in here looked so normal.

But the more she thought about it, the more she realised that someone in that restaurant was prepared to pay money to have someone else killed.

And suddenly she didn't have much of an appetite.

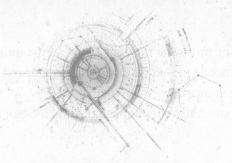

CHAPTER FIVE

Kieron woke up next morning not knowing quite where he was. He lay there, in the middle of the softest and largest bed he'd ever known, staring at a ceiling covered in ornate plaster decorations, thinking, Am I dead? Is this heaven? It's certainly not my bedroom.

There was a small chandelier hanging from the centre of the ceiling. An actual *chandelier*.

And then he heard Sam snoring, and he remembered. They were in Venice.

He got up and padded barefoot across the thick carpet to the window. The sun was already up, and he could see out onto the wide flagstoned expanse between the hotel and the waters of the lagoon. *Vaporetti* and gondolas bobbed up and down on the choppy water, which had been grey yesterday when they'd arrived but now seemed to glow softly green in the morning sunlight. Tourists passed by, and they all seemed to be smiling. Voices were raised in cheerful shouting, and somewhere he could hear someone singing an operatic aria. At least, he thought that's what it was. He wasn't an expert on anything pre-Marilyn Manson. For a few moments he was happy, knowing he was with friends, in an exciting foreign country, and that everything was OK with the world.

And then he remembered that his mother had lost her job, and he was only there to save his friends from death at the hands of an assassin, and his mood started to sour.

'Wassup?' Sam muttered from his bed.

'Nothing. Just watching stuff.'

'OK.' Sam rolled over and started snoring again.

After showering and dressing, Kieron wandered down to breakfast. He spotted Bex over in a corner of the restaurant.

'By a wall, near an exit,' he said as he sat beside her. 'Good choice.'

She smiled. 'Well remembered. Sleep well?'

'Perfectly . . . Where's Bradley?' Kieron asked.

'I don't know – I haven't seen him yet.' She frowned. 'It's odd, but we very rarely actually go on missions together. Usually I'm alone, sometimes undercover, usually uncomfortable, and he's somewhere else, sipping on a coffee and munching on a croissant, supporting me over the ARCC system. I have no real idea of what his routine is.'

'Maybe he's gone for a jog,' Kieron suggested. 'He looks like he keeps pretty fit.'

'Possibly. If so, I'm not looking forward to seeing him in Lycra.'

'So what's the plan for today?' Kieron asked.

'The plan,' Bex said primly, 'is that you and Sam go and see the sights while Bradley and I get to work.'

'And by "work", you mean, "try to identify" –' he looked

around cautiously – '"whoever might be in town for this demonstration thing".'

'That's right.'

'And how exactly do you intend doing that?'

Bex gestured to a passing waiter. 'Could we get another orange juice here, please?'

'*Si, signorina*,' the waiter said, bowing.

'I don't like orange juice,' Kieron protested. 'I'd rather have a fizzy drink.'

'Orange juice is good for you. It has vitamins. Fizzy drinks are bad. Trust me – not only am I the closest thing to a big sister you've got, on this trip I actually *am* your big sister.' She glanced around. 'The way we intend doing that is that I'll wander around the city with the ARCC glasses on, looking as many people in the face as I can without it looking weird, and Bradley will use his end of the system to do facial recognition. He'll run their faces through classified databases of known criminals and terrorists and see if any of them match.'

The waiter brought Kieron's orange juice.

'It would probably help,' Kieron said, after sipping it, 'if Sam and I went around with our mobiles and took lots of photographs of crowds, or groups of people sitting at outdoor restaurants, and emailed the photographs back every now and then. Bradley could check those against the databases as well. That way you get three times the coverage.' The taste of the orange juice suddenly hit him, tart and sweet at the same time, and he pursed his lips. 'Ooh, that's nice. That's *really* nice.'

'Is it "bae"?'

He stared at her. 'Just don't. Adults shouldn't use teenage slang. It's embarrassing.'

He looked up to see Bex staring at him. 'This whole thing would be so much simpler,' she said quietly after a while, 'if the two of you were stupid. That way we could just walk away with no regrets. The problem is, you're not stupid, either of you. You're very clever. And I know if we send you away, we'll be losing something.'

'But you're still going to send us away,' he said softly. 'You have to, don't you?'

'If anything were to happen to you – either of you –' She caught herself, and looked away. 'I would never forgive myself. And neither would Bradley.'

'Maybe,' he ventured carefully, 'I could apply for a job with MI6. Maybe that way we could keep working together.'

'It's not that simple. You'd have to be accepted first, and there's a general rule that anyone who desperately wants to be in MI6 probably shouldn't be allowed to be. And then, even if they *do* take you on, there's the training courses. Endless training courses. And even then, there's no guarantee you'd be an agent. You'd be more likely to be put in an analyst job, looking at intelligence reports, or just basic admin or computer stuff. And even if you *did* manage to get accepted as an agent, there's more training courses. Weapons, self-defence, survival, undercover skills, defensive and offensive driving . . . By the time you got through it all, I'd have retired.'

'And you went through all that?' he said, impressed.

She shook her head. 'No, Bradley and I created this ARCC system and MI6 headhunted us.' She shrugged. 'OK, we did some of the training – it was a condition of accepting these contracts we're on. But essentially we're freelance operatives. No sick pay, no pension scheme.'

He took another sip of juice. 'In that case,' he said brightly, as if the thought had only just occurred to him, 'you and Bradley could just *hire* me and Sam – take us on your books.'

'Yeah, dream on.'

Bradley joined them shortly after that, and then so did Sam. They had the continental breakfast, which seemed to be mainly slices of cured meat and cheeses, with fifteen different types of bread, brioche or croissant you could put them on or in. Sam actually did stack up alternating layers of cheese and meat in a bagel and carried it back to the table proudly.

'You're not going to be able to get that in your mouth,' Bradley said. He was eating muesli with yoghurt poured over it and blueberries sprinkled across the top.

Sam smiled. 'You want to bet?'

'He can unhinge his own jaw, like an anaconda, so he can open his mouth really wide,' Kieron said. 'I've seen him do it.' He glanced suspiciously at the towering cheese and meat sandwich. 'What's that on the top?'

'Pineapple,' Sam replied, sitting down. 'Fresh as well. They have slices.'

While they ate, Bex briefed Bradley on Kieron's suggestion. Reluctantly he nodded. 'Yeah, makes sense. It's a pretty low-risk thing for the boys to do, and it does increase our chances of identifying faces.' He looked over at Kieron. 'Clever thinking.'

'Are you going to stay here, at the hotel?' Sam asked.

Bradley shook his head. 'Actually I think I'm going to sit outside, in an open-air cafe. There's an Italian tradition of having a shot of brandy with your espresso – I think I might join in, just so I don't look out of place.'

'Excuse me,' Bex said, leaving the table. 'Back in a minute.'

Kieron and Bradley watched as Sam squashed his loaded bagel down with his hands until it was half the size it had been. Grinning, he picked it up and took a huge bite.

'You learn something every day,' Bradley said.

Bex returned within ten minutes, carrying a bag.

'What have you got?' Sam asked.

'Mobile phones – with a pay-as-you go SIM – no contract. We each get one. If we use our own mobile phones then we risk being tracked – especially if this Asrael realises we're here. This minimises the risk.' She handed them out. 'I've got a list here of each number, so what I suggest we do is each programme everyone else's number into your contacts. Obviously you can use the camera on the phone to take all the photographs you want.' She tapped the bag. 'I've also got memory cards in case you need more memory.'

Sam held his mobile up. His face was creased into a critical frown. 'Generic Androids? Couldn't we have gone for something a little more *upmarket*?'

'You have much to learn about undercover work,' Bex said.

Sam glanced at Kieron. 'Shouldn't she say that like Yoda?'

he asked. He went on in a grotesquely strangulated voice: '"About undercover work you have much to learn."'

Kieron did his best to suppress a snort of laughter, and looked back at Bex. She was scowling at the two of them.

'The point is,' she went on, 'to blend in, not to stand out. Right – everyone had enough to eat? You two have got the maps Bradley gave you? If not, the front desk can give you colour ones. I suggest we spend the next two hours looking around, then meet back here and recharge the phones while you two give Bradley all your images, and then we can head off and find somewhere for lunch.'

A thought struck Kieron and he put a hand up self-consciously. 'Er . . . what about money?'

'Money?' Bex repeated blankly.

'Well, there might be stuff we want to buy. A can of drink, maybe. Or chocolate. Could we, like, just have a little bit?'

Bex sighed and gazed sadly at Bradley. 'I knew it would come to this – now they want to be *paid* for what they do. They'll be wanting pension schemes next.'

Bradley opened his wallet and slipped out a couple of bank notes. 'Ten euros each. Don't spend it all at once, don't buy postcards to send home and don't buy tatty tourist gifts for your families. Remember – we're not even supposed to be here.'

As he took the money, Kieron happened to glance up at an elderly couple at a nearby table. He was terrible with ages, but they looked as if they might be in their seventies. They were smiling at him.

'It's lovely to see a family together on holiday,' the woman said. She was plump, with grey hair, glasses and a kind smile.

'Especially these days,' her husband said. At least Kieron assumed it was her husband. Maybe they were having an affair and had run off to Venice together – he had no way of knowing. 'You boys are very lucky, being able to visit a place like this. Make the most of it!'

Kieron didn't know what to say, so he just smiled an embarrassed half-smile and looked back to Bex. She was handing out the memory cards.

'Ready to go?' she asked, looking at him quizzically.

Leaving Bradley still sitting at the restaurant table mulling over his options, Kieron, Sam and Bex left the hotel together, emerging into bright but cold sunlight. Bex looked around.

'Right,' she said, 'this is the Riva degli Schiavoni. Kieron: you turn right and head around the corner. Cross St Mark's Square diagonally and find your way through the alleys and streets until you get to the Rialto Bridge. Follow signs saying "Ponte di Rialto". Sam, you turn left and head along the edge of the lagoon until you get bored, then turn left again and head inwards. Just wander around. Make sure you know where you are on your maps: if you don't, there will be signs. I'll go this way –' she pointed right – 'and head across to the Guggenheim Museum. Don't take photographs of individuals if you can help it – that'll just raise suspicions. Take pictures of buildings if you can, or bridges, but try and angle yourselves so that you get a lot of people in the shot and you can see their faces rather than the backs of their heads. If you get lost, either call me or ask someone the way to St Mark's Square. OK? Everyone happy? Go!' She waved a hand. 'Be free, my minions!'

Excitedly, Kieron set off as he was instructed, turning into the large open expanse of St Mark's Square. Ornate buildings and pillared walkways lined the edges, and pigeons strutted or fluttered everywhere. There was something very familiar about the place – he guessed it was like Trafalgar Square in London or Central Park in New York: everyone had seen bits of it on TV or in films.

He stopped at a massive church, in front of which crowds of tourists milled, taking photographs or just admiring the architecture. He took several photographs himself on his new mobile but, remembering Bex's instructions, he made it look as if he was photographing the other side of the square, where a large, red-brick tower stood, so he could capture their faces.

Would international criminals attending an assassin's secret demonstration really be wandering around taking in the sights, he wondered, then caught himself. Of course they would! They also had to eat meals and go to the toilet – just because they were criminals it didn't mean they weren't human. Venice was a tourist attraction for people the world over – of course they'd use any free time they had to look around.

Maybe someone at the church was one of the super-criminals who was in town for Asrael's demonstration. He glanced around, trying to make it look like he was staring at the buildings, but actually checking out the faces. What would an international criminal look like? He imagined someone like a character from a James Bond film: tall and thin, with a dark beard and wearing a black suit with a round collar. Nobody like that was visible: it was mainly young people in jeans or chinos or shorts, with T-shirts or polo shirts, and wearing trainers, or old people in comfortable clothes and leaning on sticks. Maybe the villains were all somewhere else. Maybe they had a tour group of their own, and they were all walking around the city together!

He laughed to himself and moved on.

Rather than go on across the square, as Bex had suggested, he decided to go into the church – partly because he guessed there would be lots of people in there, looking around, and partly because he was interested in seeing what it looked like on the inside anyway.

Outside, the façade of the church facing onto St Mark's Square consisted of five arched portals flanked by multicoloured marble columns. He moved past them and through a huge pair of bronze doors into the cool and dark interior – the 'narthex', he remembered from a project at school. Every church had a narthex. This one was huge, with arches soaring hundreds of metres above his head and joining up to form massive domes, each one of which seemed to be a mosaic of tiles of gold and bright colours. Dizzy, he had to look down at his feet, where he saw that the floor consisted of many hundreds of large marble slabs.

How long had it taken to build this? he wondered. How long had it taken to carve all the statues, and paint the various artworks? Hundreds of years of focus and dedicated effort. How much would it cost to rebuild it these days? Probably more money than any country could afford to spend. And what better use could the money it originally cost to build have been put to – relieving poverty, perhaps?

He spent a while admiring the way the arches led into the domes in sweeping curves. The architectural knowledge it must have taken to be sure that the domes wouldn't fall in amazed him. He was studying engineering at school, reluctantly, but now, suddenly, he could see what it was all for. He could imagine how the shapes of the arches and the domes could be represented by equations, and how the equations would *show* if it was safe. It wasn't like he suddenly *understood* everything, but he could see *how* it could be understood.

After about half an hour he felt like he'd taken photographs of every person in the place, twice, so he walked out of the church into the open air and headed across the square to the entrance to an alleyway that led off from one corner. The colonnaded side of the square leading there was lined with shops, and Kieron stopped to browse the windows. These were *expensive* shops, and the prices on the tickets were enough to make him draw in his breath sharply. Even though they were in euros, the euro and the pound were more or less equivalent – at least that's what Bex had told them – and there were pairs of shoes here that cost more than his mum made in a month, or that he could ever expect to get in pocket money in a year! And pens – old-style fountain pens – costing more than a week's groceries. Masks as well: shops selling nothing but masks. Some of them were cheap, plain white plastic ones that simply covered the face anonymously, but others were extravagant affairs made out of varnished leather, with massive beak-like noses and exaggerated foreheads. Why would there be mask shops in Venice?

Heading down the alley, he found himself passing a strange, eclectic mixture of clothes shops, food shops and shops selling glass plates and glass-handled cutlery. The smell of roasting garlic and tomatoes drifted into his nostrils at every turn. And so many people! He kept having to move to one side to avoid them, or detour around groups of tourists who had stopped to look at something: a carving, a statue, a fountain or just a crumbling patch of old bricks.

Kieron had once heard Sam say, about some Shakespeare play they'd been reading in English class, 'This thing is chock-full of quotes!' He was beginning to feel the same way about Venice: it was full of history, all stuck together randomly.

He spent the next forty-five minutes or so just wandering, confident in the knowledge that he had a map and a mobile phone if he got into trouble. He passed through squares, past churches and houses and restaurants, across tiny arched bridges and along the footpaths beside canals. And he was almost never alone – there were people everywhere, staring around in wonder and taking incessant photographs. The only time he *was* alone was in a small square with an ancient fountain in the centre, but as he crossed it he realised that several cats, lounging on the steps around the fountain, were watching his progress.

Every now and then he even saw people wearing masks like the ones he had seen in the shop. They wore robes as well: long black or white robes reaching down to the ground. And strange hats with three peaks. There were usually two or three of them together, and they were always standing posing for tourists to take photographs. This was just like a pantomime.

The people wearing masks made him feel uneasy. He had a feeling they were just part of the whole Venice 'experience', some reference back to its ancient history, but given that he was supposed to be searching for potential criminals or terrorists, he found it disconcerting that some people were actually hiding their identities.

Just when he thought he was completely lost, he emerged from a narrow alleyway onto a wide canal. He thought it might be the one that the *vaporetto* from the airport had taken to get through the centre of Venice to St Mark's Square. Ahead of him, a large and ornate stone bridge swept up and across the canal. Unlike any of the other bridges he'd seen, it was covered by a stone roof. And it looked old: so old that the stones seemed to have gradually been worn away by centuries of rain.

This was probably the Ponte di Rialto: it seemed like a good bet.

Still taking photographs as he went, he climbed the ramp up to the middle section, then descended to the other side. It was wide enough that there were shops on either side, and at both ends were stalls selling fruits and vegetables.

The bit of Venice on the other side of the bridge had a different 'feel' to it: more upmarket, more sophisticated. Kieron chose left-hand alleys whenever he could, trying to direct his path back towards the big canal. When he got to its side again he couldn't see any other bridges across its width, so he walked back alongside the canal to the Rialto Bridge again, and from there he gradually retraced his steps, with several diversions, back to St Mark's Square.

He headed towards the Hotel Danieli with a sense of accomplishment. He'd found his way around a strange city, by himself! At least, that's what he thought, until he realised he was lost. He had a feeling he'd overshot somehow, and ended up in an area he wasn't familiar with. He found himself on a bridge, staring along the flat, cliff-like walls of the buildings on either side of the water, looking at another bridge that crossed the canal further down. This bridge, however, was entirely encased in stone: a walkway from one side to the other with stone scrolls on top, stone masks carved into the arch underneath, and only two trellised windows through which whoever was on the bridge could see out.

'It's called the Bridge of Sighs,' said a voice.

He turned his head. A woman stood beside him, probably only slightly older than Bex. She had a rucksack on her back, a bandana around her neck and khaki shirt and shorts. She seemed to be shortsighted: the glasses perched on her nose had very thick lenses, and she peered through them. She looked like a Girl Guide leader.

'Why do they call it that?' he asked, intrigued.

'Because it connects the interrogation rooms in the Doge's Palace to the cells in the prison on the other side of the canal. The view from those windows was the last view of the city that convicts saw before their imprisonment.' She smiled.

'It was supposed that prisoners would sigh at their final glimpse of the beauty outside before being taken down to their cells, and never seeing the light of day again.'

'Wow,' Kieron said. It was all he could come up with.

'It's just a pretty story invented by Lord Byron, the poet,' the woman added. 'The days of inquisitions, torture and summary executions were long over by the time the bridge was built, five hundred or so years ago.'

He glanced back at the bridge. 'Five *hundred* years? And it's still in one piece? It hasn't fallen into the canal?'

'They knew how to build things properly in those days.'

'Can you point me back towards St Mark's Square?' he asked.

She gestured in the direction he'd been crossing. 'It's literally two minutes away, that way,' she said.

'Thanks.' He smiled his gratitude, and left.

When he arrived back at the hotel, he found Bradley sitting outside with a pastry, a large coffee and a small glass of transparent liquid on the table in front of him. He turned to face Kieron through the ARCC glasses, but Kieron had worn those glasses himself, for long periods of time, and he wasn't entirely sure whether Bradley was seeing him, or was looking at something visible only in the glasses, or both – looking *through* something visible only in the glasses at Kieron.

'Hi,' Kieron said uncertainly. 'Can I sit down?'

'Go ahead,' Bradley said. 'Have you had fun?'

'It's an incredible place,' Kieron said honestly. 'It's so busy, and so old. Do people actually live here as well, or is it just like a kind of historical theme park?'

Bradley laughed. 'That's actually a really good description, but no, people actually live here. I've sometimes dreamed that if I make enough money I'd buy a place here and retire in comfort, just sitting around drinking grappa and eating pastries.'

'Even though it's sinking?'

Bradley shrugged. 'That could be a problem from an insurance point of view. Maybe I should try Miami instead.'

'What about sinkholes? I saw a documentary about it. Holes just opening up in the ground and swallowing houses, cars, whatever.'

'Fair point. How about Japan?'

'Earthquakes and volcanoes.'

Bradley sighed. 'Looks like I'm stuck in England then.'

Kieron put his new phone on the table. 'Here's the photos I've taken. Do you want me to take the memory card out?'

'Don't worry.' Bradley waved his hands in the air for a few seconds. 'Right – I've forced a Bluetooth connection, and I'm downloading the photographs now. And while I'm at it – yes, I've also linked your old mobile number to this one, so any phone calls to you just transfer across automatically, and any phone calls you make or texts you send will look like they came from it.' He slid the phone back across the table. 'Right – there you go.'

'Where are the others?' Kieron asked, looking around.

'Not back yet.'

'OK. Is it all right if I just go for a wander? I'd like to see a bit more of this place while I've got the chance.'

'That's fine.' Bradley sounded like he was already half distracted, and his fingers were still moving. 'Be back in half an hour?'

'OK.'

Bradley pointed vaguely towards where the *vaporetti* were arriving and leaving. 'If you go that way you'll find Harry's Bar. Ernest Hemingway used to drink there. So did Charlie Chaplin, Orson Welles and Alfred Hitchcock.'

'I don't know any of those names. Except for Charlie Chaplin. Isn't he a comedian?'

Bradley sighed. 'Kim Kardashian?'

'Yes, I've heard of *her*,' Kieron said dismissively. 'I don't care where she drinks, though.'

He set off in the direction Bradley had indicated. A little way along the Riva degli Schiavoni he came across a large group of tourists gathered around four street musicians, three of whom had steel drums slung around their necks, while the fourth had a drum. They were playing something with a pounding rhythm and a strong melody – Kieron thought he recognised it as the theme from some American TV show he'd caught on cable. He stopped for a few minutes, listening with his eyes closed, feeling the pulse of the drum vibrating through the ground and up into his body through his feet.

'It's good, isn't it?' someone said beside him in an accented voice. He opened his eyes and turned his head. A girl stood by his side. She looked to be about the same age as him, but her hair was so blonde it was almost white.

'It is,' he said honestly. He smiled shyly.

'It makes me want to dance.'

'Not me. I don't dance.'

She nodded, smiling. 'That's sensible. Boys shouldn't dance. They have no sense of rhythm. They just look stupid, but they don't know it.'

'At least I know how stupid I look,' Kieron said.

'You don't look stupid now,' the girl said. 'Just don't dance and ruin it.'

Kieron felt slightly nervous. Excluding Bex, it had been a long time since he'd talked with a girl for this long. *To* a girl, yes, but that was just him blabbing. Real conversations didn't happen very often. 'So, are you from around here, or are you a visitor like me?'

She laughed. 'Do I sound Italian?'

'No,' he replied. Without thinking, he went on: 'Your accent sounds beautiful though.'

Internally he cringed at the stupidity of the comment, but the girl's eyes widened in surprise and pleasure. 'Thank you. I am from Norway. My name is Katrin.'

'Are you with your family?'

'With my sisters.' She took a step back and waved a hand to two girls on her other side. They had very pale blonde hair too, but no freckles. 'This is Eva, and Hekla.'

'Hi.' Kieron nodded and smiled. 'I'm Kieron.'

'Are you here with *your* family?' one of the girls asked; Kieron wasn't sure if it was Eva or Hekla.

'No.' He caught himself, remembering the cover story that Bex and Bradley had drilled into him. 'Well, yes – my two brothers and my sister. We're staying at the Hotel Danieli.'

'Ah.' Katrin nodded. 'So are we!'

'Perhaps we could look around Venice together?' Kieron blurted nervously, before he could stop himself.

Instead of sneering and turning away, Katrin smiled. 'That would be nice.'

The warm tingle of mixed triumph and happiness that ran like lightning through Kieron's body suddenly got extinguished by the sound of his mobile. He knew it was his mobile because it vibrated as well. Unfortunately, the ring tone it had been set to was the theme from the kids' TV series *Thomas the Tank Engine*. Bradley's idea of a joke? He just hoped the girls took it to be ironic, rather than a declaration of his taste. 'Sorry – I have to get this.'

'Sure,' Katrin said.

Keiron answered the phone. 'Yes?'

'*It's Bex. Can you come back now? We need to have a conference.*'

'OK.' Shutting it off, he turned to Katrin. 'Sorry – I need to go. Maybe I'll see you in the hotel lobby later?'

Katrin smiled, and Kieron thought his heart might actually melt. 'That would be nice,' she said.

The warm glow inside him lasted all the way back to the hotel.

CHAPTER SIX

Bex had located a decent-looking trattoria during her exploration of the city. It had a small frontage on a corner overlooking one of the canals, but it went back for a long distance and had various arched areas off to the left and right. Although it was lunchtime, most of the tables were unoccupied and the waiters stood around looking bored. The four of them sat down at a table beneath one of the arches, away from any prying ears.

'Right,' she said, once the waiter had taken their order, 'Bradley's going to update us on what he's found. Go, Bradley.'

'Go, Bradley!' Kieron and Sam chorused, pumping their fists. As they giggled, Bex stared them down. 'Quiet, you two – this is actually serious.'

Bradley had brought along a tablet. He positioned it so that the others could see the screen but it couldn't be seen from the main body of the restaurant. Bex knew that he would be seeing the same view in the ARCC glasses.

The first image was a mosaic of tiny photographs.

'You all provided me with a lot of data to work with,'

he said. 'Between you, there were about six hundred photographs, containing five thousand individual faces. Plus several close-ups of Sam's thumb.'

'Yeah, sorry,' Sam muttered. 'It took me a while to get used to where the lens was.'

'Funny,' Bradley said, 'but luckily nobody else had that problem. Anyway – moving on. I used a search app to pull out each face and consider it separately, then I used a recognition app to characterise each face mathematically – taking things like the distance between the eyes, the slope on the cheekbones, the width of the mouth and the shape of the face, and then converting that into a unique mathematical equation.' As he spoke, the thumbnail images vanished – replaced by a grid of very small faces. A tiny net of green lines appeared on each face. 'What I *then* did was to compare each of those unique mathematical equations with the equations held in the databases of known criminals and terrorists held by the major police and intelligence organisations around the world. That identified several hundred faces of people known to those organisations.'

Most of the small faces in the grid disappeared. The remaining faces moved around and expanded to form another grid. The faces this time were large enough that Bex could tell them apart. Probably three-quarters of them were men, with ages ranging from teens to pensioners.

'That's still a lot of people,' Kieron pointed out. 'Surely they can't *all* be here for Asrael's demonstration?'

'Probably not,' Bradley agreed. 'Let's be honest, even criminals and terrorists go on holiday. What I did next was remove all of the pickpockets, jewel thieves, thugs, insurance scammers, bad drivers and other irrelevant characters from the list, on the assumption that anyone wanting to hire an assassin would probably be: a) fairly well-off, and b) wouldn't be involved in petty larceny or any crimes that were accidental or spur-of-the-moment.' More faces disappeared, and again the ones that were left swelled in size and rearranged themselves into yet another grid. 'This leaves us with twenty-eight people. Twelve of them are known to be members of criminal organisations like the Russian mob, the Japanese Yakuza, the Chinese Tongs and the various Italian crime families that are still clinging to power in New York. Ten of the others are linked to terrorist groups such as ISIS and the Taliban. The remaining six either work for big international companies suspected of using highly illegal tactics against their competitors or for firms that supply mercenaries or bodyguards for dodgy missions in dangerous countries, or are otherwise suspected of involvement in serious crimes.'

'They won't be the only people here for the demonstration though,' Kieron said thoughtfully. 'There'll be some attendees who aren't on any watch list – maybe because they've never been caught or suspected of anything.'

'And we didn't get photographs of everyone in Venice,' Sam added.

'Point taken.' Bradley nodded. 'Points taken. In fact, I think we were fortunate to get twenty-eight people who might – just *might* – have been invited along to this very select gathering.' He made small typing gestures with his fingers, and most of the faces on the screen faded away. Six remained. 'These people are staying in our hotel.'

'I think I saw two of them at breakfast,' Kieron exclaimed. 'Those old people on the right-hand side. They actually said something to me!'

'That's Eric and Joan Lysander,' Bradley said. 'They're suspected of embezzling millions of pounds from a shipping company Eric worked for. They went on the run before they could be arrested. They've been pretty much living on cruise ships since then.'

'Why would they want to hire an assassin?' Bex asked, intrigued.

Bradley hesitated, retrieving the information from the ARCC system, before responding. 'Ah – yes, they had a co-conspirator, but he ran off to Barbados with half the money. They probably want revenge. Or maybe they want to threaten him so he gives the money to them.'

'And then they have him killed anyway.' Sam nodded wisely. 'It's what I'd do.'

'Good to know,' Bex said, staring at him and raising an eyebrow. Once he'd seen her and looked away, blushing, she looked at the six remaining faces on the screen. 'Then again – a rich elderly couple, in Venice – chances are they *are* actually here on holiday. What about the other four?'

Bradley swiped away the Lysanders' faces. That left a young woman with dyed blonde hair and exaggerated fake lashes, an older man with a shaven scalp and two men with dark skin and beards. 'I think,' he said thoughtfully, 'that our best bet is the woman: Bethany Wilderbourg. According to the information I've been able to glean about her, she's married to a billionaire businessman who's been having a string of affairs. She wants him dead so she can inherit his fortune. She's apparently done that several times before, although nobody's been able to prove anything to the satisfaction of the courts.' He shook his head sadly. 'She's here with her yoga instructor, name of David Harringdon. He's married to an older former client named Linda. I think we can presume that he wants her dead as well, so the two lovebirds can get married. It's like a reality-TV show.'

'There's nothing like true love,' Bex said. 'And of all of them, she's probably the lowest risk to us if we're caught.'

'Caught doing what?' Kieron asked.

'Caught sneaking into her room.'

Bex nodded at Bradley, and he continued: 'I went back to the twenty-eight people we suspect are here to attend the demonstration, and I used the ARCC equipment to remotely access their emails and their text messages – not just the obvious ones, but also any covert accounts or burner phones they might have, plus anything they deleted but which could still be retrieved from their systems. Obviously they had to have communicated with this Asrael somehow – I doubt they just bumped into each other at the supermarket. I also doubt they would be careless enough to leave any messages unencrypted, so, I looked at any common messages, things they *all* had that seemed innocuous but which might contain a secret message.' His fingers twitched, and the grid of faces on the screen was replaced by a painting Bex recognised. Or rather, she didn't recognise the painting itself, but she recognised the style of the artist.

'That's a Jackson Pollock,' she said.

'Correct,' Bradley replied. 'It's called *Alchemy*, and it's on display at the Peggy Guggenheim Museum of Modern Art here in Venice.'

'It looks like someone's flicked paint onto a canvas,' Sam said critically, 'and then drawn shapes in the wet paint with a stick. I could do that.'

'Jackson Pollock's paintings sell for millions of pounds,' Bradley said severely, 'while I doubt you could swap anything *you* did for a hamburger.' As Sam bristled, he continued: 'Anyway, each of the twenty-eight people we've identified received an email containing this image.' He looked around the table. 'Now, does anyone know what "steganography" is?'

'It's a type of dinosaur,' Sam said, still scowling.

'That's a "stegosaurus".' Kieron frowned. 'Isn't it something to do with codes?'

'Kind of.' Bradley nodded approvingly. 'Well done. Steganography is a way of hiding information in a digital picture so it can't be seen.'

Sam made a *huff* noise. 'You could hide an elephant in that picture,' he muttered. 'In fact, it looks like it was *made* by an elephant.'

Bradley went on as if he hadn't heard. 'I checked the image, and I found a hidden message in the digital data. It confirmed that each of the recipients was invited to what was described as: 'A demonstration of skill by the international assassin Asrael', and it gave them a date, a time and a location. It also said that each recipient would be sent, through the post, an identification card with a radio-frequency identification chip, like you get in passports or those security tags they use in shops. The RFID chip on the card would be their entry pass. Actually, it's –'

'You said "date, place and time",' Bex interrupted. 'When, and where?'

'The date is today, the time is nineteen hundred hours local time and the place is here in Venice, although the exact location hasn't yet been revealed. Apparently the attendees will be collected at eighteen thirty at a particular pier on the Grand Canal, and if their IDs check out they'll be taken across the lagoon somewhere.' He paused. 'All attendees are required to wear Venetian masks to protect their identities. You probably saw masks like that as you were wandering around taking photographs.'

Kieron nodded eagerly. 'Some of them looked really weird – like birds with really exaggerated beaks.'

'There's a tradition in Venice of wearing masks at what they call *Carnivale*,' Bradley explained. 'Carnivale happens once a year, around Easter time. Some of the masks are just simple things, meant to hide the face, while others represent characters from medieval theatre. The ones I think you mean are actually based on masks that doctors in the Middle Ages used to wear in an attempt to stop themselves from catching whatever horrible diseases their patients had. The beak part would be filled with a mixture of herbs that were supposed to ward off the disease. Whether or not it actually worked was anybody's guess. Probably frightened half the patients to death, which kind of defeated the object. Anyway, those masks have become part of the whole "Venice experience" now.'

'So,' Bex summarised, leaning back in her chair and thinking as she spoke, 'we know that this woman – Bethany Wilderbourg – received an invitation and an RFID chip. She'll have it with her, obviously. What I need to do is sneak into her room this afternoon and steal it. What *you* need to do –' she looked at Bradley – 'is make sure she doesn't suddenly come back to her room and catch me. Can you do that?'

'I certainly can,' he said.

'Won't she have the RFID chip with her?' Kieron asked. 'I mean, if I were her, I'd want to keep it close to me so it didn't get lost or stolen.'

'Good point,' Bex replied, 'but like any other Italian city, Venice is a hotbed of pickpockets and handbag thieves who prey on tourists. The handbag thieves in particular can slice through the strap of your bag with a razor blade and take it off you as they pass without you even realising. No, Bethany will have left the chip in her room, probably in the hotel safe.' She thought for a moment. 'I'll probably need half an hour, Bradley. Can you get me that?'

'Sure. I might need the boys though – I can cover the front entrance of the hotel, but there's at least one other way in. Is that OK?'

'What room is she in?' Bex asked.

'Third floor – room 319.' Bradley sniffed. 'It's one of

the cheaper ones in the hotel. She's obviously being careful with the money she's "inherited" from her dead husbands.'

'Right,' Bex said firmly – more firmly than she felt, 'let's go.'

The four of them headed back to the hotel. While Bex went straight up to the third floor, Bradley sat down in the lobby to watch the main entrance while the boys went to cover the other ways in.

The corridor was deserted, and her shoes made no sound on the thick carpet. Bex passed an open door with a trolley of towels and toiletries outside. She caught a quick glimpse of a maid making the bed. The room she wanted was ten doors down – even if the maid was working her way *towards* the target room rather than away from it, Bex should have finished by the time she got there.

She stopped outside room 319. Taking a breath, she knocked. No answer. She knocked again. 'Room service!' she announced, but there was no sound from inside. The door remained closed.

Right – it looked as if Bethany Wilderbourg was indeed out, which meant that the operation could go ahead. If she'd answered then Bex would have had to apologise and say she'd got the wrong room, then wait until Bethany did actually leave, and that might have taken a while.

She checked left and right down the corridor. Still nobody.

The lock on the door was a simple key card type. Bethany would have a card with a magnetic strip which would be read by a sensor inside the lock when she pushed it into the slot above the door handle. If she'd had more time then Bex would have tried to get a new card created by whoever was on the front desk, telling them that she was Bethany Wilderbourg and she'd dropped her card into a canal by accident. Hotel reception staff very rarely remembered what guests actually looked like – they saw so many of them. But time was tight, and Bex had another way in.

She took a device out of her pocket, about the size of a magic marker. It had a short cable attached with a thin jack at the end. She felt with her fingers beneath the metal lock for the small DC power socket. Those types of locks weren't connected to the mains, so they had to have a means of being recharged – and also a means for changing the security code on the chip inside, if necessary.

Once she found the socket, she plugged the jack of her device into it and clicked the small button on the other end. The device beeped once, then again a few seconds later. The first *beep* meant that it had successfully copied the security code from the chip, the second that it had transmitted that code back to the lock again.

She offered up a quick prayer to a deity she didn't believe in, on the basis that it couldn't hurt.

A green light flashed on the lock, and the door clicked open.

Quickly she pushed it open, slipped inside and softly closed it again. She glanced at the bed, just in case Bethany was in there asleep, but it was empty. It was also made up, which mean she wasn't at risk of the maid deciding to skip a few rooms and interrupting her.

106

Bex knew what kinds of tricks people like her used to see whether anybody had searched their room – a hair stuck with saliva across closed drawers and shut suitcases; items slightly misaligned and their positions memorised or photographed so that the room's occupant would know if they'd been moved. Bex deliberately didn't touch anything. She didn't have to: if Bethany was sensible then she would have put the invitation to Asrael's demonstration, and the identifying RFID tag, inside the room's safe. Either that, or she would have taken it out with her, in which case they would need another plan, and quickly.

The safe was where Bex expected it to be: on a shelf in the wardrobe. The shelves ran up the left half of the wardrobe space, with a hanging rail taking up the right-hand side. A selection of dresses hung from the rail. It looked as if Bethany had expensive taste: the clothes were designer items well out of Bex's price range. Ignoring them, she concentrated on the safe and was relieved to see it was also the kind she expected: thick steel walls, a thick steel door (shut) and an electronic lock with a keypad and an LED display. Instructions for setting the code were on a card Blu-tacked on the inside of the door. When a new guest arrived in the room, the door of the safe would be open and the security code set to 0000. If they wanted to store anything, they would do so and close the door, then type their own security code into the keypad. That code would work any time the guest used the safe, until they left. Assuming they left the door open, the code would reset to 0000 after a set amount of time. Obviously the hotel had ways of getting into a safe if a guest forgot their code, but again Bex didn't have time for that. Fortunately she had a better way.

Below the keypad, near the edge of the closed door, she noticed a small, oval plate with the manufacturer's logo engraved on it. Two small hex screws secured the plate to the door. Using a small tool on her key ring, Bex undid one screw and rotated the plate by ninety degrees. That revealed a hidden hole. This, she knew, was a failsafe lock – a way of getting the safe open. The management of the hotel would have the key for the lock, but part of Bex's extensive agent training had been in the theory and practice of lock-picking. She was good at it, and more importantly perhaps, she enjoyed it.

She bent down to get a better view of the lock, and pulled a hairpin from her hair. It wasn't really a hairpin – it was a malleable piece of metal wire – but it *looked* like a hairpin to anyone searching her.

She unbent it into a straight line and poked it into the hole, and then beneath it, in the space left, she pushed the thin screwdriver tool from her key ring. The two together took up all the space. After that it was a case of breathing lightly, putting tension on the lock by turning the screwdriver shaft slightly and fiddling about with the wire. As soon as she felt the spring-loaded pins that held the lock shut she pushed them as delicately as she could until they moved up, out of the way. Once she'd done that for all four pins, it was simplicity itself to turn the screwdriver as if it was a key and unlock the safe.

The LED display flashed *UNLOCKED*, and the door swung open.

Inside was Bethany Wilderbourg's passport, a stack of euros, two pieces of card with scalloped edges the size of a party invitation, two sealed white envelopes and two black plastic discs that looked like casino chips.

Why two? Bex wondered. No time to worry about that now. The passports and money she would leave behind: they obviously had nothing to do with the demonstration and she didn't want to steal Bethany's own stuff. The cards and the discs looked like they could be relevant, so she slipped them into a pocket. The envelopes she wondered about. Maybe they were part of the puzzle, or maybe they were just invitations to dinner from someone Bethany knew in Venice. Eventually she put them in her pocket with the tokens and the invitations, just in case they were important, closed the door to the safe and pressed the lock button. The safe buzzed, and the word *LOCKED* blinked on the display.

Job done. Time to go.

She heard a *beep* from the room door, and a *click*.

Damn, she thought. This keeps happening to me. I should stay out of other people's hotel rooms.

Before it could open, she stepped into the wardrobe, pushing the dresses out of the way, and pulled the doors closed.

Through the crack left between the two doors she saw the door to the room swing open. A woman entered. This wasn't the maid; it was Bethany Wilderbourg: Bex recognised her from the image on Bradley's tablet. Her hair was wet and she carried a rolled towel. She hadn't been out doing tourist stuff in Venice at all; she'd been in the hotel pool!

Bethany went into the bathroom. A few seconds later – not long enough for Bex to get out of the wardrobe and out of the room – she came back in without the towel. She'd probably hung it up to dry.

Please let her go straight out and do some sightseeing! Bex thought. *Please!*

Bethany approached the wardrobe.

Damn – she's going to get changed, or she needs a jacket or something! I am so screwed!

With horror, Bex realised that she'd left the metal plate that had hidden the security keyhole hanging loose. Bethany would spot it any moment!

She reached sideways with her right hand, feeling for the safe. Her fingers touched the edge. Quickly she slid her hand sideways until she reached the rotated metal plate. She turned it back to the right position – just in time!

Bethany opened the left-hand wardrobe door – the one that revealed the shelves, the safe and about three inches of the hanging space, but thankfully she didn't pull the second door open. Bex held her breath and pressed herself back against the back wall of the wardrobe, trying not to rustle the dresses. She must have disturbed them though, because suddenly she smelled a waft of perfume that must have been left behind from the last time the woman had worn them. The odour tickled her nostrils, and she tried not to sneeze.

Bethany tapped in her security code, and the safe door beeped and opened.

Don't let her notice that the invitation and the RFID fob have been taken!

The strong, floral scent of the perfume was tingling at the back of Bex's nose now. She reached up and pinched her nostrils shut, but that just seemed to make the tingling worse, like some small insect was trapped in there and was desperate to get out. Bex screwed her face up, trying to suppress the urge to explosively sneeze.

Bethany reached in, pulled out her wad of banknotes and peeled three from the top. She threw the rest back inside and closed the door again, locking it with a push of the button. Then she closed the wardrobe door, retrieved her jacket from where she'd put it on the back of a chair and left the room.

The itching in Bex's nose was almost intolerable now, but she forced herself to count to ten before she sneezed the loudest sneeze she'd ever managed in her life.

Fortunately the sound didn't bring Bethany back to investigate, but it sounded to Bex as if it might.

Patting her pocket to make sure she still had the card and the fob, she opened the room door a crack and listened. Somewhere down the corridor she heard the *ding* of the lift. That was probably Bethany, heading downstairs and out. That, Bex thought as she slid out into the corridor, was going to shock Bradley, or the boys. They'd been looking out for Bethany coming *into* the hotel; seeing her suddenly going *out* would throw them completely. She just hoped they didn't react; not Bradley – he was too much of a professional for that – but the boys might show their surprise and tip Bethany off.

Bex caught herself and shook her head. Those boys had proved themselves over and over again. They weren't going to go all amateur on her now and give the game away.

She took the stairs down to the lobby. Bradley was where she'd left him, in a comfortable chair. He looked like he was reading something on his tablet.

She sat down beside him.

'That was interesting,' she said quietly.

'Yes, I saw our target leave. What happened?'

'She'd been for a swim.'

'As the poet Robert Burns said, "The best-laid schemes o' mice an' men gang aft agley". That means –'

'I know what it means. The military equivalent is: "No plan survives contact with the enemy." My dad used to say that all the time.'

'Did you get what we came for?'

'I did. At least, I got something that fits the description, and it was in the right place, although there were two sets, not one. Let's not look at them now, just in case she comes back and sees us. We can go to your room. Oh, and let's get the boys on the way.'

Five minutes later they were all in Bradley's room.

Bex bought out the cards and the RFID fobs. 'Apart from cash and a passport, these were the only things in the room's safe. If these aren't what we're looking for, then we're in trouble.' She tossed the fobs to Bradley. 'Have you got the equipment to check this out?'

He laughed. 'Have *I* got the equipment? What do *you* think?'

'Have you?' Kieron asked, frowning.

Bradley sighed. 'Yes, I have. Just give me a few minutes.'

While he set up his tablet, Bex looked at the first card. It was thick, ivory in colour, and its edges were scalloped. Just like any high-class party invite. Even the lettering on it was just what she would have expected – a font that looked like exquisite handwriting. She ran her fingers over it: the ink stood out from the card, embossed. All very impressive.

The words printed on the card were simple and direct:

You are invited to a demonstration of the skills of Asrael. Be at jetty 13 at St Mark's Square at precisely 18:30 on the fifth day after you receive this invitation.
Bring this card, and the token that arrived with it. These are the only identification you will need and that will be accepted.
Tell nobody. Bring nobody. No weapons or recording devices permitted.
You will see something you will not believe.

She glanced at the second card. It said exactly the same as the first.

The two white envelopes seemed to stare up at her challengingly. They were blank, made of card. Feeling a slight twinge of guilt, Bex opened the first one.

113

The only thing inside was a slip of card with a name handwritten on it: *Charles Wilderbourg*. Bethany's husband? It seemed likely.

The second slip of card bore a different name: *Linda Harringdon*.

Each card had an address beneath the name. Both addresses were in the more exclusive parts of Los Angeles.

'I've checked out the fobs,' Bradley said, distracting her. 'Each one has a different code – no extra information. I can't tell where the demonstration is taking place. The only way to know is to go.'

'Yes, but we have a problem,' Bex said. 'She's got a friend, and they've been invited too. If I turn up alone, it might make Asrael suspicious. At the very least it'll draw attention to me. I need a plus-one.' She held the second card up and waved it at Bradley. 'Play nice. You're it.'

'As long as there's a glass of wine and a few vol-au-vents,' he said. 'Good thing I packed a decent suit and shirt.'

Bex met his gaze, and she could see that he'd come to the same conclusion she had. He nodded slightly, and she nodded back. She turned to Kieron and Sam.

'We're going to need your help, boys,' she said.

They both smiled, and she couldn't help smiling back.

'As you heard, I have to take one other person with me to the demonstration,' she went on, 'but it can't be either of you. I doubt Asrael would believe that my partner was a teenager. Ideally I'd go alone, with Bradley supporting me from here with the ARCC kit, but that's not an option this time.' She paused, and looked from Kieron to Sam and back again. 'We're going to need the two of you here, giving us any support that we need. Are you up for it?'

Kieron glanced at Sam. 'Are we? What do you think?'

'Aren't we getting a little old for all this mucking around?'

Kieron nodded. 'Actually I met a girl earlier. She's from Norway. We said we might meet up later, down in the lobby. She's got a friend. In fact, she's got two friends.'

'Sounds good to me.'

Kieron and Sam kept straight faces for another few seconds as they turned to look at Bex and Bradley, but they couldn't sustain it and they burst out laughing.

'Of course we'll help!' Kieron said through the laughs.

Three hours later, after Bex and Bradley had both grabbed a catnap in their rooms so they were fresh for the mission ahead, and after they'd both got changed into smarter clothes – a black suit in Bradley's case and a smart trouser suit for Bex – they met up in the lobby and headed out to the jetties.

'Did you see that?' Bradley asked as they left the hotel.

'What?'

'Bethany Wilderbourg. She was in the bar, arguing with a man. I'm guessing she's saying he's got the invitations and the ID chips and he's saying she has them. Just keep moving.'

It was cold outside. Far across the lagoon, lights glittered on the other islands.

'Which one of us is going to wear the ARCC glasses?' Bradley asked.

'I'm more used to them and, frankly, I look better in them. Hand them over.'

Without saying anything, Bradley passed her the glasses and an earpiece. 'So, my job is just to stand beside you and look decorative?'

'Your job is to stand beside me and look like a bodyguard.' She slipped the glasses on, nestled the earpiece in her right ear and pressed the tiny button on the right-hand arm of the glasses. As she did so, she noticed Bradley slipping an earpiece into his own ear – one of their spares. 'Kieron – are you there?'

'I'm here,' his voice murmured in her ear. 'Just turn your head so I can check out the focus and the infrared functions? Yeah – that's OK. All working perfectly.'

'Right. Let's go.'

They walked along the side of the lagoon together. Bex slipped her arm through Bradley's. 'Just so we blend in,' she said. 'Don't get any ideas.'

'Wouldn't dream of it. Besides, I've still got a girlfriend back in Newcastle.'

'You haven't said anything to Courtney yet?'

'When have I had a chance?'

'Oi!' a voice shouted over the ARCC glasses.

'Sorry,' Bradley murmured. 'Oh, that's jetty thirteen up ahead.'

Bex looked in the direction he was pointing. Instead of a *vaporetto* or even a gondola, a black yacht was tied up by the quay. It must have been thirty feet long, with a bridge area rising up above the back half. The bow came to a sharp point. Nobody stood near it, but a gangplank led from the jetty up to its deck.

'Sunseeker, according to the boat-recognition website I've found on the glasses,' Kieron said in her ear. 'Sunseeker 75, to be precise. Very nice. Very, very expensive. Being an international assassin must pay well.'

'OK,' Bex said. 'Here we go.'

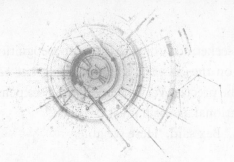

CHAPTER SEVEN

Kieron watched as Bex and Bradley walked up the gangplank and onto the black yacht. As they moved, the ARCC glasses overlaid a glowing green wireframe schematic of the yacht's innards over the actual picture, showing him the location of every cabin and storage area, as well as the engines and the fuel tanks. Simultaneously, the infrared sensors highlighted every hotspot: the engine and the transmission shafts, but also every single person there.

'You've got two people up in the bridge area,' Kieron murmured, 'plus another two below decks.'

'OK,' Bex said calmly, as if she was talking to Bradley. Kieron knew, though, that she was acknowledging his information.

The image transmitted from Bex's glasses showed a bearded man in white jacket, shirt and trousers, and wearing a white peaked cap, approaching her and Bradley. A red box appeared over the top of the image, with a line linking it to the left side of the man's jacket. Inside the box, the words *Probable weapon, based on pattern of fabric wrinkles in jacket* flashed in red.

'Please, your invitations?' the man said, holding out his hand. He had a slight accent.

Georgian accent, the glasses confirmed. *Probably from area south of Tbilisi.*

Bex reached into her jacket to retrieve the invitations. 'Here,' she said, handing them over.

'Thank you.' The man scanned them. 'This all seems to be in order. And your RFID tokens, please?'

This time it was Bradley who held them out. Rather than taking them, the bearded man pulled a scanner from his belt and passed it across Bradley's palm, where the tags sat. The scanner beeped twice.

'That all seems fine.' The man nodded at them. 'Now, if you don't mind being scanned for weapons and communications equipment . . . ?'

'And if we do . . . ?' Bex asked smoothly.

'Then I will have to ask you to leave this vessel,' the man said calmly.

Bradley stepped forward.

'Either via the gangplank or over the side,' the man continued, just as calmly. 'Your choice.'

With an exaggerated movement, Bradley pulled open his jacket on both sides to reveal his shirt. The man ran his scanner over him, starting with his chest then moving to his back, arms and legs. Once he was satisfied Bradley wasn't armed, he turned his attention to Bex. She calmly submitted to being scanned, and even held her tiny clutch bag out for inspection.

'Thank you. I apologise for the inconvenience, but

Asrael is very particular about the arrangements for this demonstration.'

'Understandably,' Bex said. 'Where exactly are we being taken?' She turned her head so that Kieron could see the gangplank. A man was just walking up towards the deck: mid-thirties, swarthy, with a scar on his cheek.

'Not far. Please, make yourselves comfortable in the lounge. There are cocktails available, if you wish. We will be setting off soon.'

The bearded man moved to greet the newcomer. Bex kept staring at his face, making sure Kieron got a good look. The swarthy man scowled at Bex, and finally she looked away. Kieron imagined her smiling sweetly.

'Was that long enough?' she asked quietly.

'Just checking now,' Kieron said as the ARCC software checked the man's face against its many databases. A match flashed up. 'He's not one of the people we photographed earlier,' Kieron said, reading quickly through the information, 'but he's linked to Bosnian separatists. Not a nice man.'

'I suspect,' Bex murmured in his ear, 'that we are on a ship of not-nice people.'

'Still,' Bradley added, 'there's cocktails. So that's good.'

Kieron watched as the two of them entered the main cabin. A bar stretched across the far side, with two stewards behind it, and there must have been fifteen other people already there. It was like a school dance, Kieron thought. Everyone stood around the sides of the cabin, not talking. The ARCC software went into overdrive trying to identify all of the faces. If Kieron had been prone to epilepsy then he probably would have had a fit from all the flashing images.

'I'm not going to bother reading it all out,' he said, 'but you're sharing a room with a bunch of international criminals, terrorists and rogue intelligence agents. Be very, very careful.'

'Anyone fancy a game of poker?' Bradley said brightly. As the occupants of the cabin stared at him, he added, 'No? Maybe later then.'

The swarthy newcomer joined them, pushing past Bex and heading straight for the bar.

'Cocktail?' Bradley asked Bex.

'Thank you. Something non-alcoholic.'

'Oh,' he said, looking crestfallen. 'Yes. Good idea.'

A vibration ran through the glasses, and Kieron heard a deep thrumming noise through the loudspeaker in the glasses he wore.

'Casting off,' Bex said, as if talking to Bradley. 'I think that's the technical term.'

'I have the location of the glasses pinpointed,' Kieron told her reassuringly. 'They're transmitting a location signal which I'm picking up via satellite. I won't lose you.'

'Unless the signal gets jammed,' Sam said from behind him.

The scene Kieron was looking at in the ARCC glasses shifted, as Bex moved towards the side of the cabin. She leaned in close to a porthole. Through it, he could see the retreating lights of St Mark's Square and the quayside. Two figures stood there, a man and a woman, staring angrily at the departing boat. He wasn't sure, but he thought the woman was Bethany Wilderbourg.

'All dressed up and nowhere to go,' Bex murmured. 'So sad.'

As she turned back to take her drink from Bradley, Kieron called up a map of the lagoon area. It took up most of the image space in the lenses, but he didn't think much of interest was going to happen until they reached their destination, and he wanted to get some idea of where they were going.

'Right,' he said, watching the movement of the little blinking light indicating the position of the boat, 'you're heading south-east. The main block of Venice is on your left, and the Lido, which is the beach area, I think, is on your right. My guess is that you're going to be turning north and heading between Isola Sant'Elena and Isola la Certosa. You'll be passing the island of Le Vignole in a few minutes.'

'That's good,' Bex said, sipping at her drink. 'I think.'

The track of the blinking light bore east again, heading around the curve of Le Vignole, and then straightened out. A scattering of small islands, some named and some apparently anonymous, filled the lagoon ahead. Past them, in the distance, was the Italian mainland.

Pretty soon it became clear that the boat was heading directly for a small, irregular island that sat apart from the others, like a child at a party being shunned by its friends. Kieron selected its image with his forefinger and called up whatever information he could find about it. There wasn't much.

'It looks as if you're going to be docking at an island called Isola San Zan Degola,' he said, reading from the screen. 'It's small, and it's uninhabited. It was apparently a cemetery from the sixteenth through to the eighteenth century, but it was abandoned due to an outbreak of bubonic plague.' He hesitated. 'I'm sure it's all right now though. But locals still avoid it. Nobody goes there at all apparently. It's got a reputation for being haunted by the ghosts of an entire regiment of Italian soldiers who were stationed there in the early 1800s.' He whistled as he read the words from the insides of the lenses. 'Ooh – apparently their commanding officer on the mainland lost contact with them. He sent out messengers to re-establish contact, but when the messengers got there they discovered that they were all dead.' He paused dramatically. 'And there wasn't a mark on their bodies!'

'Whooooo!' Sam whistled from behind him.

The sound of the boat's engines changed, and the picture in the ARCC glasses shifted slightly as the boat rocked and Bex had to catch her balance.

'So,' she said brightly to the various terrorists and criminals standing around the cabin, drinking silently, 'are we looking forward to this?'

No reaction.

The boat slowed down, and the picture jerked, presumably as the bow bumped against a quay or pier.

'Please,' a voice said from the doorway, 'come this way.'

As Bex turned to see who was speaking, Kieron saw the bearded man. He stepped to one side to leave the doorway vacant. One by one, the occupants of the cabin stepped out. Bex and Bradley were the last to leave.

Outside on the deck, the boat bobbed on the calm black waters of the lagoon. Bex looked up momentarily, and Kieron saw a bright scattering of stars. As she looked down again, at the gangplank that led off the boat and onto a concrete quay, he noticed an irregular mass of black a few hundred yards away across the concrete. Bright light spilled out from behind it: red and blue and purple. Through the tiny loudspeakers in the arms of the ARCC glasses he heard music as well: a pumping rhythm that wasn't so bad through the remote link but which was probably deafening where Bex was.

As if in confirmation, he heard her say to Bradley: 'If I'd known we were coming to a dance I would have worn my party dress!'

'She's got a party dress?' Sam said from close behind him. 'Who would have guessed?'

'Play nice, you two,' Bradley growled.

'Can you hear what's going on?' Kieron asked Sam, behind him.

'If I lean close enough, yeah. And if you turn your head slightly I can see the screens as well.'

'I'll bear that in mind.'

A path led away from the concrete area, up a slope towards the lights. The group from the boat headed along it in single file.

Bex turned her head. Behind her and Bradley, the four men from the boat were following them. Each one carried an assault rifle. Kieron realised with a sinking sensation in his chest that there was no going back.

Over the crest of the rise, the sudden flood of light caused the ARCC glasses to blank out for a moment. When they came back, with a flare that made Kieron wince, he saw a circular area of ground a few hundred metres across. Chairs had been set out, facing a stage and a massive LED screen like the ones that were used at rock concerts. Speakers beside the screen pumped out pounding dance music. Spotlights around the edge cast red, blue and yellow light across everything. The screen showed a logo like a stylised dragon, with the word *ASRAEL* beneath it.

It seemed obvious what was required. Bex and Bradley followed the others from the boat down towards the improvised auditorium and sat down.

Bex looked slowly around, giving Kieron a perfect view of the surroundings. What he immediately spotted was that the four crew members had taken up positions around the edges of the circle, behind the spotlights. Their guns were held low, but ready.

'I really don't like the look of this,' Kieron said, quietly enough that he hoped Bex couldn't hear.

'Me neither,' Sam whispered, his breath stirring the hairs on the back of Kieron's neck and making him shiver.

'If anyone here has managed to smuggle a weapon in,' Bex murmured, apparently to Bradley but loud enough for Kieron to pick up, 'then the lights will blind them long enough for the armed guards to act. We're at a tactical disadvantage here. It's all very well planned.'

The thudding dance music suddenly stopped, leaving a silence that seemed paradoxically even louder than the noise.

Bex glanced towards the stage.

Where a line of fireworks exploded upwards in towers of sparks.

'Very theatrical,' Bradley observed, shielding his eyes. 'I hope there's some steak along with the sizzle, otherwise I'm going to be bitterly disappointed.' As Bex turned her head partially towards him, and Kieron caught his shadowed profile, he added, 'It's only just occurred to me that, rather than being a big advertising opportunity for Asrael, this might be someone's way of clearing out a whole lot of their own competition. I mean, maybe we've been so focused on identifying the people who are here that we forgot to look for the people that *aren't*. Maybe they've got the whole place wired up with explosives.' He made a huffing sound, and shook his head. 'Hey, maybe this is our bosses in MI6, or the CIA, or someone similar, trying to clear the decks. Might not be legal, or even moral, but it *would* be effective. And ironic, if they ended up killing us as well.'

'Nervous?' Bex asked gently.

'Why do you ask?'

'Because you're talking too much. Are you feeling OK?'

She turned to face him. He kept staring ahead, at the stage.

'I'm not used to being out in the field, all right?' he said suddenly, in a rush. 'I'm used to being somewhere safe, with a coffee and a pastry, watching you going through dangerous situations and doing my best to help you –'

'And doing a damn good job,' Bex said.

'– But I'm sitting here, and there are men with guns, and I'm not entirely sure I know what I'm doing.'

'You're helping me in a difficult situation,' Bex said. 'Only a lot more closely than usual. Just follow my lead. I'll get us out of this, I promise.'

'And I've got your backs,' Kieron added.

'And I've got Kieron's back!' Sam called.

'Yes,' Kieron said, turning his head, 'but who's got *your* back.'

The huge Roman candles all subsided at the same time. Standing on the stage were three figures, silhouetted by the spotlights behind them. After a dramatic moment of silence, a few of the other spotlights swung around, remotely controlled from somewhere behind the scenes, to point at the stage and illuminate the new arrivals.

Kieron gasped.

'What is it?' Bex said, concerned.

'You're not going to believe this,' Kieron said, hearing the surprise and shock in his own voice, 'but I know them.'

He zoomed the ARCC glasses in on the stage so he could get a better look, but he was already sure. The three people standing there in front of the screen, staring challengingly out at their captive audience, were the Norwegian girls he'd met earlier that day.

'Who are they?' Bex asked, as if it was a rhetorical question. A rumble of conversation rose from the assembled crowd as they exchanged surprised comments.

'The girl in the middle is called Katrin. The ones on either side of her are Eva and Hekla.' He felt flat; let down.

He'd thought that maybe, just maybe, if there was some spare time during their trip, he might have been able to meet up with Katrin and wander around, maybe get a coffee somewhere, exchange email addresses or connect on social media. You heard about people falling in love on holiday all the time. It was a cliché, popularised by too many films to count. Stupid to think that it might have come true for him.

Sam's hand squeezed his shoulder in sympathy. 'She's actually very nice to look at,' he said. 'They all are.'

Kieron sighed. 'A shame they're apparently international assassins. They're a little out of my league.'

'Hey,' Sam said, 'you're a top-secret service operative. *They*'re out of *your* league.'

Kieron quickly typed instructions into the virtual screen. 'I'm running their faces through the ID software,' he said, 'just like I'm running the faces of everyone in the audience, but I'm not coming up with anything. Whoever they are, they're not known to any police organisation or intelligence service.'

'They're barely out of school, surely?' Bradley said.

'I think they're older than they look,' Bex replied coolly.

The girl in the middle – Katrin – stepped forward.

'Good evening,' she said, that entrancing Nordic accent that Kieron remembered. It sent a shiver down his back. 'Thank you all for coming here tonight. We are Asrael, and we want your business. We want to be your preferred suppliers of death.' She smiled confidently. 'It is a crowded market, we know. The dark web is filled with adverts for ex-mercenaries, ex-gang members and ex-terrorists who will tell you they can kill anyone you want.' She looked around her audience. Bex did too, and Kieron saw a lot of doubtful faces. 'They can't, of course,' Katrin continued. 'Yes, they might be able to break into someone's house and shoot them in their sleep, or cut the brake cables on someone's car so that it goes out of control and it crashes, but that only works if they have no bodyguards and no security systems. The kinds of targets that most of you will be seeking to get rid of will be cleverer than that. They will take precautions. They will be surrounded by an impenetrable shield of electronics, well-armed humans and old-fashioned concrete, brick and stone.' She paused dramatically. 'Impenetrable to anyone except for us. We – and *only* we – can break through your target's shield. Anywhere in the world, at any time.'

'I don't believe it,' Bradley's voice said sceptically.

'Remember my car, and our flat?' Bex murmured. 'They may be on to something.'

'They're certainly talking themselves up,' Sam said, behind Kieron's head. 'They'd better be able to deliver, after all this hype.'

Kieron snorted. 'You sound like you actually want them to kill someone.'

'I'm just saying.'

'We asked you all, when you were invited, to think about someone you wanted out of your lives,' Katrin said. 'Gone. Dead. We gave you cards and we asked you to write the name and the location of that person on your piece of card

129

before you came and seal it in the envelope. We also told you to keep those envelopes with you at all times.' She paused dramatically. 'We are going to select one person from the audience and kill their person now, while you watch. That will prove to you that we can reach anywhere, at any time, and deal sudden death.' She smiled. 'Maybe you gave us the name of someone you actually *wanted* killed, or maybe you gave us the name of some stranger you'd randomly chosen because you were suspicious of us and didn't want to give anything away. It doesn't matter. For one of you, your chosen target will die. If it *was* someone you wanted killed, then you get a free assassination out of us. If you chose a random stranger, then –' she shrugged – 'well, it's bad luck for them and for their family, I suppose.'

'Can they really do this?' Kieron asked nervously. 'I mean, it sounds unlikely. And it sounds so *cold* as well. Don't they even care about killing random strangers?'

'Assassins aren't generally known for their scruples,' Bradley murmured.

Katrin glanced around the audience, meeting each person's gaze in turn. For a moment she looked directly at Bex, but to Kieron, staring at the scene through the ARCC glasses, it looked as if Katrin was staring straight at him.

He shivered.

'It has probably occurred to you that someone in the audience is a "plant", put there by us so that we can select them as if by chance and then they give us the name of a target we have already prepared for. Just to prove that's not the case . . .' She gestured to Hekla, who took a pace forward and held up her hand. She was holding a red ball, the size of a tennis ball. 'Low-tech, I know,' Katrin said, 'but it's effective. Please – if the ball comes your way, catch it for us.'

Hekla turned so that her back was to the audience and threw the ball up into the air, as hard as she could.

'She'd be rubbish at cricket,' Sam muttered.

'*You're* rubbish at cricket,' Kieron pointed out. 'And so am I.'

The ball arced towards the middle of the audience. As it came down, the audience members underneath stirred, craning their necks to see it in the dim light. A man wearing a dinner jacket and bow tie caught it in two hands and held it up.

'Now, please throw the ball again,' Katrin instructed.

The man shrugged, looking slightly disappointed that he wasn't the one to be chosen, but he threw the ball backwards, over his shoulder, without looking.

An older woman in a black leather jumpsuit that was designed for someone far younger that her caught it one-handed. She stood up and waved the ball excitedly.

'Please also throw the ball in any direction you wish.'

The woman clapped a hand theatrically over her eyes and chucked the ball to her left. It hit a man wearing a black leather jacket and sunglasses, even though it was dark, on the back of the head and bounced off. He swore loudly as a thin, dark-skinned man in military fatigues grabbed it. He held it up, grinning, so that everyone could see.

'Thank you,' Katrin said. 'Please – give us the name of your target.'

131

The man frowned and glanced around suspiciously, then called out, in a strong accent, 'The President of the United States of America!'

The audience laughed.

'Very good,' Katrin said, clapping her hands together in appreciation. 'Unfortunately I don't believe you. Who is your *real* target? Who did you name in your envelope?'

'Oscar Fernandez Marroquín,' the man shouted.

'Do we know who that is?' Bex asked, as if speaking to Bradley. Kieron, however, knew that she was actually talking to him.

'Working on it,' he said, moving things around on the virtual ARCC screen and selecting particular options. 'Ah, yes, Oscar Fernandez Marroquín: head of the Medellín Cartel, which is a massive drug-smuggling network operating out of Colombia. He's worth approximately thirty *billion* dollars, according to the FBI, and has the nickname "The Emperor of Cocaine".' He paused, checking facts rapidly. 'This looks as if it might be some kind of power struggle within the cartel. The man with the ball is one of Marroquín's deputies, name of Pablo Eliente. I reckon he wants to get rid of his boss and take control of the cartel himself.'

'Thank you,' Katrin called to the man in the military fatigues, 'you can sit down now.' She looked around the audience challengingly. 'Does anyone not believe that this name was chosen completely randomly? Can anybody see any way we could have rigged this choice so that a name we had already prepared was chosen?'

Bex looked around as well, and Kieron looked around with her. People in the audience seemed to be shaking their heads or shrugging.

'Very well – if you all agree that this name, this Oscar Fernandez Marroquín, was chosen by chance, then let us proceed.'

Hekla had somehow obtained a tablet computer while nobody was looking at her. She now held it in front of her with one hand and tapped instructions into it with the other.

The picture of the list of names had vanished from Kieron's screen by now. Suddenly an image appeared. For a moment Kieron thought it was a map of a forested area with a clearing in the middle, but then he realised it was actually a real image, taken from above but in daylight. Today's date had been overlaid in the corner of the screen, along with a time, but the time said '14:25:38', with the seconds clicking up as he watched.

'The time's wrong,' he said.

'That's the time in Bogota,' Bex responded. 'It's six hours behind Venice. That means it's a live image.'

The picture zoomed in slowly, revealing that the clearing had a building in the centre, surrounded by a wall.

'This is the estate of Oscar Fernandez Marroquín,' Katrin said, waving at the screen. 'The image is live, being transmitted now, from above the estate.' She pointed at the man whose target had been selected. 'Do you recognise it?' she called.

He nodded, then shouted, 'Yes! It is where the pig lives!'

133

'And are you content that we go ahead with the assassination now?'

'Yes!' he shouted enthusiastically.

A sudden thought struck Kieron. He manipulated the image on the ARCC glasses, overlaying an infrared filter. 'I'm just looking for heat sources,' he said, staring intently at the picture. The skin of Katrin, Hekla and Eva's hands and faces glowed orange and yellow, with their clothes a more subdued palette of blues and greens. Hekla's tablet computer glowed red, because the battery and other electronics inside were generating heat, but each of them also had a red spot in their right ear.

'They've each got an earpiece,' he said. 'You probably can't see it from where you're sitting, but I think they're getting instructions from someone behind the scenes.'

'Or just information,' Sam pointed out. 'They could still be the ones in charge.'

Katrin nodded to Hekla, who typed commands into her tablet.

The picture on the screen slowly zoomed in closer. The building swelled until Kieron could make out details. Cars sat outside – jeeps, a limousine and several sports cars. Moving dark dots were probably armed guards patrolling the grounds. There were more dark dots, stationary this time, on the corners of the building's flat roof. More armed guards? It seemed likely.

'I wonder what's transmitting the image,' Bex mused. 'A reconnaissance satellite maybe?'

'The resolution is too good for that,' Bradley pointed

out. 'I'm sure a drug cartel could afford a satellite, but how would they launch it?' He paused for a moment, apparently thinking. 'Reconnaissance aircraft, maybe. Or perhaps a drone.'

Kieron noticed a vivid blue swimming pool in the centre of the flat roof, surrounded by green blotches that were probably potted plants or trees. A rectangular object in the pool itself was probably an inflatable lilo. There seemed to be a pinkish blob in the middle of the lilo. It took him a few seconds to realise –

'That's a man, isn't it? Sunbathing? And I'm not sure he's got any trunks on.'

'Maybe he's wearing tight Speedos that we can't see yet,' Sam said optimistically. 'Move your head a bit, Kieron – you're blocking my view.' He hesitated a moment. 'Maybe he's wearing pink trunks . . . ?' he suggested uncertainly. 'He's very fat, isn't he?'

A glowing square box appeared on the image, around the face of the floating man. A second picture appeared, inset within the first, showing his face: heavily jowled, unshaven, with little piggy eyes which were screwed shut against the bright sunlight.

'Is this Oscar Fernandez Marroquín?' Katrin asked. 'Do you recognise him?'

'It is him,' Pablo Eliente called back from the audience.

'He's right,' Kieron said, highlighting the face of the recumbent man using the ARCC software and running an identity check. A thought suddenly struck him. 'Hey, you know, I've just realised I'm watching an image of an image which has a third image inserted into it. That's a bit weird.'

Bex coughed warningly, but before she could tell Kieron quietly to concentrate, the close-up of Marroquín vanished, leaving the long-distance shot from above the house, the dots that were probably guards and the swimming pool with the lilo floating in the middle. Something seemed to *whoosh* in from the edge, speeding down past the source of the image. Suddenly the entire swimming pool vanished, replaced by an expanding fireball. The entire audience gasped as one. The tiny dots all started speeding towards where the swimming pool had been. As the fire died down, thick smoke started to expand outwards.

'And just in case you doubted us,' Katrin said, 'let us take a look at that again, from a different perspective.'

Hekla entered more commands into her tablet. The picture on the screen seemed to flicker. It took Kieron a moment to work out what had happened.

'That's a different picture,' he said. 'It's taken from slightly to one side of the last one.'

The screen image shifted, as if whatever was transmitting it was falling towards the house. Kieron assumed it was another camera zoom, but this one seemed rougher, less professional. The swimming pool grew larger and larger, as did the lilo in the centre and the man on the lilo. The rate of zoom increased as the focus continued towards the vulnerable drug lord. Kieron could see his face now, just like before, but something was wrong. The man on the lilo realised that as well: his eyes opened as Kieron watched. His expression was almost comically confused, and then his eyes opened wide in terror. He started to scream.

The picture cut to black, and then back to the previous view. Amid the drifting smoke, Kieron could clearly see a hole in the roof where the swimming pool had been.

'Oscar Fernandez Marroquín is dead,' Katrin announced. 'You will each find a tablet computer beneath your chairs. Please start bidding on how much you would pay to have us do the same to *your* enemies. The highest bids will get our services first – you can choose between speed of service and price. Thank you for your time and your attention.'

The view in Kieron's ARCC glasses shifted as Bex leaned forward to grab something from beneath her seat. It turned out to be a small tablet in a hard shell, almost military-grade. It had been wrapped in a transparent ziplock bag, presumably to protect it if the weather turned bad. She turned her head, and Kieron saw that Bradley had done the same thing. As they both straightened up, holding their tablets, Bex said quietly, 'I suppose we need to at least *look* like we're joining in.' She unzipped the bag and pulled the tablet out, folding the plastic bag up and putting it in her pocket. You never knew when those things might come in useful.

She touched the screen with her finger. It lit up immediately, displaying the Asrael logo. 'I hope there's nobody you hate enough to actually nominate,' she said quietly.

'Well,' Bradley murmured, 'there was this boy back at school. He made my life hell. I could put his name in, just for fun.' As Bex glanced at him, he added, 'Only joking. I wouldn't do that to him. Actually, he's fat and bald now, and he's got two ex-wives and five kids to support. I like to think I won out on the "success in life" game.'

'Not so you'd notice, my friend,' an accented voice said from behind them both as a large hand came down on Bex's shoulder. 'You're coming with us!'

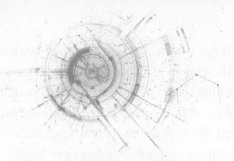

CHAPTER EIGHT

Bex felt the fingers of her captor digging hard into her shoulder. From beside her she heard Bradley gasp: the same thing was happening to him.

'The minute you touched the screens on the tablets,' a voice behind her growled, 'your fingerprints were scanned, and we checked them against all the databases we can access. Apparently you both work for the British Secret Intelligence Service. Who knew? Bad luck for you that we're technologically literate. Good luck for us that you're not.'

'What do you want me to do?!' Kieron shouted in Bex's ear.

'Just wait,' Bex said, trying to make it look like she was talking to the man who was now dragging her away, then added, 'We can explain everything!'

'Including how you stole the invitation from two of our guests and faked your way into this demonstration?' The fingers clamped hard on the soft tissue of her shoulder, biting into the nerve. 'We look forward to seeing how you do that. I have to admit, we wondered about those two people standing on the pier as we left.'

The thugs twisted Bex's arm behind her back and pushed her to the end of her row of chairs. They shoved Bradley ahead of her. He kept casting anxious glances back at her. Bex had to remind herself that, despite the fact that Bradley had been through the same training courses she had, he'd never actually operated undercover before. He knew the theory, but he'd never had to put it into practice.

'Stay strong,' she mouthed to him. 'We'll get out of this.'

The audience of criminals, terrorists and foreign intelligence operatives watched them go, glowering suspiciously. A couple of them seemed to want to head for the quayside and get out of there, but the remaining guards gestured to them with their guns, indicating they should stay where they were.

'Do not be alarmed,' Katrin said over the loudspeakers. 'This wouldn't be a decent party without gatecrashers. They will be dealt with, please rest assured. Now – let the auction continue!'

The thugs dragged Bex and Bradley across the space between the first row of chairs and the stage. Rather than take them up to the stage itself, with all the attendant publicity, they dragged them around the back of the screen.

Bex's mind raced, trying to work out ways of getting out of this. The problem was, she couldn't think of any. Every plan she came up with got them away from the immediate threat but landed them in more trouble with the other armed guards, or left them exposed to the entire audience of bad guys.

Being behind the screen was like being backstage at the

theatre while a production was taking place. People with headsets walked back and forth, muttering intently. A table had been set up with an audio-video mixing desk on it. Cables led off in all directions, like a multifunctional and technological octopus. Off to one side, a portable generator quietly chugged away.

In the midst of it all stood Hekla – tall, blonde and with perfectly sharp features. She'd left the stage to Eva and Katrin, and she still held her tablet.

The thugs threw Bex and Bradley down in the middle of an open space and stepped back, weapons raised.

'What shall we do with you?' Hekla asked, shaking her head sadly, walking casually over. 'We had assumed that *someone* would try to infiltrate our little gathering, but you were cleverer than we expected.' She smiled. 'I don't suppose we could interest you in a deal? Half-price on your first three assassinations?' She glanced from Bex to Bradley and back again. 'No, I didn't think so.'

She hadn't recognised them. That was interesting. The small changes Bex and Bradley had made to their appearances must have worked.

'So what now?' Bex asked, feeling grit and stones beneath her knees.

'Now we kill you,' Hekla said. 'You have disrupted our carefully orchestrated demonstration. We can recover it, of course, but as part of that we need the audience to see you punished.' She shrugged. 'It's business. Sorry.'

'Bex,' Kieron's panicked voice said in her ear, 'try to play for time. I've found an Italian police helicopter near the coast and I've hacked into their comms and mission system. I've told them there's an incident occurring on the island. They're flying towards you now. Just hang on.'

'You can do that?' Bex asked, surprised.

'We're in charge of everything on this island,' Hekla replied, eyebrows raised. 'Of course we can do this.'

'Hey, I'm an expert at this thing!' Kieron protested in Bex's earpiece at the same time, sounding wounded. 'I *can* do this!'

'Can I just ask,' Bex said, trying to stall long enough for Kieron's plan to work, 'how that remote assassination thing is done? I mean, it's very impressive, but I can't see how the technology works.'

'It's secret,' Hekla shrugged. 'Obviously.'

'Well, yes, but if you're going to kill us you can tell us, and we'll just take the information to our graves. That way we die happy and you get the satisfaction of knowing that we can't tell anyone.'

Hekla just smiled down at the two of them.

'My first thought,' Bradley said slowly, picking up on the plan even without knowing about Kieron's rescue scheme, 'was some kind of satellite weapon. We saw that the video feed of that drug lord was taken from above, with I think a slight slant on it. That immediately suggests to me that maybe it's a satellite weapon. The US developed some laser satellites during the Cold War.'

'Would that work?' Bex asked.

'Between satellites, probably. From a satellite to the ground, highly unlikely. The hundreds of miles of atmosphere

142

would blur the laser beam to the point where it would be useless for any destructive purpose.' He frowned. 'I suppose a reconnaissance satellite could be used as a targeting system for another weapon, but that feed we were watching didn't show any evidence of the camera system moving, and reconnaissance satellites orbit pretty fast. No, on reflection I think it's more likely to be something much lower in the atmosphere – an aircraft, or a drone.'

'Sounds plausible,' Bex said, nodding. She glanced up at Hekla, who was watching the two of them with supercilious interest.

'We saw the picture switch from one camera to another one just before the drug bloke died. That probably means there was one drone watching, probably hovering high up in the atmosphere, and another drone nearby with a warhead on board. Once the first system had acquired the target, the second system stopped hovering and guided itself down to the pool.'

'But,' Bex pointed out hurriedly, noticing out of the corner of her eye that Hekla was looking bored and had been about to interrupt, 'the target was chosen at random. That means Asrael must have explosive drones hovering in the atmosphere all across the world, above every country. Hundreds of thousands of drones, just waiting to be ordered to locate a target and kill them. Millions of drones maybe, just hovering in the clouds. Surely someone would see them? Aircraft, radar systems, amateur astronomers with telescopes . . .'

'Unless the drones are somehow transparent,' Bradley said with the air of someone laying down a winning card.

Bex turned back to Hekla. 'So – as far as we can tell, either Asrael has launched a million transparent drones fitted with high-definition digital cameras and explosive charges into the skies without anybody noticing, or it's all a massive trick. Do you want to tell us which one it is?'

'I think it's a good thing you're going to be dead soon,' Hekla said.

'How long until something happens?' Bex asked, speaking slightly louder so that Kieron would know that she was actually talking to him.

Kieron was on the ball. 'Less than a minute,' he said in her ear.

Hekla shrugged. 'We're not going to torture you – there's no point. Something quick, I think, and then we dump your bodies in the lagoon.' She smiled. 'Don't worry – you'll be dead before you know it.'

'Given the levels of pollution in the lagoon,' Bradley said, voice calm, 'I wouldn't be at all surprised.'

'There's something you're not taking into account,' Bex said to Hekla.

The girl frowned. 'What's that?'

Bex smiled. She wasn't sure if this was going to work, but she had faith. She also had very good hearing, and she had picked up what sounded like a deep *thrum* that was half-sound, half-vibration in her hands and knees.

'You have customers,' she said, 'but we have friends.'

Suddenly the whole area behind the stage, behind the screen, lit up. The light was so bright that Bex had to screw her eyes shut and peer through her slitted eyelids.

144

'*Tutti, per favore, rimaneti dove sieti!*' a loudspeaker blared, shivering the very air.

'That's the Italian police helicopter arriving,' Kieron said in Bex's ear. 'Get out of there.'

Bex looked left and right, at the two thugs who stood there with guns in their hands, pointing down at where she and Bradley knelt on the soil of the Venetian island.

She glanced over at Bradley. His left hand rested on the dirt, but she saw that his fingers were curled, digging in. His head twisted slightly, and she saw the gleam of his eyes. He was waiting. Waiting for her.

She put her hand down, fingers clenching in the dirt. The dirt that might, for all she knew, contain the ashes of centuries of dead Venetians and the seeds of bubonic plague, but what the hell. She closed her fingers around a good handful, then said, 'Give us a countdown.'

'What?' Hekla said, frowning.

'Three . . .' Kieron said in her earpiece. 'Two . . . One . . . Go!'

Bex threw the handful of dirt up into the face of the nearest thug with a gun. To her left, Bradley did the same.

The two thugs staggered backwards, hands rising to their faces, fingers clawing to get the grit out of their eyes. Bex sprang up and launched herself at the nearest, wrestling the gun from his hands and kneeing him in the groin.

'Go!' she shouted, grabbing hold of Bradley's arm as he was getting up from the ground and pushing him backwards, but using the impetus to throw herself forward, towards Hekla. 'Party dress!'

As her shoulder hit Hekla's chest, driving the Norwegian girl backwards, Bex heard Bradley's footsteps running unevenly across the ground. She hoped he'd got the hint. If she'd yelled, 'Meet up again at the quayside, where we joked about my party dress!' then the Asrael crew would have known where they were going. By shouting what to them must have been a meaningless phrase, she hoped she'd given the two of them a chance. Hoped. It all depended on how on the ball Bradley was.

Hekla's heels caught on the rough ground and she stumbled. Bex grabbed the tablet from her hand, only belatedly aware that she herself was still holding the one from beneath her seat. She quickly swiped upwards, catching Hekla beneath the chin with the twin tablets. Hekla's teeth slammed together with an audible *click* and she fell backwards, spreadeagled on the bare earth, eyes wide open and shocked.

Bex started running before looking around to check the tactical situation. She deliberately ran in the opposite direction to Bradley: if they were going to be chased, it made sense to split the enemy's forces. Stones rattled away as her feet caught them. She glanced over her shoulder.

Behind her, one of the guards was pulling Hekla back to her feet while the other one pointed his weapon up at the hovering police helicopter. As Bex watched, his finger twitched on the trigger. A spray of bullets zipped upwards. Aware that he'd come under fire, the helicopter's pilot must have pulled on the cyclic control stick. The helicopter veered away, gaining height to get out of range of the gunfire. As it slewed sideways the bright spotlight swung around, momentarily illuminating Bradley as he ran past the massive screen and into the audience. Nobody seemed to be pursuing him. That, at least, was one piece of good luck.

Bex sprinted as fast as she could through the near darkness. There seemed to be no other lights on the island apart from the helicopter spotlight and the ones that Asrael had brought with them. All she could see was what was illuminated by the stars and the half-moon that sat glowering near the horizon.

The ground rose steeply under her feet. Somewhere up ahead she sensed, rather than saw, a low ridge in the ground. At the very least that would give her something to hide behind, and maybe she could crawl along in its shelter if it led towards the quayside.

She hoped Bradley would be all right.

'Kieron?' she said suddenly, remembering that he was still there.

'Ye-es.' He sounded hesitant. 'Are you both OK?'

'So far. The party's probably over though.'

'Good thing you're not wearing that party dress – you wouldn't be able to run properly.'

'You'd be surprised,' she said. 'I once chased down a guy wearing a wedding dress. Me – not him.'

'Thanks for the clarification,' Kieron said, sounding a little bit more cheerful. 'But you're not married, are you? *Are* you?'

'I was undercover,' she said. By now she'd got to the top of the hill and was sliding down the other side. 'And

I don't think the ceremony ever got to the end. We were at the "Does anybody know just cause or reason" bit when it all kicked off.'

She took a moment to look around. The ridge curved away to either side, but it was what the ridge surrounded that took her breath momentarily away. Rows of blocky tombs stretched away, made out of a white stone that almost glowed in the moonlight, with avenues of cracked tilted paving slabs and grass separating them. The tombs weren't individual ones, like you might see in an English graveyard – each row was maybe eight feet high, and had five small doors, one above the other, running from the ground to the ornately sculpted top. The doors were made of the same white stone, but had little scalloped ledges where plants or candles could be placed. It was, Bex thought almost hysterically, like looking at an endless row of marble filing cabinets, but knowing that each drawer probably had a dead body in it. A very old dead body.

'Are you seeing this?' she asked Kieron. 'I'm not hallucinating, am I?'

'If you are then so am I. I think I saw this film once. It doesn't end well.'

From the other side of the ridge she heard footsteps. She quickly moved diagonally across the open ground towards the shelter of one of the rows.

'Bradley's still got his earpiece, hasn't he?' Bex said, thinking.

'Probably.' Kieron didn't sound confident. 'I suppose it could have fallen out in the confusion. And he hasn't got a microphone. So even if he can hear us, we can't hear him.'

'Understood.' She kept her voice low, so that her pursuer – if there was a pursuer – couldn't hear her. 'I want you to check the video on the ARCC glasses from when we arrived on the island. Apart from the boat that brought us here, are there any other boats? Bradley and I will need something to get away on, and I want to know what our options are. I don't think we can rely on the police – they'd just take us into custody along with everyone else and sort out who we are later on.'

'Will do.'

She slipped down the wide avenue and along the nearest row of tombs as quietly as she could, listening all the time for the sounds of movement. Every ten metres or so she noticed a narrower gap between the blocks, running at right-angles to the wider avenues. That was useful – if there hadn't been anything like that then anyone standing at the end of the avenue could just look all the way along it and see her. At least she had a way out.

Something howled in the distance. Probably the wind whistling through the alleyways, she told herself. Nothing to worry about. And definitely not a werewolf or a ghoul. Those things didn't exist.

Breathing fast, she slipped into one of the gaps and poked her head back around the edge, looking in the direction from which she'd come. She couldn't see anyone there, but in the distance, beyond the edge of the tombs, the cone of light from the police helicopter shone down on the amphitheatre where the demonstration had been taking place. It was flying higher now, and moving around jerkily. Bex thought she heard rapid gunfire, but she couldn't tell if it was coming from the ground or the helicopter. Maybe both.

'I guess at least we disrupted Asrael's little party,' she said. 'Maybe they'll be so concerned with repairing the damage to their reputations that they'll leave us alone for a while.'

'Let's hope,' Kieron said.

'I know,' she went on. 'It would be nice to have a bit more certainty.'

She knew she had to find her way to the quayside and hoped Bradley was there. She turned and moved to the other end of the alley between the blocks of tombs, to the next avenue. She glanced out quickly, looking rapidly left and right. The avenue stretched out in both directions: deserted. She slipped out into the unnervingly open space and headed back towards the ridge, and the amphitheatre. If she went the other way she risked getting lost among the tombs. They all looked the same. She had to get back to a landmark she recognised.

Many of the flat stone doors that sealed the tombs were cracked. Some were broken, and a few were missing entirely. Inside the ones she could see into, she made out box-like spaces with a lot of dust, and sometimes a rough shape wrapped in old cloth. In one or two of the tombs she thought she could see bones, and in one she was convinced a rounded skull sat, staring outwards through shadowed eye sockets.

That dust . . . Her mind kept on going back to Kieron's casual statement about bubonic plague victims. How long could plague bacteria live? A year? Ten years? A hundred?

What was the risk of breathing it in?

To be fair, that was probably the smallest risk she currently had to worry about.

She paused as a distant screech echoed back and forth between the stone walls of the mausoleums, making it hard to judge distance or direction. Just an owl, she told herself. Really, it's just an owl. Not a werewolf or a ghoul.

'Do they have owls in Venice?' she heard herself asking Kieron.

'What?'

'Never mind.'

A noise – behind her. Pebbles hitting a stone wall. She turned quickly, scanning the empty spaces between the rows of tombs that lined the avenue, but she saw nothing. She backed herself up against the nearest tombs, trying to minimise her silhouette to anyone who might step out. Her head was beside a tomb with a cracked door: the stone broken, with a large chunk having fallen to the ground.

She held her breath, waiting.

Nothing. No movement, no sound.

She relaxed, just a little bit. Maybe it had just been a bird, or a cat, looking for food. Mice, running away from an owl swooping close overhead.

Something reached out from the cracked door of the nearest tomb and touched her hair.

Bex's whole body tensed in shock. She suppressed an instinctive scream, took a step away and turned, hands raised, ready to fight whatever was trying to pull itself out of the darkness.

The pointed, whiskered nose of a rat sniffed suspiciously at the air, then pulled back into the shadows.

Bex let out a breath she hadn't even known she was holding. Rats and cemeteries. She supposed she shouldn't even have been surprised.

'Are you OK?' Kieron said suddenly. 'Only, your heart rate has suddenly shot way up.'

'Just a little taken aback,' she muttered. 'It's very – Gothic – here. Very atmospheric.'

As she looked back towards the amphitheatre, she saw that the police helicopter had flown even higher, and its spotlight swung back and forth erratically, trying to pick out some kind of sense in all the activity she suspected was going on. The gunfire seemed to have stopped though.

'The Italian police are sending more helicopters,' Kieron said in her ear. 'I'm intercepting their communications. They think it's some kind of terrorist activity, or maybe a war between rival drug gangs. Either way, they're taking it seriously.'

'Did you manage to look at the ARCC camera images?' she asked.

'Yeah – as well as the Sunseeker boat you came in on, there's a couple of motor launches moored there. You and Bradley should be able to get away – if you can get to them before Asrael do.'

'Then I need to get moving.'

She took three decisive steps along the row of tombs, making sure she stayed at least one rat's body length away from the dark holes of the broken doors. As she came alongside one of the alleys that ran perpendicular to the avenues, she glanced across the far side, then back to the alley by her shoulder.

Where a dark shaped suddenly lunged at her.

The shoulder stock of an automatic weapon caught her cheek. For a second all she could see was glowing stars swimming in a blood-red sea. A sudden impact knocked the breath from her body, and it took a moment before she realised that she'd fallen and her shoulder had hit the ground. Belatedly, pain washed through her body like a cold wave. She took a deep breath through clenched teeth. No time to recover, only time to react. Story of her life.

Her legs were bent, facing towards the alley between the rows of tombs. She suddenly straightened them, pushing her feet straight out. She was lucky: her heels connected with the ankles of the man who'd hit her with his gun. She heard him grunt in pain, and moments later his weapon clattered on the ground as he fell forward, hitting the ground beside her.

Stay or go? Take his weapon, or just get the hell out of there?

She rolled over, reaching out for the gun. Her fingers touched a metal barrel. She grabbed for it, tearing it out of the man's hands.

He turned over and scrabbled away, trying to get to his feet. Bex used the gun as a crutch, pushing herself up with it and launching herself at him. As she dived forward she bought the gun swinging around. The thug was on his knees by now. The weapon caught him on the temple, knocking him sideways. He hit the wall of the narrow alleyway and slid down it, apparently unconscious.

Bex ran to the end of the alley, quickly checked the next avenue, and then, once she'd established it was empty, ran out into it and back towards the clearing where the demonstration had taken place.

'Do you have a map of this island?' she asked Kieron.

'Kinda – I mean, I know its shape. There's not much more detail than that.'

'Can you overlay the stuff you know about – the quayside, the clearing with the seats in and the tombs – over the map? Just to get an idea of where I'm going.'

'Already done.'

'Good work. I don't want to go back through the demonstration area, for obvious reasons. Am I better off going right or left?'

A moment's pause, then: 'If you go left you're getting close to the edge of the island. There's a chance you might get pinned down. Right gives you plenty of space to circle around it.'

He was thinking tactically. Bex felt a sudden flush of pride. Not the time to tell him though. 'I'll do that then.'

She emerged from the avenue between the blocks of tombs. Ahead of her, the ridge was silhouetted by light spilling over from the arena. She climbed over the banked earth and angled right, keeping away from the lights. She could see the space behind the screen, where she'd confronted Hekla, but it was deserted now. The technicians had gone. Even the mixing desk had been removed. The screen was still there though, and as Bex passed it she got a good look at the rows of seats where the audience of criminals and terrorists had previously been sitting. It too was deserted now; half the seats lay on their sides, knocked over in the chaos. Two of the spotlights had been knocked over as well, their lenses cracked and their bulbs burned out. Bex had the impression that the audience had panicked: with the Italian police circling overhead the whole Asrael thing must have looked to them like some elaborate trap, some way of getting them all out into the open where they could be arrested. The problem was, they had no way off the island except for Asrael's Sunseeker yacht. There was probably a crowd trying to force their way on board right now. Well, at least this whole thing meant Asrael were probably a spent force in the assassination business, and good riddance.

Kieron would probably be sad about the way that events had turned out though. Bex made a mental note to have a serious talk with him when she got back. *If* she made it back. She'd got the impression that he had quite a crush on the lead Norwegian girl – Kirsten?

Past the seating area, Bex made her way through the relative darkness. She could hear muffled shouting from up ahead and to her left – probably the audience of potential assassin-hirers fighting their way onto the boat. She aimed right, heading for where Kieron had indicated the motor boats were tied up. If she was lucky – *really* lucky – some of the technicians and guards wouldn't yet have made it back there. Well, she knew that at least one guard was flat out back among the tombs. Maybe a couple of the others had been crushed in the audience rush.

And, of course, she had to find Bradley.

She sensed rather than saw the rise of the ground between her and the quayside area. Just as she realised it was there, Kieron's voice said in her ear, 'I'm picking up an infrared glow from up ahead. I think it's people.'

'OK.' She dropped to a crouch and climbed the ridge until her head was just above the edge and she could see what lay ahead. Far in the distance, the lights of the main city of Venice glittered. Off to her left the Sunseeker yacht had just pulled away from the concrete quay. Half the criminal audience had failed to get on board – they were either shouting and waving their fists in ineffectual fury or trying to jump the rapidly increasing space before the yacht was out of reach. One Italian police helicopter hovered overhead, shining its light on the scene. In the distance, another two were en route to the island.

'The motor boats I mentioned earlier are over to your right,' Kieron said suddenly.

'OK. Any sign of Bradley?'

'I don't know where he is. Even on infrared I can't see him. He must be hidden by buildings or stuff.'

All the attention seemed to be focused on the departing Sunseeker. Bex crept across the top of the ridge, keeping low to minimise her profile to anyone who happened to be looking in her direction. Broken flagstones, gravel and patches of scrubby grass lay between her and the lagoon. Some kind of building lay ahead and to her right; just a black shape against the stars. Quietly she made her way towards it.

The building was old, with windows missing and large gaps in its walls. Half of the roof had fallen in. All in all, it was as old and ruined as the rest of the island.

Looking around the building's corner, towards the edge of the old quayside, she saw two thick coils of rope. They were tied to large, rusty rings set into the concrete. About a metre of rope joined them to the quayside itself, where they vanished over a drop rough enough that it might have been nibbled away by mythical creatures. If she was lucky there would be motor boats on the other ends of those ropes. If she was *un*lucky then it would be old rowboats, or perhaps nothing at all.

She moved past the building and prepared to make a run towards the rusty rings, the ropes and possible salvation.

'I was beginning to think I was on my own here,' a voice hissed.

'Never that,' she whispered back as Bradley appeared by her shoulder. 'Do you still have your bidding tablet thing from the demonstration?'

'Nice to know you're more concerned with my welfare than with any evidence I might have kept on my person.' He held up his clear ziplock bag that had held his tablet. 'But you know me and technology – I can't let it go. Yeah, I've still got it. Have you got yours?'

'Yes. I'm thinking there might be material on there that will lead us back to wherever Asrael are based, so we can find out who hired them to kill us.' She shrugged. 'Assuming they actually did get hired to kill us, and we weren't just part of some other demonstration.'

'Well, let's hope it ended better than this one.' He tapped his ear. 'I've still got the earpiece in too. I've been monitoring your communications with Kieron. I'm guessing the motor boats are just over there?'

'Seems likely. Are you up for a little trip over the water?'

'Ooh – do I have a choice?'

'Well, you could see if the Italian police helicopters would give you a ride . . .'

'Thanks – I think I'll stick with you.'

Bex ran across the gap between the ruined building and the lagoon. She glanced over the edge. A rusty metal ladder with several missing rungs led down to where two sleek, black motor boats bobbed on the black water. She waved a hand to beckon to Bradley. 'We're in business,' she called in a low voice. 'Come on.'

As she heard his footsteps running across the concrete to join her she slipped down the ladder and into the nearest motor boat. Moments later Bradley was beside her. Quickly she pulled the cover off the starter switch. There were six terminals underneath. She delved into her pocket for the piece of wire she'd used to break into the safe back in the Hotel Danieli. She looped the wire around the 'B' and the 'S' terminals to make an electrical connection, and the engine behind her roared into life.

'Cast off,' she said.

Bradley looked blank. 'What?'

'Untie the rope that's holding us!'

'Oh. You should have said. I'm not a nautical person.' He moved to the back of the boat. After a few seconds he said, 'Done.'

'Hold on to something.' She gunned the engine, and the motor boat pulled smoothly away from the island, its bow rising out of the water. She heard a sudden scuffle from behind her, but no splash or yell, so Bradley was probably OK. Probably.

Glancing to her left she saw the blaze of lights in the distance, from where the yacht and the helicopter were involved in some kind of complicated interception out on the waters of the lagoon. A lot of terrorists and criminals would be spending the night in police custody – and possibly longer, if there were any outstanding international warrants out on them. Hopefully, in all the confusion, nobody would notice that she and Bradley had left.

'Kieron?' she said, as a sudden thought hit her.

'Yes.'

'Get on to room service. We're going to need a bottle of wine and some sandwiches. It's been a long night.'

'Will do.'

She guided the motor boat in a smooth curve away from the island and towards the historic city of Venice. Salt-tinged wind blew her hair back from her face, and spray from the lagoon dampened her skin. She felt absurdly happy. It wasn't like they'd actually accomplished much, but at least they'd disrupted the Asrael meeting and got away with some more information, so it qualified as a success. And she was in a very expensive motor boat, which had to count for something.

'Ah, Bex?' Bradley called from the back of the boat.

'Yeah?'

'You know that other motor boat – the one moored beside this one?'

'Yeah . . .' She had a bad feeling that she knew what was coming.

'Someone's climbed down into it, and they've started it up. I think they're coming after us.'

'Do you "think", or are you sure?'

A pause. 'I'm sure.'

Bex pushed the twin throttle levers forward, keeping one hand on the wheel to maintain a straight course. Her heart started beating faster. She should have known this wouldn't be quite so easy. Life never was.

The bow of the boat rose further out of the water and it surged ahead. That engine was powerful. She supposed it made sense. An organisation as well-prepared as Asrael – and they were an organisation, she was sure, not just three girls from Norway and some friends – would buy or rent the best.

She glanced over her shoulder. Phosphorescent wake boiled and bubbled behind them as they raced through the water, forming a white line that pointed right back to the cemetery island. The wind dried her eyes out, and she had to blink a couple of times so she could see properly.

'What's happening?' she called.

'Two people in the boat,' Bradley called. 'One driving – looks like one of the blonde girls. One with an assault rifle – looks like another of the blonde girls. I don't know where the third one has gone.' He paused, then: 'Whoops!'

'What?'

160

'They're firing at us!' he shouted. 'But they're bouncing up and down on the waves, so their aim is off!'

'Yeah – for future reference, that's an "Oh hell!", not a "Whoops!"'

'Duly noted!'

Bex's thoughts raced as she checked and double-checked all the possible futures that fanned out from that point in time. Could they make it to St Mark's Square before the other boat caught them? Possibly, but while they were slowing to dock at a pier the other boat would close the gap. Would Asrael shoot, even at the edge of St Mark's Square? Probably, if they thought they could get away. Alternatively, if they caught up with them before St Mark's Square, what would they do? Disable their boat by shooting into the engine probably. That was if they wanted Bex and Bradley alive. If they didn't care if they lived or died, then they'd probably fire into the fuel tank and watch as it exploded.

So – one chain of logic led to them probably being shot as they disembarked at St Mark's Square, while another chain of logic led to them being caught or blown up in the middle of the lagoon. The chances of them getting to safety were vanishingly small. And the Italian police? They were completely occupied with taking the yacht and its occupants into custody. They weren't concerned about two motor boats. No help there.

The whole process took less than a second, and by the end of it she knew there was a high chance that she and Bradley would be intercepted, and either captured or killed.

So . . .

'Bradley?'

'Yeah?' he called back.

'Your tablet – it's still in that sealed plastic bag?'

'Yeah. Why?'

'Put your ARCC earpiece in there, then come and get my earpiece and glasses off me while I'm steering. Oh, and I snatched Hekla's tablet as well – it's down by my feet with my one. Put everything into the plastic bag, breathe some air into it and reseal it, then make sure it's watertight.'

'OK – then what?'

'Then throw it in the water.' Before Bradley could ask what she was doing, she called, 'Kieron?'

'Yes.' He sounded scared.

'We're going offline. There's a fair chance that the other motor boat is going to intercept us, and if that happens I want to make sure one of Asrael's tablets gets to you so the two of you can analyse it.'

'WHAT?!' That was Kieron shouting.

'Don't argue, and don't protest.' She spoke fast, overriding his natural teenage inclination to argue. 'Just accept it. This is the hardest lesson any agent has to learn: suck up what can't be changed, and move on, taking it into account.'

She could hear a tiny voice in the back of her head saying, *God, grant me the serenity to accept the things I cannot change, the courage to change the things I can, and the wisdom to know the difference.* Her dad used to have that saying framed on his wall.

'Don't try to change the things that can't be changed,' she went on. 'I'm going to leave the tablets floating in the water

162

just off the coast of this cemetery island, in a waterproof plastic bag filled with air. You and Sam need to come and get them. You can locate it via my ARCC glasses – they've got a homing chip, and I know you can find it.'

'And what then?' he shouted.

She took a deep breath. This was hard. Harder than anything she'd ever done. Asking someone to abandon her – that was easy. She'd been rehearsing that all her professional life. Asking someone to risk their lives to continue the fight – that was *hard*.

'Listen to me very carefully. Bradley and I are out on a limb here. Nobody in MI6 knows we're in Venice, for very good reasons. It's just the four of us – me, Bradley, you and Sam. I could tell you and Sam to go back to England and forget about us, but I know you well enough to know you won't do that.' She took a deep breath, closed her eyes, prayed momentarily, then continued. 'So given that I know you're going to ignore any instructions to leave us, if we're not back at the hotel within the next forty-five minutes you're going to have to get those tablets, and you and Sam are going to have to electronically take them apart and see what evidence might be in there about where Bradley and I have been taken. I don't think they're going to hang around Venice. It's too hot for them here. Thanks to your actions – which I thoroughly approve of – the Italian police are going to be crawling over everything local. I think Asrael are going to take us back to their base to find out who we are and why we're so interested in them.'

If they don't kill us straight away, she thought. Which they might.

'I don't know how the two of you are going to do it, but I'm hoping that you can find a way of saving us. Use the ARCC glasses, and use your intelligence and your natural ability to do surprising things. The glasses will give you access to our bank account. Try not to spend it all on concert tickets and T-shirts. And –' she took a deep breath and tried to force down the lump in her throat – 'if you don't manage to rescue us, then don't let it drag you down. Get over it. I'm asking the impossible here, so don't fret if you can't manage it. If we're not rescued then it doesn't mean you've failed – it means I was asking too much.'

She stopped, the lump in her throat too large to get words past.

'Bex,' Kieron said.

'Yes.'

'This is us. This is Sam and me. Of *course* we'll rescue you.'

'Bex out,' she said, pulling the earpiece from her ear and the glasses from her face before her sudden, heartfelt sob could travel across the airwaves between her and the two kids she had come to love so much. She passed them one-handed to Bradley, who had moved up to stand behind her.

'Did you hear any of that?' she asked.

She thought he reached up and plucked an earpiece from his ear, but it wasn't easy to tell as she fought to keep the motor boat steady as it ploughed through the waves.

'Not a word,' he said. She also thought he slipped the earpiece into the transparent bag he held, but she couldn't be sure. He threw the bag over the side.

A sudden *rat-a-tat-a-tat-a-tat* probably meant that their pursuers had fired on them. The motor boat jinked left, the steering wheel fighting her hands for control.

'What do you think?' she said, as Bradley threw the bag over the side. 'Keep running, or just give up?'

'Oh, keep running,' he replied steadily. 'Why make it easy for them?'

She glanced at him, meeting his gaze. 'Good advice.'

Something pinged off the metal frame of the windscreen, leaving a gash of bright metal that shone in the moonlight. A bullet. Bex hauled on the wheel, pulling the boat around in a loose curve, then turned the wheel the other way. The boat obediently swerved back again, leaving a wavy trail of white wake behind it. The manoeuvre cost them a bit of the lead they had, but if it put off the marksman in the boat chasing them then it was worth it.

'The boat that's chasing us is the same make and model as the one we're in,' she called to Bradley. He'd moved to the back of the boat, where she presumed he was throwing the plastic bag over the side. 'That means we have to assume it's just as fast and just as manoeuvrable. So – we can't outrun it and we can't out-turn it. That limits our options.' She turned her head briefly and glanced over her shoulder, just checking that he hadn't fallen in when she altered the boat's path. He was still there, seemingly kneeling at the bow and leaning over. She wasn't sure what he was doing. 'If I keep on going in a straight line they'll stay the same distance behind us, firing at us until they hit the engine or the fuel tank. Or one of us.' She looked over her shoulder again. He was still there, bent over the rail. 'What are you doing?'

'Throwing up,' he shouted back. 'I get seasick. Don't worry about me. Keep going. I'm listening.'

'OK.' She paused, gathering her thoughts. 'Our best bet is for me to keep weaving this boat back and forth in the water. That'll leave a wake behind us. If they're cutting across our wake all the time then hopefully that'll slow them down, and maybe destabilise them as well. And if I can fool them into thinking I'm steering left, then I can steer right and build up more of a lead. It's a plan, but frankly not much of one. What do you think?'

'I think I should have skipped lunch,' Bradley called back miserably.

'Did you throw the bag overboard?'

'Oh, believe me – everything I have that can be thrown has been thrown.'

True to her plan, Bex kept turning the wheel, first one way and then, a few seconds later, the other way. From above their path must have looked like a glowing snake in the darkness. When she looked backwards she could just about see the windscreen of the black boat chasing them, flashing as it reflected the moonlight. As she had predicted, it was keeping a straight course, but whenever it hit the ridge in the water that marked their wake it nearly left the water entirely, and then smashed down into it again, like a car driving far too fast over a speed bump. She almost felt sorry for their pursuers – their teeth must be rattling in their gums. There was no way the marksman could have kept a steady aim under those conditions. The best they could do was just spray bullets vaguely in their direction, hoping that one of them would hit.

Which is exactly what was happening. Bex's windscreen suddenly developed a rash of small holes in the plastic, each outlined by a web of white cracks. Something plucked at the sleeve of her jacket. She looked down and saw a neat hole in the material that hadn't been there when she'd put it on earlier.

They were probably halfway across the lagoon now, heading towards the brightly lit areas of Venice where the city never slept. Other boats were on the water near them; she could see their lights: white on their bows; red, white and green set in a triangle on their sterns; white and green set diagonally on their sides in the internationally understood maritime code. She wondered what the crew and passengers on those boats made of the two unlit black motor boats zipping past them.

The windscreen was bowing towards her now, the plastic under pressure from the headwind generated by their rapid passage. Small bits of plastic detached and flew off into the darkness.

She felt an itch right between her shoulder blades. Any minute now, she thought, a bullet is going to hit exactly in that spot. Any minute now.

The black bulk of a *vaporetto* loomed up ahead of her. As they passed it Bex hauled on the wheel, bringing them into a tight curve around the *vaporetto*, using it as cover. Rather than coming back to her original route, she kept going at a right angle, hoping that their pursuers wouldn't notice.

They were cleverer than that. Where Bex had gone one side of the *vaporetto*, the other motor boat had gone the other side and ended up heading straight for Bex. She turned her head briefly, cursing, and clearly saw the face of the girl at the wheel, and the other girl standing beside her, one hand braced around the back of her chair and the other hand holding an automatic weapon. As Bex turned her head back, snarling and checking ahead of her for any other boats before she hit them, she saw in the corner of her eye flashes of light from the muzzle of the weapon. Moments later it was as if people were hitting the side of the motor boat with hammers. Lots of people; lots of hammers.

The engine coughed and died. One of the bullets must have severed a fuel line.

The motor boat slowed dramatically, pitching and yawing as the waves of the lagoon hit it. The other motor boat slowed as well, but under power; bringing itself alongside.

The chase was over. She and Bradley were Asrael's prisoners.

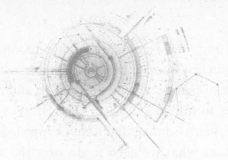

CHAPTER NINE

'Oh hell. Oh no.' Kieron leaned back in his chair and put the palms of his hands over his eyes.

He heard Sam breathing heavily behind him. 'What happened?' his friend asked.

'The video and audio feed from the ARCC glasses stopped when Bex took them off. You heard what she said – she's put them into a plastic bag and thrown them into the lagoon.' He hesitated, feeling a churning mix of emotions bubbling up within his chest, threatening to block his windpipe. 'She's gone, Sam. She and Bradley – they're actually gone! They're not there any more.'

'If I heard Bex correctly,' Sam said calmly, 'they told us to wait forty-five minutes to see if they get back here. Just because they've thrown the kit into the lagoon doesn't mean they didn't manage to escape. Look on the bright side.'

'OK.' Kieron tried hard to push down the feeling in his chest. 'So we wait forty-five minutes. Then what?'

'Again, if I heard Bex correctly, she's given us instructions to track them down and rescue them.'

'If they haven't been killed on the spot and their bodies

thrown into the lagoon!' Kieron said, his voice much higher-pitched than he was comfortable with. He was on the edge of panicking, and he knew it, and he couldn't do anything to stop it.

'Well, yes, assuming that hasn't happened,' Sam agreed. 'And that's what we need to do over the next forty-five minutes –'

'Forty-four now,' Kieron muttered.

'OK, the next forty-*four* minutes – we need to get eyes on the ground. Or the water. Whatever. We need to find out what's actually happening out there – whether Bex and Bradley have been shot and their bodies dumped, or whether they've been taken prisoner.'

'And how exactly do we do that, genius?'

'We've got the ARCC kit,' Sam pointed out in a steady, level voice that Kieron's mind grabbed hold of like a drowning man would grab hold of any piece of flotsam or jetsam floating past. A drowning *agent* . . .'And you were plugged into the Italian police force, remember? They'll know what's happened. They'll be swarming around there like wasps around a pot of jam. If any bodies are discovered in the water, they'll know about it. Just keep monitoring their communications.'

'OK.' Kieron breathed in and out a couple of times, trying to steady his pounding heart. 'I can do that.'

'Yes, you can.' Sam reached out and put his hand on Kieron's shoulder. He squeezed it reassuringly. 'Winning the cross-country race, that's not important. Dressing like everyone else and listening to the same music they do, *that's*

170

not important. It doesn't matter that we've always failed at things like that. But *this* is important, and that means we have to step up and do it, regardless of how hard it is and how it makes us feel. Because that's who we are – we're the kids who know what's important and do it, while the rest are posing in their hoodies and showing off their bling. We can do this, bro. We *are* that good.'

'That,' Kieron said, 'is probably the worst motivational speech I've ever heard.'

'Worked though, didn't it?'

'Yes. It worked.'

Kieron dived straight in, using the ARCC glasses to scan video feeds and audio inputs, watching the flickering images projected onto the lenses and using his hands to select options and move data around. Pretty quickly he established that the Italian police –the carabinieri, as they were apparently called – hadn't got a clue what was going on. Radio messages were talking about everything from a spat between criminal gangs through a terrorist attack up to a full-scale uprising by Fascist forces. Nobody had mentioned the possibility of alien invasion yet, but Kieron thought it was only a matter of time. The level of hysteria was incredible. But the good news was that no bodies had been recovered. The Sunseeker yacht had been intercepted and guided to a secure location, where the suspects on board were being processed and questioned, and two motor boats – occupants unknown – had been seen escaping at high speed, but nothing else. At least that was something. Something he could grab hold of.

'What's the situation?' Sam asked. He slid something onto

the table in front of Kieron. 'I got some food from room service while you were working. I tried to get a bottle of wine as well, but they wanted to know how old I was, so I told them to forget it.'

'Thanks. It's chaos out there, but at least there's no sign of Bex and Bradley's . . . any bodies.'

'Well, that's good. What next?'

'Next I try to locate the glasses they threw overboard while they were trying to escape. If I can find out where they are, then we can try to get them back and analyse the stuff that's with them for clues.'

With a grand gesture he swept the virtual carabinieri windows away and called up a geolocation programme. A default option quickly called up the chip in the ARCC glasses Bex had been wearing. Kieron selected the 'find now' option, and waited while the software ran. Ten seconds later it was telling him that the glasses were in the middle of the lagoon, located somewhere in between a set of small islands.

'Got them,' he said. 'Although I'm not sure how we're going to get to them.'

'They're in the water, right?' Sam said through a mouthful of food.

'Right.' Kieron felt a sudden stab of hunger. He hadn't eaten for hours.

'Then we hire a boat, we get the boat driver –'

'The captain.'

'We get the captain to take us out into the lagoon and we retrieve the floating bag of stuff. Assuming it hasn't sprung a leak so that it isn't floating any more.'

'Brilliant. How do we pay for the boat?'

'Using Bex and Bradley's bank account, remember. We can get some money out of a cashpoint. They said we should.'

'And what do we tell the captain of the boat?'

'That's easy. We say we want to get the perfect photograph of Venice, and we've calculated the absolutely perfect spot from which to take it, but it's in the middle of the lagoon. So we give him the coordinates and get him to take us there.' He paused. 'We'll tell him it's for a school project.'

Kieron shrugged. 'OK. Where's my food?'

'Extend your right hand. Now lower it. OK – your hand is now in your food.'

'You're a moron – do you know that?'

Kieron picked up the plate and a fork and shovelled food into his mouth. It was great – spaghetti in a tomatoey, slightly spicy sauce that had bits in it that looked like mushrooms but were squishy. 'What *is* this?' he asked Sam through a mouthful of it.

'It's called spaghetti alla vongole,' Sam said. 'Not sure how that translates.'

'It's good. The mushrooms are odd though.'

Halfway through the bowl of pasta, his mobile rang. He grabbed it. 'Bex?'

'Who is Bex? Is that some girl you've met?'

It was his mum's voice. 'Mum – what are you doing?'

'What – I can't phone my favourite son to see if he's eating properly and washing?' Her voice was slightly slurred. Kieron checked the time. It was late at night in Venice, but dinnertime where his mum was. He hoped she was having some food with her wine.

'How's the course going?' he asked.

'It's OK.' She sighed. 'They keep telling us stories to try and convince us that life can be better if you've lost your job. They did one today about some mice who get cheese delivered to them every day, and then one day the cheese doesn't turn up. Some of the mice stay where they are, hoping the cheese will reappear some time, but the others go off in search of more cheese – and they find it. They find better cheese than they had before, while the mice who stayed put starved to death waiting for their cheese. Quite a morbid story. Obviously the cheese is our wages, and the point is to convince us that we should go out and look for new, better jobs rather than obsess about what we had. I said I could just as easily write a story in which the mice who stayed where they were got rewarded with a double-sized delivery of cheese and the ones who left all died of starvation, but apparently that wasn't the "right" answer, so I've now been labelled a troublemaker.' She sighed. 'Still, there's this really nice guy on the course that I'm getting on well with, so who knows? Maybe good things will happen.'

'That's – lovely, Mum. I'm glad you're enjoying yourself.'

'What about you, darling?' she asked. 'Are you surviving OK without me? I'll give you a clue – the correct answer is, "No, I'm having a terrible time, and I can't wait until you're back."'

Kieron looked around the hotel room, through the ARCC glasses that were still showing him maps of the lagoon, with its complicated current patterns and the location of Bex's

174

glasses and earpiece. 'No,' he said, 'I'm having a terrible time, and I can't wait until you're back.'

'You're so sweet. But seriously – are you eating properly?'

He looked down at the bowl in his hands. 'Spaghetti.'

'Not out of a tin. Please tell me it's not out of a tin. That's not the way that Italians eat their spaghetti.'

'Mum, I can confidently say that I'm eating spaghetti in the authentic Italian way.'

'That's good. And you're sleeping OK? I don't want you staying up playing games all night. Promise me that you won't be staring at a computer screen all night.'

He looked at the images in the ARCC lenses. He had a feeling that neither he nor Sam would be getting much sleep, and that the glasses would be getting a bit of a bashing. 'I promise, Mum.'

He thought he heard a man's voice say something in the background.

'Got to go,' his mum said. 'Love you. Take care. Brush your teeth. And do your homework.'

'Will do.'

The line went dead. He slipped the glasses off and ran a hand across his face. He tried to focus on the generically inoffensive artwork on the hotel room walls, but everything looked blurry. He screwed his eyes shut, counted to ten and then opened them again. The blurriness had gone.

'Homework,' he said. 'If only that was the worst thing we had to deal with.'

Sam, sitting cross-legged on the bed, smiled. 'Look at it this way – Bex asked us to get the stuff she threw overboard and use it to find her and Bradley. If that's not homework, what is it?'

Kieron considered for a moment. 'Fair point. Let's get on with it then.' He thought for a moment, trying to work his way logically through the problem the way that he knew Bex did. 'Actually, I've got a different idea.'

'What is it?' Sam asked.

'What are the odds of getting a boat captain to take us out into the lagoon at this time of night?'

Sam checked his watch. 'Slim, I guess. It's late.'

'And even if we do manage to convince someone to take us out, what are the chances of us finding a floating bag in the dark without looking suspicious?'

'Anorexia-slim. Bulimia-slim.'

'And given how late it is, what would Bex suggest, right now?'

'She'd suggest with some force that we should get some sleep, and face the problem with a fresh mind and more energy tomorrow.'

'Then that's what we should do.'

Sam gazed down at the patterned duvet on Bradley's bed. 'And do you really think that either of us will get any sleep?' he asked quietly.

Kieron tried to inject his voice with as much certainty as he could. 'If Bex and Bradley have been taken hostage, then they'll still be alive tomorrow. If we stay awake trying to find them, we'll burn ourselves out. Let's at least get four or five hours' rest. Even if we don't actually sleep, our bodies will recharge some of their energy and our brains will be fresher.'

Sam nodded, reluctantly. 'Look,' he said, 'I don't want this to sound creepy or anything, but I really don't want to go back to my room to sleep. It's kinda lonely there. Can we, like, just curl up under the duvet here in Bradley's room and doze for a while?' He shrugged, embarrassed. 'We've got enough pillows to build a wall between us, if it bothers you.'

'I wouldn't worry about that,' Kieron said, smiling. 'If I find you snuggling up to me while you're asleep, I'll just punch you.'

'Yeah, and the other way round.'

They finished their food quickly, put the trays outside the door, then lay on the bed, fully dressed. With the air-conditioning on, the temperature was perfectly comfortable. Kieron stared at the ceiling, head nestled in the feather pillow, listening to Sam breathing heavily beside him, and wondered what events the new day would bring. His brain started to fill with possibilities, and he felt himself getting tenser. Deliberately he forced himself to relax, using a technique that he'd learned in drama lessons. He tried to imagine that all of his worries were a dark, heavy liquid running through his body like black mercury. Gradually he imagined that the heaviness of the liquid was making it sink through his body, trickling through nooks and crannies until it pooled wherever his skin touched the bed. Breathing deeply and steadily, he then pictured the liquid draining out of his body through those points and seeping into the bed, leaving his body lighter and more free than it had been before. As he concentrated on the mental images, his body did actually seem to become lighter. He felt almost like he was floating above the bed, rather than lying on it. The next thing he knew, the sun shone in through the windows, illuminating the room with a cheerful glow, and he could hear a cat squalling outside somewhere. It was morning, and it was time for them to get to work.

Kieron checked the location of Bex's ARCC glasses using his own glasses. They had drifted perhaps half a kilometre across the lagoon with the tide. A sudden panicky hand clutched at his heart as he realised that both he and Sam had completely neglected the possibility that the inflated floating bag might have been carried out of the lagoon completely and be bobbing up and down out in the Adriatic Sea by now, but fortunately the flashing light was still inside the lagoon's boundaries. He had noticed the day before that the hotel had what they grandly called a 'Business Suite' down near the restaurant, where they could get printing done, so he downloaded an image of the map from the glasses to a removable USB drive and headed down there. The woman at the desk in the Business Suite couldn't have been more helpful, and within five minutes he had several paper copies of the map in an envelope.

He and Sam grabbed a quick breakfast and then got some money from the cashpoint conveniently located in the hotel lobby. It luckily had an option that allowed them to change the language of the display from Italian to English, although Sam accidentally switched it to Danish first. The cash that came out was euros of course. Feeling suddenly rich and very adult, they walked out into the warmth and humidity of St Mark's Square. The stones had been washed overnight, and the place smelled fresher than it had done the day before. They headed along the quayside to where the gondolas and the *vaporetti* bobbed on the blue-grey waters of the lagoon, and ducks and seagulls floated between them looking for scraps of food. Gondoliers and boat crewmembers glanced at them, evaluating their potential as customers and good tippers with harsh, experienced eyes.

'What do you think?' Sam asked.

'I think we'll need something small, and with an engine,' Kieron said. 'So not a gondola and not a *vaporetto*. Let's go on a bit and see what we can find.'

After a few minutes they came across exactly what they needed – a small boat, just large enough to take a family sitting on two rows of benches, with an outboard motor at the back and a cabin at the front with a steering wheel and controls. The grizzled man sitting on a bollard near the edge of the quayside stared at them curiously as they approached.

'*Dove sono la tua madre e il tuo padre?*' he asked.

Sam and Kieron glanced at each other uncertainly. 'Do you speak English?' Kieron asked.

'Where are your mother and father?' the boat's owner repeated in an accented voice.

'We're on . . . on a school trip,' Kieron said, repeating the story they'd agreed. 'We need to take a perfect photograph of Venice, and we've worked out the best place to take it from.' He held one of the maps out. 'Can you take us to the place that's marked with a red dot, please?'

The boat's owner stared at the map without taking it. 'Too far to get a good photograph,' he said eventually, shrugging,

179

'unless you have a zoom lens, but then why not stay closer and use a normal lens?'

Kieron felt his heart shrink a little. It had all seemed so easy when they'd talked it through, back in the hotel room. Trust them to have found someone argumentative. 'It has to be done from here,' he said, trying to sound insistent and tapping the paper. 'It's to do with the position of the sun.'

The boat's owner glanced up at the sun and then back at them sceptically. 'Fifty euros,' he said after a few moments. 'You want to go now?'

'Please.'

He stared at them. 'Do you need to get your cameras?'

Kieron's brain froze. Fortunately Sam came to the rescue. 'We're using our mobiles,' he said.

The boat's owner shook his head sadly. '*Turisti stupidi*,' he muttered, and gestured to the benches. 'Sit down. I take you there now.'

Kieron waved the map. 'Don't you need this?'

The man tapped his forehead. 'I have it in here,' he said. 'I live on this lagoon all my life. You take me blindfolded to a place, put my head over the side and let me look at the waves, I tell you exactly where we are.'

Once they were settled in the boat, he took the controls and yelled to someone on the quayside to undo the mooring rope. A few seconds later the engine sprang to life and the boat was chugging its way through the throng of arriving and departing gondolas, *vaporetti* and other vessels and heading out into the heat haze that had already started building up across the lagoon.

The regular up-and-down motion of the boat, combined with the smell of diesel fumes, made Kieron regret the cheese, scrambled egg and sausage that he'd shoved into his mouth and washed down with orange juice for breakfast. Glancing sideways he could see that Sam was looking pale and sweaty.

'Fifty euros extra if you are sick!' the boat's owner called back over his shoulder without looking at them. 'It is a clean-up cost.' Relenting slightly, he added, 'There is a bottle of lime juice and water in the locker by your side. That will help you.'

Sam quickly pulled the bottle out of the locker and took a swig, then passed it to Kieron. 'It helps,' he said.

Kieron gulped from the bottle. The sharp tang of the lime juice made his mouth pucker and his face screw up, but within a few seconds his stomach felt better.

The main bulk of Venice receded behind them, along with the shouting, the ringing of bells, the music and the general hubbub of Venetian life. The lido lay on their right, low and dark, while other islands slipped past them, one by one. The breeze picked up, cool on their faces. Hopeful seagulls followed them, waiting to see if they might throw some scraps of food overboard.

After perhaps twenty minutes, the boat's owner brought them to a halt. 'Here,' he said, waving at the water around them. 'Your perfect spot.'

Kieron gazed over the side in one direction, while Sam gazed over the other. No sign of any floating bag. Kieron slipped the ARCC glasses on and quickly called up a map of their current position, with an overlay showing where

Bex's ARCC glasses were still *bleep*ing their position away merrily. They were perhaps two hundred metres away.

'Not quite perfect,' he said, standing up and staring around at the islands critically. 'Can you take us a little way in that direction.' He pointed off to the left.

The boat's owner stared at him in disbelief. Then, muttering under his breath, he revved the engine slightly and manoeuvred the boat, first backwards and then forward again at an angle. 'Here, maybe?'

Kieron glanced at the map, then focused on the man beyond the translucent image. 'Maybe just a few metres forward?' he suggested gingerly.

The owner closed his eyes, shook his head and swore, then nudged the boat slowly forward. He kept glancing at Kieron. Kieron, in turn, zoomed in on the image in the glasses until he could see that they were virtually on top of the bag. It was on the far side, so Kieron coughed sharply, attracting Sam's attention, then gave a meaningful look over the side of the boat. Sam took the hint and moved across.

'Stop here!' Kieron said suddenly.

The boat halted. Its owner looked around, mystified.

'The view here is same as view just back there!' he protested.

Sam suddenly stood and leaned over the side.

'Lime juice not working?' the owner asked.

Sam pulled himself back into the boat, clutching a transparent plastic bag that had been blown up so that it resembled a balloon. Several small objects rattled around inside. 'Nearly dropped my bag!' he called. 'But it's OK now.'

The boat's owner stared at him, a frown on his face, obviously trying to remember if Sam had actually come on board with this bag. After a few seconds he shrugged, probably deciding it wasn't his problem.

Kieron took his mobile from his pocket and theatrically took several photographs of Venice and the other islands. After he thought he'd taken enough to make it look realistic, he called, 'Thanks – that's perfect. Can we go back now, please?'

The owner was immune to surprises by now. He restarted the engine, turned the boat around and headed back to St Mark's Square. Kieron had to stop himself from grabbing the bag from Sam and opening it up, but there would be time for that later. Sam just let a little bit of air out to make it look less suspicious.

Back on the quayside, they paid the owner of the boat and made their way to the hotel, and straight to Kieron's room.

Once there, they emptied the contents of the bag onto his bed, which had magically been made up while they'd been out. Quickly Kieron inventoried what they had. One pair of ARCC glasses, check. Two earpieces, check. And three computer tablets of similar design– Bradley's, Bex's and Hekla's – in ruggedised cases, check.

'OK,' he said. 'Let's get to work.'

The tablets still had power, but they were password protected. That didn't really matter – the computers running the ARCC glasses had enough anti-encryption programmes available to them that Kieron was pretty certain he'd be able to get through. He linked to the tablets via the hotel Wi-Fi and set to work.

Within half an hour he'd managed to crack their encryption and gain access to the secrets inside. In his mind it was like getting through the shell of a chocolate egg to the creamy filling within. Maybe that was a bad simile, he thought. Maybe real agents didn't think that way.

'Right,' he said eventually. 'Those ones –' he indicated two of the tablets – 'aren't much use. They're just loaded up with the software that the people at the auction were using to make their bids for the first assassination that Asrael would carry out. I think they'd been thoroughly electronically scrubbed and factory reset before being put out for the audience. *This* one –' he pointed at the other tablet – 'is a lot more interesting. This is the one Bex grabbed off Hekla just before she and Bradley ran for it. It's got all the stuff Hekla was using to control the auction and also, more importantly, to control the drone.'

Sam nodded. 'Does it give you any hint as to how they actually managed to pull off an assassination in Colombia within a few seconds of randomly choosing the target from the audience? Because – and I think I speak for all of us here – that's just stupid. Even the President of the US of A can't do that, because if he could then there's people in the top levels of various terrorist organisations who would be dead now. So – how did they do it?'

Kieron had been mulling that same question over since the previous evening, and somewhere along the line his subconscious mind had come up with an answer. Or, at least, a possible answer. 'OK,' he said cautiously, 'you heard Bex suggesting that there were two remotely

184

piloted drones involved: one drone watching through a high-definition camera, probably hovering high up in the atmosphere, and another drone near it carrying a bomb.' He frowned, thinking. 'They're probably powered by solar panels and with some kind of sophisticated artificial intelligence on board. Once the first drone had acquired the target, the second system turned itself into a guided missile, heading straight down for that poor bloke in the swimming pool.'

'That poor drug lord,' Sam pointed out.

'Yes,' Kieron agreed. 'We can be fairly sure the actual target was chosen at random, but it's also unlikely that Asrael has hundreds of thousands of drones wafting around in the clouds waiting for instructions. And unless they've cracked the impossible problem of travelling faster than light or backwards in time, they couldn't get two drones to Bogota within a few seconds.'

'You're just telling me how impossible it all is,' Sam pointed out. 'We need to know how it was actually *done*.'

Kieron reached out and picked up the envelope with the name of Bethany Wilderbourg's target for death within. He stared at it through the ARCC glasses, choosing various filters and sensors with his fingers. Suddenly he saw a mesh of small wires buried within the card: invisible to the naked eye but obvious when you looked at them using a combination of microwave sensor and thermal imager. A small computer chip appeared to have been embedded in one corner. 'This envelope is actually an electronic device in its own right!' he exclaimed. 'It can be tracked and located, just like we did with Bex's ARCC glasses.' He waved the envelope. 'Everyone at the demonstration brought one of these with them, naming their target and their location. Asrael must have broken into their houses or apartments before they flew out here, opened the envelopes, copied the names and locations down, then sealed the envelopes up again so nobody would know they'd been opened.' He frowned. 'They must have had as many burglars as there were invitees – this was a large-scale operation. But that means that before the demonstration took place they had a complete list of the potential targets. So, they positioned their drones above each target, so that no matter which one was picked they would have sensors and weapons available.'

'There were – what? – sixteen other people at the demonstration. So that's –' Sam looked confused.

'Thirty-two drones needed,' Kieron said. 'A much smaller number than the hundreds of thousands it would have taken if there wasn't a trick.'

'Expensive.'

'But well worth it. Just look at the bidding frenzy that erupted after the demonstration. They spent a lot of money so they could make back an eye-wateringly *huge* amount of money.'

'So it's a scam?' Sam leaned back in his chair, an admiring expression on his face. 'A very big, very clever scam. Asrael have no intention of killing anyone: they're just going to run off with the money.'

Kieron sighed. 'All that cleverness, directed in completely the wrong direction. Just think what they could do about

186

poverty or world hunger, if they put their minds to it.' He glanced over at Sam, but his friend's face had fallen into a frown. He didn't look convinced.

'But it didn't work. Their demonstration was interrupted by Bex and Bradley being caught, and then by the Italian police arriving. Their customers are all under arrest. But Asrael haven't been arrested – we know from accessing the police computer, of course.'

Kieron nodded reluctantly. 'I suppose. But the demonstration *was* a success, and rumours will leak out. They almost certainly videoed it, and they'll use that as an advert. They'll have to find some more customers, but that shouldn't be hard. The world is filled with people with money who want other people dead. The trouble is, they'll need more than that. They'll need to re-establish their credibility.' He shut his eyes and sighed as he realised where his thoughts were taking him. 'If I were them, I would pull off some really *big* assassination – something guaranteed to grab headlines. And if I were them, I would also kill Bex and Bradley, video it and use the video as part of their next advert, just to show that they can deal with anyone who infiltrates them.'

'Then we need to find Bex and Bradley, and fast. We need to rescue them.' Sam indicated the tablet. 'Any hint on there as to where they might have gone?'

Kieron quickly accessed the GPS chip built into Hekla's tablet and used the ARCC's mapping capability to flush the data out. He scrolled through the list of latitudes and longitudes, using another app to convert them into real locations.

And felt his heart sink.

'You're not going to like this,' he said quietly. 'Before the tablet got to Venice it was in Berlin for a few hours, probably on stop-over. And before that . . .'

'What?' Sam asked, leaning forward, eyes wide. 'Where?'

'Bergen.'

'Where's that?'

'Don't you know anything? It's in *Norway*! If they've gone anywhere, they've gone there. They've gone to *Norway*!'

CHAPTER TEN

Bex awoke, not knowing where she was. Keeping her eyes closed so she didn't give away the fact she'd woken up, she tried to work out what her other senses were telling her. She was sitting on a hard surface – probably plastic, judging by the way her buttocks slipped on it when she wriggled slightly. Her hands rested on curved metal tubes about the width of her thumb. Well, 'rested' was an exaggeration. They were fastened to the tubes, and quite tightly as well, judging by the way her fingertips tingled. The tight bonds were cutting off the blood supply. Probably plastic cable-ties – it's what most captors used these days: they were easy to obtain, quick to fasten, almost impossible to break if they were fastened tightly enough, and didn't raise suspicion if they were found during a search in the same way that ropes, chains or padlocks might do.

She tried surreptitiously to move her feet. They didn't budge an inch. Either the hard edge of the seat was cutting off the blood supply to her legs in the same way that the plastic ties were doing to her hands, rendering them numb, or her ankles had been bound just like her wrists. Or possibly both. She couldn't rule that out.

Right – fastened to a metal and plastic chair by cable ties. That was bad: the only reliable method for getting out of those things without help depended on clenching your muscles when they were put on and tightened, so that when you later relaxed those muscles there was some flex in the ties, some looseness which you could then exploit by twisting around until the plastic wore down and snapped. Yes, you'd need to be a contortionist, but it was possible. The problem was, she'd been unconscious when the ties had been applied, which meant that her captors had been able to pull the ties very tight indeed. Not much hope there.

Eyes still closed, she put her feet flat on the floor and pressed them down, hoping that the chair would lift up. If it did then she might be able to push it over backwards and something might break. Something that wasn't her skull or her neck, she hoped.

The chair didn't move. Probably screwed to the floor. Her captors were really taking no chances.

The floor. Hard – probably wood. No carpet. File that away for later investigation. And she could feel it vibrating slightly beneath the soles of her feet. Maybe there was a generator running nearby.

Nothing her shoe could touch or reach was going to be of much help. If she was going to get out of this then she was going to have to expand her boundaries – look for something nearby she could influence.

She opened her eyes, but everything was still as black as pitch. For a moment she panicked, thinking she'd been somehow blinded, but as her breath came more quickly she realised that she could feel some of it bouncing back onto her lips and cheeks. It seemed like someone had put a hood on her – maybe to stop her seeing what was happening around her, or who was now holding her prisoner. Black cloth, and thick to boot. And now she came to think about it, she couldn't hear anything either. Earphones? Probably, and surprisingly comfortable ones as well: form-fitting, foam, and, judging by the strangely 'dead' quality of the silence in her ears, with some kind of noise-cancelling technology built in. That didn't sit comfortably with the hard plastic-and-metal chair though.

Sit comfortably. She forced herself to suppress a laugh: no point in alerting her captors to the fact that she'd actually woken up. She *wasn't* sitting comfortably, and judging by the lack of sensation in her buttocks she hadn't *been* sitting comfortably for quite a while.

How long? That was a good question. Obviously she couldn't look at her watch, but judging by how hungry and thirsty she felt, and the vague feeling that she needed to go to the toilet, she'd been out of it for a good few hours. Maybe as much as ten or twelve.

A sudden flash of anger at her own helplessness made her clench her fingers on the metal tubing, and she noticed that she could feel the vibration through the arms of the chair as well as in the soles of her shoes. A motor, maybe? An engine? Was she in a vehicle? Not a boat, she was sure, despite the fact that she and Bradley had been cornered in one. An aircraft, perhaps? No sign of the dry mouth and the pressure in the ears she normally got on aircraft though. Maybe a car. No – more likely a van, given the materials of the chair she was sitting on and the fact that it was fastened to a wooden floor.

She sniffed. The hood didn't help, probably blocking most of the smells that would otherwise hit her nostrils, but she thought she could detect the sweet tang of diesel fumes. Most likely a van then, and an old one.

The sudden memory of her and Bradley in a boat that was drifting to a halt, its fuel line severed by a bullet, brought back a whole raft of other memories. Katrin, Hekla and the other girl – Eva – running their bizarre and inexplicable demonstration. Kieron vectoring the Italian police helicopter towards the island. Escaping on the motor launch. The scary chase through the tombs. Gunfire. And then drifting until another motor launch came up alongside them, with the three Norwegian girls and several armed thugs pointing guns at them. And then what? Darkness.

She clenched her fists, angry that she couldn't remember what had happened next, but as her muscles went hard she felt a stab of pain in the crook of her elbow, exactly where someone would inject her with, say, a sedative. Was that what had happened? Had she and Bradley been drugged to keep them quiet while they were being moved?

Something tapped against her right foot. She kept still, not wanting to give anything away. Something hard, knocking against the sole of her boot. And again! Maybe an object on the floor, rolling back and forth as the van moved? Or maybe one of her captors, sitting beside her and shifting position, occasionally touching her by accident.

Or maybe it was Bradley, sitting secured by her side, inches away in space but a galaxy away in terms of being able to communicate. She moved her foot a millimetre to the right, and her boot contacted something solid.

Whatever it was, it knocked back, but this time there was a pattern to it, a whole sequence of thuds against the edge of the sole of her boot. Her instinct was to pull back, but there was something almost familiar about it, something she should be able to identify. Four rapid taps, then a gap, then two more rapid taps. A longer gap, then four rapid taps again, three slower taps, then a quick tap and two slow taps.

She felt herself relax, and beneath the hood she smiled. Morse Code, nearly two hundred years old now, and yet something that every agent knew off by heart. Four rapid taps – 'H'. Three slower taps – 'O'.

She checked off each letter as it was transmitted, painstakingly slowly, and managed to piece together the short but oh-so-sweet message:

HOW ARE YOU?

Bradley. Alive, and sitting right beside her. Almost certainly tied up, hooded and temporarily deafened with earphones, but still able to get through to her. Bless him. For a moment she wondered if it might not be Bradley at all, but one of her captors, trying to *convince* her that they were Bradley. Maybe they were going to try and interrogate her subtly, letting her talk to what she thought was her friend.

No, it was Bradley. Anyone else would have used textspeak to shorten the message – HW R U? – but Bradley hated textspeak. He always spelled every word out, and spelled them correctly as well. And used semicolons. He was the only person she knew who used semicolons in text messages. This was him.

After it became obvious that Bradley had finished, Bex used her own boot to transmit a message back to him:

FINE BUT ALL IS DARK AND QUIET. WE ARE IN A VAN I THINK.

His response came straight back, spelled out at length:

I AM BY WINDOW. BASED ON FLASHES OF HEAT AS SUN SHINES THROUGH ON MY HOOD WE ARE HEADING NORTH.

HOW LONG UNCONSCIOUS? she tapped back.

MAYBE EIGHT TO TEN HOURS. I NEED A TOILET BREAK.

She remembered a childhood refrain, sung during long car journeys, and couldn't resist. STOP THE CAR I WANT A WEE-WEE! she messaged.

WHAT IS NORTH OF VENICE? he asked.

LOTS OF GERMANY, THEN DENMARK.

THAT WOULD MAKE SENSE, GIVEN WHERE THOSE GIRLS TOLD KIERON THEY CAME FROM.

Maybe the Asrael team was taking them back to their home base. It seemed likely, although Bex didn't like to speculate on why, or what might happen to them when they got there. At least they didn't want her and Bradley dead – not yet anyway. Part of her hoped that Kieron and Sam had managed to follow her rushed plan and rescue the ARCC glasses and the Asrael tablets from the dark waters of the lagoon, but another part of her almost hoped they hadn't. Yes, she wanted to be rescued, but she really didn't want the boys to be put in danger.

In the end, she supposed they had to decide for themselves what they'd do. They were nearly grown up and they had to take responsibility for their own actions.

Bradley's foot suddenly jerked sideways, hitting her ankle hard. She cried out in sudden surprise and pain. What had happened to him?

Moments later she found out when her own hood was roughly pulled off, along with her earphones. The sudden glare made her blink.

Once her eyes had adapted, she looked around, trying to take in information as quickly as she could.

They were indeed in a van – an old one, with a driver's seat and passenger seat up front, and four rows of crude chairs in the back. The kind of thing you'd see schools transporting kids around in in old black-and-white films. The sun was indeed low on the horizon on their right. They'd slept their drugged sleep all through the night.

Two of the armed thugs sat in front. Hekla and Katrin were in the first row of what Bex thought of as 'the cheap seats', with Eva behind them, and Bex and Bradley behind Eva. It was Eva who had pulled their hoods off. She sat there, smiling gently, holding the hoods now. Glancing quickly over her shoulder, Bex saw two more thugs in the last row. They were both asleep. Professionals: they knew that you should always sleep when you could, because you never knew when you might get the chance again. The same thing held true for eating.

The view through the windscreen was of one of Germany's incredibly straight autobahns. Traffic on the road was fairly light. Looking to her left and right, Bex saw that the world outside looked grainy and grey – probably because the windows had been covered with a sticky plastic film that she guessed made them look like mirrors from the outside. So – no chance of a passing motorist having seen two hooded figures in the back and calling the police.

The view through the side windows was of a flat, boring landscape where trees marked divisions between fields. The occasional farmhouse or barn that flashed past probably hadn't changed much in fifty years.

Looking back to the windscreen again, Bex saw that they were fast coming up to a road sign. As it passed by she thought it said Hamburg, or possibly Hanover. She desperately tried to remember her German geography. They were probably on the A7 – like Bradley had said, heading north through Germany towards Denmark.

'Sorry to wake you up so abruptly,' Eva said, smiling sweetly, 'but I was getting seriously bored and I wanted someone to talk to.'

Bex glanced sideways, at Bradley. He gazed back at her. He seemed uninjured.

'What shall we talk about?' Bex asked. Her voice was croaky, and she coughed to clear it. 'Needlepoint? Netball tournaments? Or con artists who create the illusion that for a small fortune they can kill anyone in the world, anywhere, any time, for a price, while in fact they can only kill some specific people they know about in advance – a service they are only too happy to demonstrate?'

'Are you absolutely sure of your conclusions?' Eva said, right eyebrow rising slightly in a surprise she was trying hard to mask. 'Perhaps we are the next generation of assassins. Techno-assassins.'

'I doubt it. Too much doesn't add up. I don't know how you arranged to have your drones in the right place at the right time, but I really don't see you having millions of them all in the air at the same time, ready to rain fire and destruction down on anyone at a moment's notice.'

'We did hit your apartment though,' Eva pointed out. 'And your car.'

'Yes,' Bex said smiling calmly, 'we wanted to ask you about that. It's obvious you used the same type of drone, but that was before your demonstration on the island. Why take a contract before you'd even got all your potential customers together and demonstrated your capabilities? And who on earth would risk employing you before you'd even proved what you could do?' She tried to make the question sound casual, as if the question about who had hired Asrael to kill them was just something tacked on the end, but that was what she really wanted to know. Often, getting someone to answer a question meant hiding it behind another question, one you were less interested in.

'We were approached,' Eva said, smiling back, 'by someone who had heard about us. We were preparing our demonstration, and frankly we were amazed – and slightly worried – that they knew as much about us as they did, but they assured us they just wanted to get ahead of the game – pay us for a job. They said it would be a private, covert test of our system before we exposed it to our customer base. We gave them a significant discount, but it worked, didn't it? Your apartment and your car were destroyed, and you had no idea how.'

'But you didn't get us,' Bex pointed out. 'None of us.'

Eva tilted her head to one side curiously. 'You said, "*none* of us". Interesting. My English is rough, but surely, as there are two of you, you should have said, "*neither* of us"?' She closed her eyes briefly and nodded. 'There are more of you. Thank you for that information. We need to look into that. It seems we have left some loose ends behind. We need to clear them up.'

Bex tried not to react, but inwardly she cursed herself. Still woozy from the drugged sleep, she'd inadvertently given away the fact that Kieron and Sam were part of the team.

'So what happens to us?' she asked. 'Where do we go from here? You obviously need us for something, otherwise you'd have shot us and dumped us in the lagoon.'

Eva stared at Bex for a long moment. '*Someone* wants you dead. Admittedly, we failed in that, back in England, but we might be able to persuade whoever your enemy is to pay us a little bit more to kill you now, properly. If not, well –' she shrugged – 'you're almost certainly working for MI6, which means you have secret information in your heads that other people will want. The Russians will offer us a decent sum for you. So will the Chinese. Who knows – MI6 might beat their offers if we hand you back to them.' A long pause, then: 'Or maybe they'll pay us to kill you, just to stop you falling into the hands of their enemies.'

Bex wanted to glance sideways at Bradley, but she stopped herself. They both knew there was at least one person in MI6 who would pay to have them dead – presumably the same person who hired Asrael to kill them in the first place, although Asrael had no way of knowing that. Instead she said, 'You've got it all figured out, haven't you?'

'It's a business,' Eva responded, 'and, as with every successful business, we have to leverage our assets.'

Bradley suddenly spoke, surprising Eva. 'I presume the auction process has ended. Do you mind telling us who won?'

Now Eva laughed: a genuine, full-throated laugh. 'Ah,' she said through the last few chuckles, 'so this is the point where the evil team of assassins reveal the full enormity of their plans?'

'That would be nice,' Bradley said seriously. 'I mean, who are we going to tell?'

'I *will* tell you, but mainly because I want to see your faces as you realise what's going to happen, and how you've completely failed to stop it.' She gazed delightedly from Bradley to Bex and back. 'A far-right group in England, backed by a billionaire businessman, has secured our services for a fantastic sum of money. They want us to kill your entire royal family, in order for a fascist regime to be established. The police raid on the island has dented our credibility a bit, so we're going to have to actually *do* this one, just to prove we can. So – that's what you failed to stop. Enjoy your knowledge.'

Eva looked as if she was going to say something else, but one of the girls in the front seats turned around and shook her head warningly. Eva glowered, but turned away and stared out of the window.

ANY IDEAS? Bex tapped out in Morse Code against Bradley's foot.

LOADS, he tapped back, BUT THEY ALL INVOLVE NOT BEING HERE. YOU?

NOTHING.

AT LEAST THEY HAVEN'T PUT THE HOODS BACK ON US.

DON'T TEMPT FATE.

The van drove on for another hour or so. Bex's mind churned with ideas, but none of them were any use. Maybe, when she and Bradley were untied at the end of their journey, they'd be able to do something, but it was pointless planning for it. Neither of them had any idea what situation they'd be in then.

Abruptly the van left the wide road, taking an intersection that seemed to lead them through a wilderness of flat countryside covered in scrubby bushes and the occasional dilapidated concrete building. If this was leading to a secret base, Bex thought, then it would have to be very impressive to make up for its surroundings.

There was no secret base. Instead they turned off onto a dirt track and drove for maybe twenty minutes before emerging from a clump of scraggy trees onto a flat expanse of cracked concrete that seemed to stretch towards the horizon.

OLD AIRFIELD, Bradley tapped.

YES, Bex tapped back, BUT WHAT THE HELL IS THAT?

The van stopped beside a helicopter that appeared to be waiting for them, but it was unlike any helicopter Bex had ever seen. Its body was long and thin, with a cockpit at the front – more like a small commercial airliner – with two massive tubular engine cowls running along its upper surface, but the really bizarre thing was that it was raised high off the ground on four thin, skeletal legs. A National Express coach could have driven comfortably underneath it and out the other side. Its long rotor blades curved downwards from their hub, hanging lower than its underside. If it hadn't been for the crane-fly-like legs they would have scraped the ground. Its upper surface was painted a sickly green, and its underside was, strangely, a dull orange. The paintwork seemed old and faded.

MIL MI-10, NATO CODE NAME 'HARKE', Bradley tapped. CARGO HELICOPTER. 1960'S TECHNOLOGY. I USED TO HAVE A DINKY TOY VERSION. I LOVED THAT THING.

'It's a bit old, isn't it?' Bex said, raising her voice. 'I mean, are you sure it's safe?'

'It does the job,' Eva said without turning around. 'That's another principle of successful businesses – only spend money where you need to, and to make yourselves look impressive to your customers. You two are not customers.'

Several crew members who had been waiting jumped to their feet and gestured to the driver to approach. Bex noticed with a sudden jolt that a flat metal pallet lay on the ground immediately beneath the helicopter's belly. Chains

201

led upwards from its corners to chunky brackets on the helicopter itself.

'You have to be kidding,' she said, aghast.

'We're Norwegian,' Eva called back. 'We have no sense of humour.'

Their driver cautiously manoeuvred the van onto the pallet. He turned the engine off, and the crewmembers moved in to secure the wheels with more chains.

'Er, forgive me,' Bradley said hesitantly, 'but are we going to de-bus? Get on board? Get comfortable?'

Eva shook her head. 'No, we're staying here.'

Glancing outside again, Bex saw that the crew had vanished. From somewhere above them a coughing roar broke out, like an asthmatic and elderly lion. A cloud of black smoke drifted across the concrete. The tips of the blades, which now surrounded them on all sides, began to rotate, slowly at first, and then with increasing speed.

'Is there an at-seat trolley service?' Bradley asked. His voice was higher pitched now, with what Bex recognised as an edge of real panic. 'Or maybe, you know, just a *toilet break*?'

'Suck it up,' Eva said.

The chains holding the pallet clanked as they pulled taut. Moments later the pallet jerked upwards and began to sway.

'Travel sickness pills?' Bradley asked weakly.

The ground dropped away below them as the Harke lurched into the air. The rotation of the blades – a flickering blur above them, silhouetting the helicopter's body – had straightened them out now. Stomach lurching, Bex gazed out of the window at the rapidly receding concrete. She couldn't see the pallet the van was attached to; as far as her jangling nerves could tell, they were hanging in space, swinging from side to side.

This was not going to be a pleasant journey.

KEEP YOUR EYES OPEN AND FIXED ON THE HORIZON, she tapped. IT'LL HELP WITH THE TRAVEL SICKNESS.

Bradley didn't reply. When she looked sideways at him, his face was pale and sweaty.

Off to the right, Bex saw what looked like glittering blue water, with the orange-and-purple sky of a beautiful sunset beyond. They seemed to be flying along a coastline.

GERMANY STILL?

It took a few moments before Bradley tapped back: STILL HEADIN NORTH, I THNK. PROBLY DENMARK.

She noted the dropped letters and felt a twinge of worry. He must be feeling pretty bad.

After a while there was more water than land in sight, and then just water. The further north they flew, the colder it got. Even the blue of the sea took on a harder, sharper edge, and when finally land appeared again, she saw patches of snow among the green of vegetation; patches that grew larger and larger until everything through the windows on both sides was either snow or rock, punctuated by the snaking dark lines of roads.

Her breath turned to steam in front of her face and her fingertips tingled.

NEXT TIME, she tapped, THERMAL UNDERWEAR AND GLOVES.

NEXT TIME? Bradley tapped back. When she glanced sideways at him he was staring straight ahead, blankly.

The swaying of the van was beginning to get monotonous, lulling her to sleep. When the pitch of the Harke's engines changed she snapped out of a doze, unsure how much time had passed.

It was difficult to tell whether they were flying over spits of land separated by water or water interrupted by random stretches of land. On the few occasions Bex thought she saw the gleam of a light go past, she couldn't tell whether it was a building or a boat.

The helicopter got lower and lower, and then suddenly she saw a building rising up towards them: all wood and white stone, gleaming in the last rays of the sun. No straight lines: just curves everywhere, like a stranded sea creature; an artificial starfish perched on the edge of a steep hillside, almost a cliff, at the bottom of which waves crashed against rocks in explosions of white spume. Then the legs of the helicopter touched ground, and seconds later the pallet bumped roughly a couple of times before grating to a halt. The helicopter settled around them, and the rotor blades began to slow down to a point where they could be seen individually again rather than as a blur.

DOSNT MATTER IF K AND S FIND ARCC KIT, Bradley tapped. He was noticeably slower than earlier, and less precise. TOO FAR WAY. NOTING HEY CN DO.

THEN WE RESCUE OURSELVES, Bex replied.

IF U SEE CHNCE, TAKE IT. LEAVE ME BHIND.

NO WAY.

Outside, the helicopter crew had disembarked from their high cabin and seemed to be unfastening the van.

'Put the snow chains on,' Katrin ordered from up in front – the first thing Bex had heard her say for hours.

The air inside the van had turned bitingly cold.

WHERE DO YOU THINK WE ARE? she asked, trying to keep Bradley engaged with what was happening. Stop him from sinking into catatonic depression. He was still too close to the concussion he'd suffered only weeks ago: he didn't have the physical or mental reserves to cope with the trouble they were in. That was a problem, because Bex might have to depend on him if they were both to escape.

NORWAY. WEST. BTWEEN STAVANGER AND BERGEN.

The van began to move, snow chains biting into the frozen ground. The driver accelerated slowly, picking his way across the flat surface that lay between the helicopter and building ahead of them. It was the size of a manor house and glowed with warmth and light, like a beacon in the night. Skirls and flurries of snow surrounded them as they drove, stirred up by the bitter wind that managed to insert its fingers in through cracks and gaps in the body of the van.

Something moved, off to one side. For a moment Bex thought it was another helicopter, but it seemed too small: an object like two barrels fastened together, with a rotor blade spinning around the narrower waist where the two sections joined. It had just lifted off from a strip of concrete where, Bex realised with a growing disquiet, a row of a few hundred similar objects sat beneath tarpaulins.

'I suppose it saves treating guards for frostbite and chilblains,' she said to Eva, nodding her head towards the object as it rose smoothly into the air.

'Well, we have them, so we may as well use them.'

'How are they powered?' Bex asked curiously.

Eva shrugged. 'I don't know. Small nuclear batteries maybe? Not my area.' She turned around and clicked her fingers at one of the thugs sitting behind Bex and Bradley. They'd been so silent and motionless that Bex had forgotten they were there. 'You two – take these two into the lodge. There's a storeroom in the basement, near the stairs – put them in there.' She glanced at Bradley, then at Bex. 'And find a portable toilet from somewhere and put it in with them. If you can't find one, a bucket will do.'

'Welcome to Norway,' Bradley said weakly. 'We hope you enjoy your stay at the lodge.'

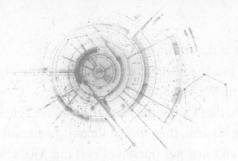

CHAPTER ELEVEN

'OK,' Sam said, 'what resources do we have?'

'What?' Kieron asked.

'It's the kind of thing Bex would say. "What are our resources? What tools do we have in the toolbox? What have we got that we can use?"'

'OK, I understand. We have you, me and whatever is in this room, including the ARCC kit. That's it. Oh, and we're stuck in Venice. Oh, *and* we need to get to Norway. We think.' He shook his head in dismay. 'You know that bit in movies when things are as bad as they can be? That moment when the villain's escaped with the secret plans and kidnapped the hero's girlfriend, the hero's car has crashed, he and his best friend are crawling from the flaming wreckage with cuts, bruises and broken bones miles down a remote country road in the middle of nowhere, not knowing what to do or how to get the girl and the secret plans back, and the hero's friend says, "Hey, it could be worse – it could be raining," and then it starts raining? You know that moment?'

'Yeah?'

'This is that moment.'

Sam punched him in the arm. Hard. Really hard. 'Man up, mate. We've got a job to do.'

'Yeah, that's what the hero always says.' He breathed out, rubbing his arm, then took a long, slow breath in. 'Actually, we haven't *just* got ourselves and the ARCC kit – we're in one of the most expensive hotels in one of the most exclusive locations on Earth. That means that within ten metres of where we're sitting there's probably someone with a lot of money and access to a private jet. All we have to do is persuade them to take us to Norway.'

'Persuade?' Sam said, in a tone of voice that suggested he thought Kieron was mad.

'Stay with me on this. Yes, we have to persuade them. I don't know how, but we'll think of something.'

Within a few minutes Kieron had pulled up images from the hotel's security cameras, concentrating mainly on the restaurant and lift areas. He cross-referenced the photographs with the record of arrivals at the local airport and archives of style and gossip magazines, trying to identify anyone who had an executive jet. At the back of his mind while he worked, his brain was trying to figure out what plausible argument two teenagers could come up with to persuade a complete stranger to fly them to a different country – *Our friends are going to die if you don't!* seemed a bit overdramatic, although it was true – but he couldn't come up with anything convincing. Still, one problem at a time.

Which was when he found something interesting.

'Take a look at this,' he said thoughtfully, handing Sam the glasses.

Sam slipped them on. 'Ooh – two people in a swimming pool.'

'Look closer.'

'OK, but we have things to do, you know?' He paused. 'Oh, hang on – isn't that the guy with the YouTube channel where he plays all the new computer games with his friends and they do a running commentary saying how bad they are? His real name is Fyn Harkess, I think, but what's his tag? GamR BlamR or something.' Kieron could practically hear Sam emphasise the random capital letters.

'I think it is,' he said.

'Isn't he married to that actress – the one who did the superhero movie last year?'

'I think he is.'

'He earns, like, a million pounds a *week* from advertising and promotions. He even has his own private jet. That girl in the pool looks like the one who won the TV talent show he was the special guest judge on last week.'

'You know, I think it is.' Kieron winced as Sam looked over at him. 'Yeah, I know – my mum was watching it, and I just happened to be in the room.'

'That's your story?'

'And I'm sticking to it.' Kieron frowned, thinking. 'Hang on – how did you recognise her? You don't watch TV talent shows, do you?'

Sam looked away. 'Same reason,' he said casually. 'My mum.'

'Right.'

'But so what?'

'So he does completely random things on a whim. He once bought a house in Alaska just because he wanted to watch the aurora borealis. He's still not been there. I reckon if anyone will fly us to a different country, it's him.'

Sam suddenly perked up. 'Oh, hang on – they're getting out of the pool.'

'Great,' Kieron said with significantly more confidence than he felt. 'Quick – we need to be outside the fitness centre when they come out. Running desperately after the person you want a massive favour from makes you look bad. Bring both sets of ARCC glasses and the earpieces.'

He and Sam got to the fitness centre on the ground floor of the hotel barely five minutes later. They stood there, unsure whether or not to go in. Just as Kieron was about to try the door, it opened. GamR BlamR – or whatever his real name was – stood there, arm around a small, pretty girl. They both had wet hair.

'Hi,' he said, staring at them. He was smaller than Kieron had expected. And, Kieron reminded himself, *considerably* richer. His hair was bleached white, but streaked progressively from ear to ear with every colour of the rainbow, from red through to violet. 'Fans? You want an autograph?' He plunged a hand in his pocket. 'I think I've got some snappable GamR BlamR wristbands in here somewhere. You want one each?'

'Actually,' Kieron said, trying to project a sense of confidence in his voice, 'we need to get to Norway, we need to go in your private jet and we need to leave now. And if you don't take us there –'

GamR BlamR nodded. 'Sounds cool,' he said, cutting Kieron off. 'Venice is boring anyway. Too many old people, and the Wi-Fi is terrible.'

'OK. Like I said, if you don't take us –'

'It's cool, we'll go now.' He patted the girl on the shoulder. She glanced up at him with an expression that was veering from adoration through confusion towards anger at an incredible rate. 'You can get a return ticket to London, can't you, babe? Actually, hey, I'll call my manager and he'll sort one out for you. Just pick it up at the airport.' He kissed her on the forehead. 'It's been great. It really has.'

GamR BlamR started off down the corridor, arms outstretched, sweeping Kieron and Sam with him. 'Let's go. I've never seen Norway.'

'Don't you . . . ?' Kieron stammered. He glanced back at the girl standing outside the fitness centre. She looked as if she was going to cry. He shrugged at her helplessly. 'I mean – shouldn't you *pack* first?'

'Nah – I travel light.' GamR BlamR had a huge grin on his face. 'I just buy new clothes and stuff wherever I end up. It's a lot easier that way.'

'But –' Kieron glanced past GamR BlamR at Sam, who just stared back, wide-eyed – 'what about the stuff you brought with you? You can't just leave it behind!'

'Of course I can. That's the fun of being mindlessly rich and young – I can do whatever I want. If the maids are smart they'll collect it all up and put it on eBay. Last I heard, a hotel in Bratislava made *thousands* selling my used T-shirts and underwear. I've got a lot of fans out there.' He frowned, thinking. 'Norway. That's like, *cold*, isn't it?'

Kieron couldn't quite believe how easy this had been. 'Are you *sure* about this?' he asked, earning a punch on the arm from Sam.

'Hey, you gave me the perfect excuse to drop the girl and move on – I was getting bored here anyway, and I pretty much live my life by taking random decisions. I don't know who you guys are, but you've done me a favour.' He grinned and punched the air. 'We're going to Norway!'

Five minutes later they were in a small motor launch, pulling away from the quayside at St Mark's Square. Judging by the way the man with the peaked cap standing beside it saluted GamR BlamR as the three of them approached, the launch was on permanent standby in case the young millionaire needed it.

'We left all our stuff in our rooms,' Sam pointed out.

'We're living in the fast lane now.' The wind blew sea spray into Kieron's face and he blinked. 'I guess we can get it all sent on. The important thing is – have you got your passport?'

Sam nodded. 'Back pocket. You?'

'Same.'

'Norway's a big place, you know?'

'We'll figure it out when we get there.'

GamR BlamR spent most of the time on his mobile phone – which, Kieron noted jealously, was an iPhone with a customised case embossed with his logo. Fifteen minutes later they were climbing up the steps of the vlogger's exclusive aircraft, and five minutes after that they were taking off. It seemed that the jet, like the motor launch, was on constant standby.

'Help yourselves to anything you want,' GamR BlamR said, waving vaguely towards the rear of the aircraft. 'There's a fridge back there, and a microwave. I'll probably crash out for a while – I always do that when I'm flying, and I haven't slept for three days, so –' He puffed his cheeks out. 'You did say Norway, didn't you? Cos that's what I told the pilot.'

'Yes,' Kieron said firmly. 'Norway.'

'Great.' GamR BlamR's head lolled backwards, his eyes closed and he started snoring.

'Is this really happening?' Sam asked.

'If it's not, then we're both having the same hallucination.' Kieron shook his head. 'I didn't even get around to threatening him with exposure!' he said, sounding aggrieved.

'We should probably get some sleep as well.'

Kieron nodded. He stared at Sam. Sam stared back.

'Hungry?' Sam asked eventually.

'Yeah.'

Sam got up and walked back to the galley area. Kieron heard the sound of locker doors being opened and closed.

'I can't help thinking,' Kieron called out, 'about that girl. I hope she's not still standing there, in the corridor, staring after us.'

Sam came back a few moments later. He had a strange expression on his face – one which Kieron couldn't quite decipher.

'Judging by the ingredients I've found back there,' he said, 'your boy here's favourite snack appears to be peanut butter and jelly sandwiches with crispy bacon. You up for it?'

'Seems rude not to,' Kieron replied.

They ate, they explored the amazing entertainment system on the aircraft and then they slept. When they woke up, GamR BlamR was on his laptop, playing a game and narrating his way through it in a constant stream-of-consciousness.

'Broadband Wi-Fi in flight,' Sam observed quietly. 'That's what money can get you.'

'What's he playing?'

Sam shuffled round until he could see diagonally over GamR BlamR's shoulder. He shuffled back a few moments later. 'You know that game your mum got you for Christmas?'

'Yeah?'

'It looks like the sequel.'

Kieron was aghast. 'But it hasn't even come *out* yet!'

'I know. I think he's playing a beta-level demo.'

Kieron closed his eyes and shook his head. 'I so need to be rich.'

'You and me both, bro.'

Customs officials were waiting at the foot of the jet's fold-down stairway. They took a cursory look at Kieron and Sam's passports and waved them through. They were more interested in GamR BlamR. The moment his feet touched Norwegian soil they clustered around him, clamouring for autographs and taking selfies.

Kieron looked around. A cold wind blew against his cheek, freezing his ear. The air felt crisp and clean, like it was freshly made. Little feathery trails of cloud had been brushed onto the deep blue canvas of the sky.

'There's a lot of Christmas trees out there,' Sam said dubiously.

Kieron looked around. His friend was right. Every single tree was a perfect cone. All they needed was twinkling lights.

A futuristic black limousine swept up to the aircraft and coasted to a silent halt. Kieron presumed it was for GamR BlamR, probably arranged by his management company, or personal assistant, or the invisible AI that organised his life for him. He waited for the chauffeur to get out and hold the rear door open for the teenage gaming legend, but instead the door clicked open and swung out invitingly.

'No driver!' Sam pointed out in a whisper. 'Look in the front. That car's got no driver!'

'See ya, guys!' GamR BlamR called from where he'd just finished with the customs officials. 'Looks like my ride's arrived.'

'It's got no driver!' Sam squeaked again.

'I know. Cool, right? There's a start-up who are testing driverless cars here in Oslo. My people got in touch with them and happened to mention that I was unexpectedly coming here, so they asked if they could provide me with one of their cars, if I could mention them favourably on my YouTube channel and have some publicity photos taken with me sitting inside, actually live-streaming while being driven around. So my people said yes, and here we are.'

'I don't suppose you could give us a lift to a hotel?' Kieron asked.

'No problem.' GamR BlamR shrugged. 'You want to borrow the wheels too? I'll live-stream some stuff while we're driving into the city – after that I don't need it any more.'

'Won't the company mind?'

'They won't know. Anyway, they'll've got their publicity by then. After that, it's going spare.'

'But won't you need it to drive you places? See the sights?'

GamR BlamR laughed. 'I like you guys. You're funny. No, I've got no intention of seeing anything beyond the view from my hotel-room window. As long as I've got room service, Wi-Fi and air-conditioning, I'm happy.'

'Then what's the point of travelling?' Sam asked.

'It broadens the mind – that's what they say. So – come on. Who wants to sit in the front?'

Kieron sat in the driver's seat, behind a steering wheel that had been squashed up against the dashboard. He guessed it would suddenly expand outwards if there was any problem. He hoped not. Unlike Sam he didn't drive, and he had no intention of taking the wheel and steering them out of danger. Sam sat beside him, while GamR BlamR got in the back. Even before he'd sat down he had his laptop out and was talking excitedly into the integrated camera and microphone, narrating his life as it occurred.

Kieron's seat, and the one beside him, seemed to be able to swivel around so he could face the seats in the back. Very cosy. Just like the world's smallest living room.

Sam plucked a tablet computer from a holder on the

dashboard. 'It's got a destination pre-programmed in,' he observed. 'Looks like a really nice hotel in the centre of Oslo. It's asking if we're ready to go.'

Kieron glanced over his shoulder at the oblivious GamR BlamR. 'Yeah, I think so.'

'Fastest route or scenic route?'

'He doesn't care. Let's take the fastest.'

Sam tapped the screen and the car accelerated smoothly away, heading around the side of the terminal building and towards an exit gate, which opened for them automatically. It was that easy.

The drive into Oslo took under an hour, past two-storey houses painted in the same bright colours as GamR BlamR's hair. Eventually they were heading through the city itself, over a wide river and a wider set of train tracks, and pulling into a drop-off area in front of a hotel that looked like its designers had been unable to agree what shape to make it. On one side it was wider in the middle than at the bottom or the top, while the other side seemed to slope away in several directions.

'It looks like a cereal box that's been sat on by a small child,' Sam observed, 'and I should know. My oldest sister's kid went through a phase of taking cereal boxes off the table and sitting on them.'

'Isn't he still in nappies? Remind me never to have cereal at your house.'

A small crowd gathered around the car as it stopped. Kieron saw photographers and people holding up mobile phones and tablets. They all wanted to catch a glimpse of the rainbow-haired celebrity in the back seat.

As soon as he noticed the crowd, GamR BlamR folded his laptop up, grinned at them and gave a double thumbs-up. The door opened automatically for him – like so many other things in the vlogger's life, Kieron thought darkly – and he erupted out of the car, laptop under his arm, high-fiving and shaking hands. As the crowd swept him towards the hotel lobby he didn't even look back.

'Well,' Kieron said, 'it looks like the car's ours now. Where do you want to go?'

'Let's find somewhere quiet and anonymous and make a plan. A pizza restaurant maybe?'

Ten minutes later they drew up outside what looked like a popular but reasonably anonymous place that fitted the bill. They left the car outside – taking the tablet with them along with a digital key card they discovered in a slot in the dashboard. They spent a few minutes trying to work out how it could be used to lock the car before realising that if the key card moved more than a few feet away from the car then it locked automatically.

They found a table in the corner. The waiters spoke English, fortunately. They ordered, then sat looking at each other.

'Right,' Sam said, 'we're here. We don't know if Bex and Bradley are in Norway or not, and we don't know where in Norway they might be if they are. I'll admit that I didn't expect us to get this far this quickly, but I have no idea what we're going to do next.'

'Norway seems like a very organised country,' Kieron observed, taking the ARCC glasses from his pocket and putting them on. 'Let's assume Bex and Bradley have been slipped quietly in by Asrael. We won't be able to trace them through the normal channels – border security cameras or passenger lists – so we come at the problem from the other direction. We don't look for Bex and Bradley; we look for Asrael.'

'You think they might have a website, with, like, a contact address?' Sam asked cautiously.

'No.' Kieron touched the button on the side of the glasses, activating the augmented-reality technology, and watched as a series of translucent menus appeared in front of him, superimposed on the scene of the restaurant. 'We look for the girls – Katrin, Eva and Hekla.'

The app he'd dumped the girls' faces on started accessing Norwegian government databases – driving licences, social security, student IDs, everything that an organised society kept in order to look after its people in an organised fashion.

Fifteen seconds later, he'd found all three of them. Names, and addresses. He cross-referenced the information with tax records.

'He's rehearsing a performance,' he heard Sam say to a waiter who, he dimly saw through the menu screens, had turned up with a bottle of water. 'Youngest classical conductor in the world. Very famous. Needs to run through his moves though.'

'According to this,' he said once the waiter had left, 'they all live in a town called Beitostølen, which is about a hundred and fifty kilometres north-west of here, and they all work

219

at a company called Learsa, which is based in a building overlooking Lake Olevatnet. It's in an area called Oppland. From the lake the River Oleåne flows down to a port named Javnin. It's all pretty desolate.'

'Learsa,' Sam mused. 'That's "Asrael" backwards. Very clever. What do they do?'

'They manufacture drones,' Kieron replied, reading the words from the screen displayed on the lens of his glasses. 'Not little recreational ones – big ones for use by TV broadcasters, film-makers and the military. And yes, I am reading that information off their website.'

'That makes sense.' Sam nodded. 'They specialise in making high-end drones, so they find a way of using them in assassinations to make more money. Very clever.'

'Yes,' Kieron said. 'It happens all the time.'

'Don't knock it – as business plans go, it's got a lot going for it.'

'And they need it.' Kieron was checking Learsa's finances – all diligently filed with the Norwegian tax authorities. 'The company's been in trouble for a while now. Their drones are great, but expensive. There are cheaper ones around that do mostly the same things.' More information flashed up in another screen. 'Oh – that's interesting.'

'What?'

'Learsa is a family firm, set up by one Gustav Reginiussen, but currently run by his wife Agnetha following his death – along with their three daughters, Katrin, Eva and Hekla.'

Kieron took the glasses off and stared at Sam. 'It's still

a long shot. We don't know if the girls came back here to Norway; we don't know if they brought Bex and Bradley with them if they did; and even if both of those things did happen, we don't know whether or not they've taken them to Learsa's headquarters. But it's the best information we have, and I suggest we follow it through.'

'Agreed,' Sam said. 'But we'll need help.'

Kieron held out his hands, palm upwards. 'Who from? It's just the two of us!'

'Not from a person, from a thing. We need to get eyes-on to this company building without exposing ourselves.' He smiled slowly. 'What do you say we buy ourselves a drone – with Bex and Bradley's money of course? We can fly it right up to the place.'

'Just like we did back at that hospital in Newcastle?' Kieron nodded. 'I like it. Just one thing.'

'What?'

'Can it be a Learsa drone? Because that would be poetic justice.'

'Actually,' Sam said, 'I've got an even better idea. Give me the glasses.'

Reluctantly Kieron handed them over. He felt strangely vulnerable without them. He'd come to like the extra level of reality they gave him, and he'd got used to it as well. Having to give them away, if only for a few minutes, was like realising you'd left your mobile phone at home.

Watching Sam use the ARCC kit, Kieron felt a sense of worry descend over him like a damp grey cloud. What did the two of them think they were doing? They weren't agents – not like Bex and Bradley. They were just kids. Worse than that, they were kids far from home, in a country where they didn't even speak the language, expecting to waltz right into a nest of high-tech assassins and rescue their friends. This wasn't a game! Sam could die; Bex and Bradley could die; he could die! How would his mum feel if she got a phone call telling her that Kieron had died in some foreign country he wasn't even supposed to be in? If she couldn't understand how he'd got there and what he was doing, how would she ever come to terms with losing him? And Sam – what if it was Sam who died? Kieron knew he wouldn't be able to stand in front of Sam's mother and tell her what the two of them had been up to. He wouldn't even be able to go home. He'd have to go on the run, living below the radar, moving from town to town, taking whatever jobs he could get that paid cash and kept him from being found, and all without his only real friend. He felt his mouth go dry. The room seemed to shift around him, as though it was rocking. He couldn't feel the carpet under his feet; he felt like he was floating in space, able to see everything but not feel it or hear it properly: the sounds of the restaurant and the outside world had suddenly become fuzzy and muffled. His heart raced, and he started to shiver.

'Kieron?'

'Wha— what?'

'You looked really strange there for a minute. Are you all right?'

'Yeah.' He swallowed, as things gently settled back to

normal. Well, as normal as they had been, anyway. 'Panic attack. I think the craziness of all this suddenly hit home.'

'I've had a couple of moments like that,' Sam admitted. 'Do you remember when they made us do cross-country at school last year?'

'Don't – I've been trying to forget.'

'One of the sports teachers told me it's best not to focus on the horizon, just on where your feet are going. Don't think about how far it is to the finish line; just force your feet to take one step at a time.'

'Very comforting – thanks. Can I have those words on a motivational poster?'

'Ha ha,' Sam said succinctly.

'And to you.' Kieron smiled at his friend. 'Are you finished? What have you done?'

'What I have done is two things – firstly, I have emailed a tech shop here in Oslo that sells Learsa's drones and told them that I'm GamR BlamR's agent, that he's here in Oslo, and that he wants to have a go with one of their drones and would be happy to mention them and the location of their shop on one of his YouTube broadcasts. Secondly, I have emailed GamR BlamR's people, saying that I'm a tech shop here in Oslo and I'd love to give their client a promotional gift of a high-spec drone. Each person thinks they're talking with the other, but actually it's all going through me.' He smiled a triumphant smile. 'A package will be arriving within the hour, containing a top-of-the-line, fully charged drone.'

'I love what you're doing,' Kieron said admiringly, 'but this is fraud.'

'We're just borrowing it,' Sam pointed out. 'We'll pass it on once we've rescued Bex and Bradley. He won't even know it's been out of the box.'

'OK then.' Kieron nodded. 'Shall we go across to the hotel, intercept the package, get back into GamR BlamR's robot car and drive up to Learsa's HQ then?'

* * *

The package – a heavy box about the size of a 52" LCD TV screen – was just being carried into the hotel lobby when they got there. Sam knew the name of the person he'd been dealing with, and bluffed the delivery men into giving him the box and he and Kieron carried it back out to their car. Well, GamR BlamR's car. Well, actually the robot car belonging to some Norwegian company, but for all practical purposes it was their car for the time being.

The drive out of Oslo took them through a landscape that was gently rolling to start off with but which gradually became more and more corrugated, as if the ground had been rippled like a shaken bed sheet at some point and had got stuck that way. The grey rock around Oslo turned darker and bleaker as they headed north. Low hills became larger and more jagged. The houses, which had started out close together, became more and more spaced apart, and changed their form, looking now more like what Kieron thought of as *chalets*: the kind of thing he'd only seen at holiday camps. Several times he found that they were driving alongside long narrow lakes, whose water looked almost black in the late-afternoon light. Sometimes he noticed V-shaped ripples, signs that something was swimming in there, although he could never tell what it might have been. They were moving further and further from civilisation, into the wild.

It got colder as they drove, and several times one of them turned the heating up to stop themselves from shivering. Small flurries of snow blew against the window, borne by the cutting wind, and covered the fields and the roofs of the houses they passed with a thin layer, like a threadbare blanket.

Time lost all meaning as they drove through the stark Norwegian countryside, and Kieron was shocked when Sam suddenly nudged him out of his partial sleep and fractured dreams.

'I think we're here.'

Kieron sat up straighter and looked out of the window. They had pulled up at the side of a minor road – more of a dirt track – overlooking another of the long narrow lakes. The horizon around them was filled with dark shapes that were too big to be hills but too small to be mountains. Away to their right, Kieron saw several chalets that had been painted yellow and red. But the main thing that caught his eye was the building perched on the far shore of the lake, half hidden by the snow flurries. It sat on the edge of a steeply sloping mass of rock that led down to the surface of the water. The building was huge, wooden but futuristic, with large stretches of glass, and it looked completely out of place. It had been built out over the lake so that half of its massive bulk extended out over the water, supported by several piles that stretched from the exposed underside of the building to the steep rocky slope, like tree trunks stripped of all their branches. It seemed to glower across the water at them, like some gigantic squatting ogre.

'That's Learsa HQ,' Sam said bleakly. 'So – what do we do now?'

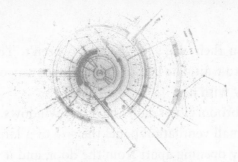

CHAPTER TWELVE

The room Bex and Bradley had been put in was basically a large broom closet filled with cleaning equipment, with hooks on the back of the door holding janitors' overalls. It was not a cell, by any stretch of the imagination, but then if this was indeed a company headquarters then holding prisoners securely probably hadn't been part of the architects' brief.

As soon as they had heard the door being locked, Bradley had pressed his back against the wall, slid down until he was sitting on the stone tiles of the floor with his legs bent, and put his head in his hands. He'd pretty much given up, Bex could tell. She didn't blame him: she felt like doing the same thing herself. The difference between the two of them was that she'd spent time on operations, and she'd been in situations that felt this hopeless before. Bradley knew the theory, but not the actuality.

She would have liked to sit down beside him, put her arm around his shoulders and tell him everything was going to be all right, but they didn't have time for that. She had to get them out of there. Maybe Sam and Kieron were on their way; maybe they weren't. They couldn't afford to wait. She had to find her own way out, and take Bradley with her.

The broom closet didn't have any windows. Why would it? A small ventilation panel the size of a large brick was the only opening apart from the door, and it wasn't large enough for Bex to get through. It wasn't large enough for a small *dog* to get through.

She scoured the ceiling and the floor in case she'd missed a trapdoor, but she had no luck. Nothing there.

OK – the door it would have to be. It was an old-fashioned wooden door, probably pine, attached by chunky hinges top, middle and bottom. The handle mechanism had a key lock in it, and she'd heard the *click* as soon as the door had closed behind them. She'd tried the handle and they were definitely locked in. She hadn't heard a bolt sliding across, so at least they didn't have that to deal with.

The lock was as old and clunky as the door. She could have picked it, if she'd had access to the several malleable wire hairpins that she always kept hidden in her hair for just such a purpose, but she and Bradley had been searched as soon as they'd entered Learsa's headquarters. Anything metal – including her rings, Bradley's St Christopher medallion and her hairpins – had been taken away, along with their belts and their shoes. Which was a shame, because she kept a back-up set of lock picks in the heel of her left shoe.

OK, she'd have to attack this problem old-school.

The door was so solid that it would take her months to scratch her way through, even assuming she could find something metal to do the scratching with. She supposed she could set fire to it, but she and Bradley would almost certainly choke to death on the smoke before the door became weakened enough for her to be able to kick her way through it. No help there.

She examined the hinges. They were massive things consisting of two tubes, each with a flat piece of metal attached. The flat piece on one hinge was fastened to the side of the door itself, probably by screws. The other piece was attached to the door frame, presumably the same way. It was difficult to tell for sure because, when the door was closed, as now, the two flat surfaces were pressed together. What stopped them from coming apart was the fact that the two tubes making up each hinge were at different heights, and they were connected by a central pin that ran right down through them. A flat head on the top of the pin stopped it from gradually working its way through and dropping out over time. When the door was opened, the tube on the door part of the hinge would rotate around the pin. All very basic. The same design had probably been used since medieval times.

So – all she had to do was lever the pin out of the top of each hinge and then the door would just fall into the room. Perfect.

If she could find some way of levering the pin out of the top of each hinge.

She glanced over at Bradley. He was slumped there, as still as a statue, with his head in his hands.

She glanced around the broom closet, looking for some

piece of metal that had been overlooked. The brooms were plastic, as were the buckets, the dustpans and the brushes. Even the *handles* of the buckets were plastic.

The hooks on the back of the door! She pulled the overalls off and threw them to the floor, but when she looked up at the hooks she felt her heart sink. They were plastic too. Even if she could have found a way to get them off the door they would have been no use, and they seemed to be glued to the wooden surface rather than screwed, so she couldn't even use the screws. If she could find something to unscrew them with.

'If we had some eggs, we could have ham and eggs,' she said quietly. 'If we had any ham.' It was something her dad used to say.

'Buttons,' Bradley said, without looking up.

'What?'

'The buttons on the overalls – they're made of metal.'

'How do you know?'

'You threw them down in front of me.' He looked up, and she was relieved to see a smile on his face. 'Take three buttons off. We can sharpen their edges on the stone floor tiles. Then, when they're sharp enough, we use them to lever the pins of the hinges out.'

'You worked all that out down there with your head in your hands?'

'Some of us don't need to keep moving around and looking at things,' he said. 'We just use our brains.'

It took mere seconds to bite through the thread fastening three of the buttons – the fabric tasted of oil and cleaning products and sweat, and Bex gagged as she tugged them away. It then took ten minutes of scraping the buttons on the floor to sharpen the already quite sharp edges to the point where they thought they could slip them between the pins and the metal tubes. And that was where the first setback occurred. The pins were held so tightly in that there was no gap into which the sharp edges could be inserted.

'The buckets,' Bradley said.

'Plastic,' Bex pointed out in a frustrated growl. 'They'll break.'

'Not if we use the base,' Bradley pointed out. 'It's thicker, and stronger.'

He was right. By holding a bucket horizontally, placing the bottom rim against the thicker edge of a button, then placing the sharp edge of the button where a pin met the tube that held it, and then ramming the top of the bucket with a shoulder a couple of times, the button could be forced into the very thin gap so that it stayed there. It hurt the shoulder involved, but that was a small price to pay for freedom. If it worked.

Bex stepped back to admire their handiwork. Three buttons sat at the top of the three hinges, wedged between the top of each pin and the tube of its hinge.

'Your idea,' Bex said, massaging her shoulder. 'What now?'

'The overalls again,' Bradley said. He picked one of them off the floor and draped it carefully over the topmost of the three suspended buttons so that it hung down. He looked at Bex. 'Fingers crossed.'

'Fingers crossed.'

He reached up and grabbed hold of the top of the overalls and pulled his feet up off the floor, so that the material – and the button – took the weight of his body. And then, very seriously, he bounced up and down.

'You look like a kid playing a game,' Bex said, trying not to laugh. Laughing hurt her shoulder.

'I feel like one,' Bradley said. 'How's the hinge doing?'

She went on tiptoe so she could see the top of the overalls, where the flat head of the pin was just visible. She thought she could see a couple of millimetres of pin showing. 'I think it's working!' she said excitedly. 'Keep bouncing!'

'This material is going to rip!' he muttered, but he kept on going.

Twenty minutes of hard work later, the three pins were half out of their hinges, which meant they were almost entirely out of the bottom sections of the tubes.

'Right,' Bex said, 'we need to get into the overalls. Disguise.'

'Bit torn, and they're missing some buttons,' Bradley observed.

'Have you ever seen a neat janitor?'

'Fair point.'

They listened for a few minutes, in case anyone was nearby. Then, when they were fairly sure the coast was clear, they pulled the whole door into the broom closet and edged out past it, then pulled it back up to a standing position. Someone, Bex thought, was going to get a shock when they next opened it – just so long as that wasn't for a while.

Dressed in their overalls, carrying a broom each, they

walked along the curved corridor outside the closet. They both kept they eyes down, just in case they passed anybody, but there was nobody around. It was late, and Bex suspected that all of the regular employees of the company – assuming there were any – had gone home. Just the criminal assassins were left.

'Any idea what floor we're on?' Bex muttered.

'I think it's the fourth floor – the top level,' Bradley replied.

'We've got to get down to the ground then.'

'Best to go right down to the basement, if there is one, then come up the stairs to the ground floor like real janitors.'

'Agreed.'

They passed a double doorway. Both doors had been opened into the room beyond. Bex glanced through as they passed.

And hesitated.

The far wall of the room was entirely glass, looking out over a night-time landscape where the half-moon, the twinkling stars and the glittering tops of the waves were the only illumination. The room was an office, with a vast pine desk in the middle of a deep pile carpet a marine-green colour. On the desk sat an advanced computer, sterile light spilling from its screen. A woman stood with her back to the doorway, beside a comfortable office chair, staring out into the darkness. It wasn't Katrin, Eva or Hekla. This woman looked like she was in her fifties, if not her sixties. Her long grey hair had been pulled back into a ponytail which hung down to the small of her back. She wore a simple but stylish trouser suit.

'Please, come in,' she said just as Bex was about to move on. She spoke in English.

'Did you want some cleaning done?' Bex asked, but she knew the game was up. If the woman had thought they were really cleaners, she would have spoken in Norwegian, and she probably wouldn't have said please.

Bex glanced down the corridor ahead. It was still empty. The same was true of the way they'd come.

'Please,' the woman said again, 'join me.'

No threat. Just a simple invitation. Bex had a strong feeling, however, that if she and Bradley tried to walk away then things would quickly turn less friendly.

Reluctantly she stepped into the room. Bradley followed.

'Can we help you, ma'am?' she said neutrally.

'My name is Agnetha Reginiussen,' the woman said. She turned around to face them. Her skin was creased, but surprisingly young-looking considering her grey hair. Her expression was tranquil. 'My husband, Gustav, set up this company, nearly thirty years ago.'

'That's . . . lovely,' Bex said, unsure what response the woman expected.

'Now I'm just a figurehead. My daughters run the company on my behalf. You have met them, haven't you? I saw them bringing you from the helicopter to here, and I saw they were not being careful with you.'

So she knew for certain that Bex and Bradley weren't the cleaners.

Bex decided to take a risk. 'Do you know what they are doing with your company?' she asked, taking a step into the room.

Agnetha Reginiussen's face didn't change. It was so pale and still it looked as if it had been carved out of ice, or some almost-white pine, but Bex could feel the pain radiating from her. 'Yes, I do. They have told me. They take great pleasure in telling me.'

'But you could stop them, couldn't you?' Bradley stepped forward to join Bex.

Agnetha smiled, but there was no humour or joy in her expression. Just more pain. 'A chauffeur picks me up in the morning and brings me here, to this building and to this office. Food is brought to me. If I make a phone call, someone is listening. If I send an email, someone reads it before it leaves the building. A chauffeur takes me home at night. The chauffeurs are changed every week so that I do not form any kind of friendship with them. And in my home there are no telephones or computers. I have no mobile. Just a television set so that I can see what is happening in the world. And if I try to leave, if I try even to book a taxi to take me anywhere, someone intervenes.' She waved a hand at the desk. 'Every so often a document is put here for me to sign. And I sign it, because if I don't –' her face suddenly seemed as though it might crack open, but she caught herself and continued, with barely a break in her voice – 'then bad things might happen to me. My daughters love me, but they love the idea of being rich even more.'

'Could you not just leave?' Bex asked. 'I mean, I saw buildings across the lake. You could walk around to there and ask for help, couldn't you?' Even as she spoke the words she knew that it wouldn't be that easy. Agnetha's daughters were too clever and too determined for that.

'There are guards,' Agnetha said quietly, 'and even if I could slip past them . . . well, you have seen those terrible things my daughters have created? Those flying devils which can bring fire and brimstone down onto anyone they choose?'

Bex and Bradley both nodded.

Agnetha slid the sleeve of her blouse up her arm. Just above the wrist, a plastic bracelet indented her skin. 'This is a tracking device,' she said. 'Even if the guards don't find me, the flying drones will. I would never make it to those houses. I would barely make it halfway.'

'And your own daughters would do that to you?' Bex asked, incredulously.

'Apparently I was not a good mother. I was too concerned with supporting my husband, and making this company work – this company they have perverted to violence. That's what they have told me, so it must be true.'

From beyond the door, Bex heard the sound of booted feet moving towards them.

Agnetha's hand moved, her fingers pointing to the desk. Bex saw a tablet computer lying on it, next to the computer monitor. It was small, with a fold-over cover: the kind of thing that looked like a book. Agnetha glanced down at it, then looked at Bex. '*I* can do nothing,' she said, stressing the word *I* slightly. 'But I have waited years for someone to arrive who *might* be able to do something.' She reached down and pushed the tablet a few inches across the desk, towards Bex.

Over Agnetha's shoulder, through the window that filled one entire wall of the room, Bex thought she saw something move. For a second she thought it was just a flurry of snow, but it hung there, in the darkness; something dark reflecting back the light from inside the office.

The boots in the corridor were getting closer. Bex glanced around, noting the small cameras in the corners of the room, covering every square inch. The girls really did not trust their mother.

She took a step forward, keeping her eyes on the thing that hung outside. A drone? She thought she could see the flicker of propellers keeping it aloft, but it was hard to make out any details. She couldn't even tell if it was armed with anything more than a camera. Was it going to suddenly fire a fusillade of bullets through the glass and into the room? Surely the Asrael girls wouldn't risk their mother like that!

She reached out towards the tablet, but instead she took Agnetha's hand. The woman's skin was dry and warm. It felt fragile, like tissue paper. 'Don't worry – we'll help you if we can,' she said. 'Can you get us out of here?'

Agnetha shook her head. She pulled her hand away. Bex let her own hand trail down to the desk. As her fingers touched the tablet she scooped it up and bought it to her side. 'The girls look after the details,' Agnetha said, but as she said the word *details* her gaze flicked down to Bex's hand. What did the tablet contain? All the details of how Katrin, Hekla and Eva were turning Agnetha's company – her late-husband's company – into a nest of high-tech assassins? And she expected – *wanted* – Bex and Bradley to take those details out into the world for her?

'Then how do we escape?' Bex said, urgently but quietly.

'I don't know,' Agnetha admitted, just as quietly, but with an underlying agony, 'but you have a better chance than I do.'

'Only slightly better,' Bradley observed as the doorway suddenly filled with security guards, all dressed in black, all holding guns.

'Please – don't let them find it!' Agnetha hissed, reaching out to clutch Bex's closed fist.

'I'm not sure what I can do!' Bex hissed back urgently, and it was true – the guards were crowding towards them now, guns raised. No way out. She slipped the tablet into a pocket of her janitor's overalls.

But outside the window the drone hovered. Watching. Watching and . . . waiting. And as Bex watched *it*, the drone suddenly moved diagonally up and left, down and right, then up and right, down and left, tracing out a cross in mid-air.

Why would an Asrael drone do that?

Bex could never work out how she knew. She just *did*. That drone out there wasn't Asrael; it was Kieron and Sam! And they had just marked the spot . . .

She stepped quickly around the desk and scooped up the computer monitor. She jerked the cables out in case they held the thing back, then lobbed it hard at the window. It hit, right in the middle of where the drone had marked the X. The glass cracked and crazed in a spider's web pattern, but there must have been a plastic film over it, maybe something to stop heat escaping from the building.

Hands grabbed Bex's arms. She lashed back with her heel, connecting with someone's leg. They cried out and let go.

She picked up the office chair and threw it at the centre of the smashed glass.

This time the plastic film tore, and the chair sailed through. Shards of glass followed. A cold wind gusted into the office, bearing flakes of snow with it.

And the drone followed.

It burst into the office like some vengeful spirit, buzzing and spinning. Bex quickly clocked that it had several cameras fitted beneath the propellers, but no obvious weapons. The only way it could hurt the guards was if the whirling propellers touched them.

Which was, apparently, a real risk. The guards all started backing away nervously, terrified of the sharp spinning blades.

Bex glanced around. There was a clear path to the door, but it would only be there for a few seconds, until the guards regrouped. She could try to leave, taking the tablet computer with her, but what if she was taken down before she made it out of the building?

She stepped back, making sure she was in range of one of the cameras, held her arm out and pointed at the smashed window. 'Go!' she mouthed. The drone was more use to her outside than in, now that it had created a diversion.

Whoever was operating the drone took the hint. It took off and veered towards the window. One of the guards, more prescient than the rest, raised his gun and fired, but all he did was clear more shattered glass from the remnants of the plastic film. The drone zoomed through the gap and vanished into the darkness.

Bradley had his arm around the neck of a guard. She ran past him, grabbing his arm and pulling him off while simultaneously punching another guard in the throat. He fell backwards, choking, as she yanked Bradley out of the room.

'I was enjoying that!' he protested.

'Escape now; fight later,' she shouted.

As they got out into the corridor she turned to look back in at the older woman. Agnetha smiled and nodded. 'Thank you,' she mouthed. 'Good luck.'

Bex and Bradley pounded down the curved corridor, hampered by the fact that they were in their socks because their shoes had been confiscated. The tablet in Bex's pocket banged against her hip as she ran. Behind them she heard shouts and scuffling as the guards pulled themselves into some kind of order and started to give chase. Glancing briefly over her shoulder, Bex saw one of the Asrael girls – Hekla, she thought, but she wasn't sure – pushing the guards roughly towards them.

'Lift or stairs?' Bradley gasped.

Bex turned her head to look past him. They were coming up to a lobby area. 'Stairs,' she said. 'Too easy to stop the lift.'

Bradley was slightly in front, and when he got to the lobby he barrelled straight through the door marked 'Fire escape' and almost fell down the concrete stairs. Coming through behind him, Bex noticed some kind of metal contraption fastened to the wall. It took her a second to recognise it as something companies had to install in order to get people down the stairs in case of fire if they couldn't walk. It was a kind of metal stretcher, body-sized, with handles along both sides. She flipped the catch holding it to the wall as she passed. It fell with a clatter. Hopefully it would delay the guards.

She and Bradley ran down the stairs together. If there were guards on the lower levels then they were done for, but none appeared. Maybe they'd all been called up to the fourth floor.

They reached the third floor without incident. Then the second.

Above them Bex heard the fire escape door burst open, closely followed by the sound of several guards falling over the stretcher. The sound of them falling over it, and each other, echoed around the concrete stairwell.

First floor. Still no problems.

As they reached the ground, the fire escape door there opened and a guard started to come through. Bex briefly caught sight of two more guards behind him. Bradley took a wild swing at the first guard's face. His jaw snapped sideways and he fell backwards, taking his unprepared companions with him. Bradley ran over the top of them and an admiring Bex followed.

They were in the ground floor lobby now, where they'd been brought in. Bex quickly looked around, getting her bearings. Going through the main doors to the outside was probably the wrong thing to do. Too obvious. Instead she pulled Bradley in the opposite direction, following signs for the car park. They were in Norwegian, but they had a helpful graphic of a parked car.

'I hope you've got a plan!' Bradley shouted as they broke through a pine door into a white-walled corridor.

'Less of a plan, more of a desperate hope!' she called back.

Ahead of them, a thick security door with an emergency bar obviously led to the outside world, and probably to the car park. Bex ran at it, hitting the bar with her elbow and pushing the door open. It scraped against a crust of snow, but she managed to make a gap wide enough for her and Bradley to get through.

It was cold outside. Desperately, ear-tinglingly, nose-bitingly cold. And they weren't dressed for it.

Bex looked around. They were in a sort of sheltered area, with a roof overhead supported by columns but no walls. Several cars sat on the dark concrete. The roof kept snow from falling directly on them, but it drifted in from the sides and piled up against their wheels and the side of the building. Bex quickly scanned the vehicles. Most of them – furthest away from the building – were ordinary Volvos, Skodas, Vauxhalls and Fords. However, the three parked closest to the building, separate from the others, were different. They were high-performance sports cars.

'Nice,' Bradley breathed. 'A Barchetta two-seater roadster, a Lotus Europa S and an MG XPower SV. I can see where the company's profits are going.'

'These must belong to the girls,' Bex agreed. 'Come on – we'll take one of the others.'

'But –' Bradley protested, 'a Lotus Europa!'

'High security,' Bex pointed out as she sprinted towards a blocky Volvo. 'Can't break in or get it started – not quickly anyway.' She smashed the window with her elbow, reached inside and unlocked the door. 'This thing is a cinch.'

As she slid into the driver's seat and let Bradley into the passenger seat, Bex was already pulling wires out from beneath the dashboard and connecting the two that would start the engine. It roared thunderously into life. 'Good, solid cars, Volvos,' she said. 'Great in cold weather.'

The security exit they'd taken burst open and guards spilled out. They had guns, and they were raising them to fire. Bex threw the car into gear and started off, wheels slipping on the thin drift of snow before they got purchase.

The gap leading out of the sheltered parking area was on the side away from the building, and Bex aimed directly for it. An enterprising – or just stupid – security guard ran in front of her, brandishing his weapon, but she just smiled at him and accelerated. He jumped out of the way just in time, and they hurtled into the open. Floodlights on poles illuminated the road, and also the wide concrete area ahead of them where the helicopter had landed with the van: almost certainly a runway so that drones could be delivered to their various military and civilian customers. Bex wasn't sure which way to go – left or right on the road or straight ahead across the runway. She glanced around, through the windscreen and the side windows, trying to orient herself. Three choices, and two of them were wrong. At least two.

Something moving in the sky caught her eye, and she glanced upwards. It was Kieron and Sam's drone. She smiled. The boys were with her, even if only in technological spirit.

The drone suddenly darted to the left, above one of the roadways. Kieron had access to maps and satellite photographs: he must be showing her the way. She followed, slewing the car around and accelerating as much as she dared on the frozen road surface. From the feel of the car, it didn't have snow chains. She would have to be careful not to skid and turn it over.

The building was on their left, the runway on their right. Ahead of them, Bex saw a gate in the distance. It was closed, but Volvos were heavy cars and she was fairly certain she could batter through it.

About three car length's ahead of them, the concrete suddenly exploded upwards in an expanding fireball, sending chunks flying high into the air and smoke in all directions. Instinctively Bex braked, her eyes dazzled by the flames. The car slid forward on the icy surface until the Advanced Braking System cut in, juddering the car to a halt.

'What the . . . ?' Bradley exclaimed.

'Bad drone,' Bex said through her teeth as she slammed the car into reverse and backed up, then suddenly jerked the steering wheel and pulled the handbrake up to send them into a skidding turn. As the car's bonnet swung round till it was facing back towards where they had started, she put it into first gear again and took the handbrake off. The car sprang forward, but now it was heading towards the armed guards who had exited the building. She aimed straight for them, and they scattered. As she drove through them she glanced sideways and saw the three blonde girls – Katrin, Eva and Hekla – climbing into the three sports cars. Maybe they were planning to catch up with Bex and Bradley, or maybe they were trying to escape; Bex wasn't sure.

Several gunshots *plink*ed across the back of the car. Bex turned the wheel, taking the Volvo into a controlled skid that ended with her heading out across the snow-covered expanse of the runway, and just in time. The roadway that she'd been heading towards suddenly turned into a ball of flame and debris.

She glanced out of the driver's side window, looking up, but she couldn't see any of the assassin drones up there. No surprise: they'd been designed to be stealthy. How many did the girls have access to?

It didn't matter. One could kill them.

The runway stretched ahead of them, a field of pure white snow hiding the concrete. Bex slowed and turned the wheel again, then accelerated so that they were screeching off at an angle. Just in time: another explosion marred the pristine whiteness with dirt, debris and flames. She actually felt the heat of that one on her cheeks.

She felt something tugging at her overalls and looked down. Bradley was pulling the tablet from her pocket.

'No time for that!' she yelled.

'Actually,' he yelled back, 'I have an idea, but you're not going to like it!'

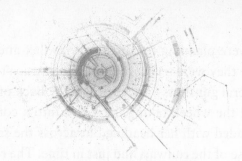

CHAPTER THIRTEEN

'Oh my God!' Sam shouted, 'they'll be killed!'

Kieron stared desperately across the lake, towards the distant Learsa HQ building overhanging the freezing black waters. A fireball bloomed like a crimson and yellow flower to one side of the building, and then another one. He thought he could hear an engine revving desperately, but then the sound of the explosions, slower than the light of the flames, rolled like thunder across the headland where he and Sam had parked their driverless car.

He couldn't tell what was going on or who was involved. Desperately, he tore the ARCC glasses from Sam's face and jammed them on himself. 'Let me see!' he said, batting Sam's hands away. 'You've had them for ages. It's my turn!'

It took him a few moments to work out what was going on. The drone was looking downwards, at a large field of snow. The snow couldn't be that thick, because a blocky car – a Volvo, he thought – raced across the camera's field of view, leaving dark parallel tracks behind it. A sudden explosion off to one side momentarily overloaded the glasses, but just before the picture whited out he saw the Volvo veer sideways.

'Asrael are using their drones,' Sam said urgently. 'They're targeting Bex and Bradley in the car.'

'Can we ram our drone into theirs and disable them?' Kieron asked, as the view in the glasses began to clear.

'No chance,' Sam replied. 'They've got access to loads of drones, and we've only got one. It's a suicide mission for the drone, and we'd only take one of theirs out at best.'

'Then what can we do,' Kieron snapped, 'apart from just watch?'

'I don't know!' Sam's voice had an edge of desperation. 'I'm out of ideas.'

'You said they took a tablet from some woman?'

'Yeah. I think that was Katrin, Eva and Hekla's mum.'

'What's on the tablet?'

Kieron heard the *huff* as Sam breathed out heavily. 'The woman indicated it was data about Asrael and what they're doing with the drones.'

'Could they use the tablet to give instructions to the drones – turn them off, make them land, or something?'

'No Wi-Fi, and no other way of transmitting the data,' Sam said, his voice close to breaking. 'I tried hacking into it with the ARCC glasses, but it was no use. It's just a flat tablet. No connectivity.'

'But we've got connectivity here!' Kieron pointed out urgently, watching as the Volvo suddenly braked and turned left.

'Yeah, but the Asrael drones need a security code before they'll accept any instructions. I've been trying, but I can't get around that. It's stupid – Bex and Bradley probably have the code on that tablet, but they can't use it to get into the drones' control functions. We can get into the drones' control functions using the ARCC glasses, but we haven't got the code!'

Again, as Kieron watched, Bex and Bradley's car slowed down. It came to a halt unexpectedly, and then reversed. 'What are they trying to do?' he muttered.

'Avoid the exploding drones obviously,' Sam pointed out.

'Yes, but nothing exploded. And if you're trying to stop someone from predicting where you're driving, you don't come to an abrupt stop.' A sudden realisation flashed across his mind, almost seeming to light his head up from the inside. 'Of course!'

'Of course what?'

'Hang on.' Kieron used his fingertips to access their drone's controls on the virtual menu he could see in the ARCC glasses. He ordered it to rise higher, increase its altitude but still look down on what was going on.

'What are you *doing*?' Sam almost screamed.

Kieron felt a smile break out across his face.

From low down the erratic movements of the Volvo – the sudden stops, the sudden turns, the gradual loops – just looked like frantic attempts to avoid plummeting explosive drones, but from higher up it was clear that whoever was driving had a plan in mind.

Kieron instructed the drone to stay at the same height but rotate around its own axis. The picture he stared at suddenly and sickeningly turned through sixty degrees, but he needed to see what Bex was doing to make sure he was right.

'Yes! She's writing the code in the snow!' he shouted triumphantly. 'Bradley must have found it on the tablet, and she's using the car to write it out for us! 1 . . . 3 . . . 5 . . . 2. It's rough, but she's doing a brilliant job.'

Sam's fingers scratched Kieron's face as he snatched the glasses back. 'Let me have that!' The abrupt sliding sideways and disappearance of the images he'd been watching made Kieron's stomach lurch. By the time he'd recovered, Sam's fingers were moving through empty air as he manipulated menus and entered instructions. 'Right – I've got a blanket input into all of the drones. There's – hell, there are *fifteen* of them left. Asrael are throwing everything at Bex and Bradley. Right – I'm typing the code in now so I can turn them all off. 1-3-5-2, right?'

'Right,' Kieron snapped, annoyed at the way his friend had taken over. He stared desperately through the windscreen and across the lake, trying to make out what was going on. An explosion suddenly flared, and then was gone.

'It's not working!' Sam shouted. 'The code's not working! Are you sure you got it right?'

'I'm sure,' Kieron said firmly, but he wasn't. Using a fast-moving car to clear snow away from dark concrete to leave numbers behind was an incredibly difficult – and approximate – thing to do. No matter how good a driver Bex was, there was room for error. Just the slightest drift or skid could change –

'What about 1-8-5-2?' he shouted. Bex hadn't completely connected the loops up!

'Trying that now,' Sam said through teeth clenched together in worry and concentration. 'Yes! I'm in! Ordering all drones to land now! Let me know if you see any more explosions.'

'Nothing,' Kieron said, and then, 'still nothing. I think you did it.'

'*We* did it. They're all grounded now. That was two lots of clever thinking you did there.' He sighed. 'Let's hope we've given Bex and Bradley enough scope to get out of the place.'

Something off to the right, across the dark water, caught Kieron's attention. Lights, moving. Headlights, splashing across the tarmac of the road that ran around the edge of the lake.

'I think someone's coming,' he said urgently. 'One of the girls. Maybe all of them. And they'll be armed.'

'We need to hide.' Sam glanced over at Kieron. 'It's going to be cold out there. You ready for this? I remember what you were like on those cross-country runs at school. You don't like the cold.'

'Do I have a choice?'

'Not really.

They exited the car, left and right. The sudden cold sent a spike of pain through Kieron's head. Sam was right. He hated the cold.

He looked around. All the rocks he could see would hardly hide a tortoise, let alone a person. No bushes close by either. The parking area they'd chosen was clear of anywhere they could hide.

'Actually –' he said, breath turning to vapour as he

spoke – 'maybe this is a bad idea. Couldn't we just drive away?' He wrapped his arms around himself to try to conserve some warmth. He could feel the cold radiating in through the soles of his trainers and up into the soles of his feet. He knew that technically cold didn't radiate anywhere, it was heat that did the moving, but it did nothing to quell the fact that his body heat was gradually bleeding away into the ground.

'They'd follow us,' Sam pointed out. He indicated the road around the lake, where the lights of the approaching car were getting closer. *Cars* plural. Kieron could see two sets of lights, maybe three.

'How do they know where we are?' he asked.

'I don't know. Maybe they could track the signal I sent.'

The cars were only a minute or two away now. Kieron felt his heart pounding. The pain in his head had spread now, from a spike to a general throbbing.

'The lake,' he said suddenly.

'What about it?'

'We're on the edge of a slope leading down to the water. It's quite steep. Maybe we can climb down a little way and hide there.'

'Worth a try.'

They moved gingerly towards the edge and scrabbled down until their feet were resting on a thin ledge and their heads were below the level of the ground. The sharp edges of the rocks cut into Kieron's hands at the same time as they sapped the warmth from them. At least the numbness stopped the pain, but he knew, as he pressed himself against the sloping cliff-face, that he would get colder even faster now.

The roar of approaching car engines distracted him momentarily. They slowed, stopped, and then several car doors opened.

Footsteps on loose gravel.

'We know you're there,' a girl's voice said. Kieron's heart sank. He was sure it was Katrin. Obviously it *had* to be Katrin. She was the one he'd liked the best. 'You're the boy from St Mark's Square, aren't you? It took a while, but we traced your friends' movements back to when they arrived on the island, and we found they'd booked into the hotel with you.' She paused. Kieron imagined her leaning her head to one side thoughtfully as she looked around. 'Did you meet us by accident in the square, or was it deliberate? Was it all planned?'

He looked sideways, to where Sam was spreadeagled against the rock. Their eyes met. Sam made a small movement with his lips and shrugged slightly. Only Kieron, who had known him for as long as he could remember, could have interpreted the message: *Hey, you really know how to choose them, don't you?*

Kieron raised an eyebrow and smiled. He knew that Sam would understand the reply: *I'll stick to fancying your sister in future!*

More crunches of feet on gravel. The girls were separating; one moving left, one moving right while the third one stayed in the middle.

'You've been very clever,' Katrin said, 'I'll give you that. You and your older friends have caused us a lot of trouble. But look, we can be sensible about this. Show

252

yourselves, and we can find a way out of this that makes us all happy.'

Sam caught Kieron's eye and shook his head sharply, but Kieron had already realised that Katrin was lying. There was no easy way out of this for all of them. It was the girls or the two boys – a stark choice.

Bang! A sudden gunshot rang out, sending birds flapping in panic from hidden nests. Seconds later it echoed back from the other side of the lake.

'Sorry.' That was Hekla, apologetically. 'I thought I saw something move. Probably a fox.'

'I don't think they are going to come out from wherever they are.' That was Eva's voice. 'I mean, would you?'

'Probably not.'

Eva's voice was so close that Kieron felt like if he just looked up he would be staring at her as she stood on the edge of the cliff. 'Keep looking. If we don't find them in ten minutes we'll set their car alight and leave them here. They won't last more than an hour in these temperatures.' She paused. 'It is a shame; I would like to have punished them.'

'What about Mother?' Hekla asked.

'Oh, she will be punished as well.' Katrin's voice had an edge of dark anger in it.

Kieron's feet had become so numb that he couldn't feel the ledge beneath them. Pins and needles had started up in his right thigh. He tried banging his leg with his clenched fist, but it didn't do any good. He tried to shift the position of his right foot, but the numbness made him misjudge the movement. His foot went back too far, and slipped off the ledge. Pebbles clattered as they fell towards the water, ending in distant splashes. Sam looked urgently at him. Checking he was OK. He tried to smile back, but his face seemed frozen. He couldn't move his cheek muscles or his lips properly.

'I think they're hiding over the edge,' Eva said.

'I think you're right.' That was Katrin. 'Clever boys.'

'Shall we just shoot them?' Hekla.

'If we're close enough to fire down at them, we're close enough that they could reach up and pull us over the edge. No, come over here. Grab some rocks, as heavy as you can manage. We'll throw the rocks over the edge and knock the boys into the water, where they'll freeze to death within a few minutes.' Katrin giggled suddenly. 'It's like those games you see in the arcades, where you have to push coins over the edge of a moving plate so that when it goes back the coins push other coins over the next edge. I loved that game when I was a kid.'

Kieron glanced urgently to his right, along the face of the cliff. The ledge they were on petered out after a little way; no hope of escape there. Sam was busy checking to his left. He turned his head back and shook it. No escape that way either.

A rock the size of a football appeared over the edge and plunged past Kieron's head. It hit the ledge and bounced, sailing out into the darkness. Moments later Kieron heard a louder *splash* from far below.

'Nothing?' Hekla sounded amused. 'Let's try another one. Just scream, boys, if it hits you.'

Kieron thought he heard a car in the distance. For a moment he thought it was random passing motorist, but then he realised that it was more likely to be Bex and Bradley. A warm feeling flashed through him as he realised they were coming to the rescue, but reality doused the warmth with a cold, sick realisation. The girls were armed. Bex and Bradley weren't. It would be a massacre, over within seconds.

He had to do something. Anything.

What resources did they have? What tools in the toolbox? Two freezing boys.

No, two freezing boys with a set of ARCC glasses.

A plan suddenly unfolded in his head, fully formed, as if it had just been waiting there for him to notice it.

He couldn't communicate this to Sam using just his eyebrows. Instead he pointed at the glasses his friend was still wearing, and then to his own face. Sam frowned. Urgently, Kieron gestured to his friend to pass them over. After what seemed like an eternity, Sam got the message. Carefully, so he didn't disrupt his own balance, he removed the glasses and handed them across.

Kieron put them on. He raised his right hand to access the menus, but there wasn't enough space in front of him to move properly. If he tried, he would push himself off the cliff!

'Put your guns behind your backs,' Katrin ordered her sisters. 'When they stop the car, Hekla, I want you to shoot out their tyres so they can't escape, and you, Eva, are to shoot the man. I'll take out the woman.'

He would have to turn around to give himself room to move his hands.

As quickly as he could, he shuffled around until his toes were hanging over empty space. He pressed his back as hard as he could against the rock. As he raised his hands to access the virtual menus he felt something press hard in the middle of his chest. He looked down. It was Sam's hand. His friend had edged closer to him and was stopping him from slipping over.

The car engine was nearby now. Only seconds remained.

The driverless car was parked only around ten feet from the edge of the cliff, and from the way the key card locked it at a distance Kieron knew it had some kind of RFID or Bluetooth technology. That meant, with the technology of the ARCC glasses behind him, he should – *should* – be able to access it. Hack it. *Drive* it.

He heard Bex and Bradley's car pull off the road and into the parking area with a spray of gravel.

'Ready?' Katrin said to her sisters.

New menus popped up as the ARCC glasses found the car's electronic brain. Views from the sensor cameras around the car's body appeared in front of him. He could see the three girls standing apparently innocently in front of it, and he could also see Bex and Bradley's car skidding to a halt behind it. The girls had their hands behind their backs. Bex's expression was furious.

Operating on instinct, Kieron tapped instructions into the cold, empty air.

The driverless car's motor roared. The girls looked confused, then suddenly worried.

The car sprang to life, aiming straight for the girls, who dived out of the way gracelessly. Kieron got a sudden view from the side cameras of them sprawled on the ground, then the car was past them and over the edge of the cliff. Looking up Kieron saw the underside of the vehicle slide overhead like some massive alien spacecraft, before it was past him and beginning its downwards arc to the lake.

He turned around and scrambled up the sloping side of the cliff to level ground, Sam doing the same by his side. Bex had already subdued Hekla, kneeling on her back and twisting her arm up behind her back. Bradley had pulled Eva into a kneeling position and had her in a headlock.

But Katrin was on her feet, gun raised and aimed at Bex.

Kieron scooped the glasses from his face and threw them at the girl as hard as he could. They caught her on the cheek. Her head jerked sideways and her hand came up instinctively to protect herself. Her gun discharged harmlessly into the air.

Bradley saw exactly what was going on. He reached into his pocket and pulled out something rectangular and black. The tablet from their mother! He threw it underarm at Katrin. It spun through the air and caught her on the bridge of her perfect nose. Her head snapped back, she took two steps backwards and her feet hit one of the rocks that she and her sisters had collected to throw at Kieron and Sam. She began to topple backwards, over the edge of the cliff. Instinctively working together, Sam snatched her gun out of her hand while Kieron grabbed her shoulder and yanked her sideways. She fell on top of him, unconscious.

Kieron lay there for a few moments, breathing heavily and staring at the glittering stars in the night sky. He heard footsteps approaching, but he was too tired to turn over. He just lay there, with Katrin's body sprawled across his chest.

'Typical,' Bex's voice said. 'We do all the hard work, and all the kids can think about is girls.'

'This one's not my type,' Kieron wheezed. 'Too violent. When we get home, there's a red-headed barista in a coffee shop in Newcastle I want to ask out.'

'Tell you what,' Sam's voice said from somewhere over to his left, 'when she asks you what your name is so she can write it on your order, just say: "Your new boyfriend".'

'And that,' Kieron said, pushing Katrin off him so he could get up, and grinning over at his friend, 'is why you never get a girl.'

EPILOGUE

A week later, back in Newcastle, Bex thought she'd just about recovered. Every now and then a shiver ran through her, but she wasn't sure if it was her body remembering the cold or her mind still trying to get rid of the stress of the mission. Either way, it was unpleasant.

Her hand shook, almost spilling her coffee. Bradley, across the table from her, reached out a comforting hand to steady it. His face looked strangely naked without the ARCC glasses. 'I'm glad it's not just me,' he said quietly.

Bex smiled at him. 'You had it a lot worse than I did. How are you feeling?'

'Surprisingly good.' He shrugged. 'Maybe I just needed a good holiday somewhere picturesque.'

As Bradley pulled his hand back, Bex glanced across the cafe. Over by the far wall, Kieron sat at a small table with a coffee in front of him. Well-placed, she noticed – good view of the door. His hands were moving animatedly, but he wasn't using the ARCC kit. Instead he was describing something to a red-haired barista who had taken her break just after they'd entered and had asked Kieron if he wanted to join her. He had. Of course he had.

'Kids,' she said.

Bradley nodded. 'How can they be so resilient, and have so much energy, when we're so brittle and so tired?'

'Oh, I've worked that one out. All teenagers are vampires. They drain the energy from any adults near them.'

He nodded. 'That actually makes sense.'

Bex took a sip of her coffee. 'Did you manage to do anything for Kieron's mum?'

'You've got foam on your upper lip.' He pointed, as if she didn't know where her upper lip was. Rather than wipe it off with a napkin, Bex deliberately poked her tongue out at him and then deliberately licked her lip.

'Yeah, very adult,' he said. 'Can you actually touch the tip of your nose with the tip of your tongue?'

She could, and she proved it.

'Fair,' he said, grinning. 'I asked for that. Now, what were you saying?'

'I asked you if you'd managed to find Kieron's mum a job?'

He nodded. 'I found a tech company who needed a senior human-resources manager, and I emailed them her CV just as they were about to post the vacancy. They were so pleased with her experience and her proactiveness that they decided to save themselves the cost of running the advert and just recruited her straight away.' He shrugged. 'Of course, it meant I had to pretend to be her to them for a while, and also pretend to be them to her, but after a few emails back and forth I stepped back and let nature take its course. She starts on Monday.'

'Brilliant. And dare I ask about Norway, and Asrael?'

'Dare away. I've been monitoring the police computers, and also the IT systems of the Norwegian secret service, which, by the way, is called the Etterretningstjenesten. Lovely word. The three girls have been arrested on terrorism and fraud charges, and their mother has retaken control of Learsa.' He smiled. 'She's also refusing to pay her daughters' legal bills.'

'Good for her.' Bex paused, and glanced again at Kieron. He'd stopped talking, and was now listening as the girl described something to him. He was smiling and she reached up unconsciously and touched her hair. All good signs. 'And what about . . . that other matter?'

'You mean, who was it who hired Asrael to kill us?' He was quiet for a moment, and looked over at the window of the cafe and the bustling life outside. 'Yeah, I've been waiting for the Norwegian police to upload all of their computer evidence to their hard drives. I'm hoping there'll be something on the Asrael system that will help us. They've been holding on – analysing the evidence offline – but they have to upload it some time.' He reached into his pocket, pulled the ARCC glasses out and slipped them casually on. 'Let me check.'

As his fingers touched the air, accessing data, Bex stopped herself looking across to see how Kieron was doing. This was his moment. This was – hopefully – something he would remember for the rest of his life. She had to leave him to it.

'Ah,' Bradley said, and took a breath through clenched teeth.

'"Ah"? Just "Ah"?'

'Ah,' he said again.

Bex leaned back and stared at him. 'I could punch you in the nose and send broken shards of bone through your brain if I wanted to. Tell me what "Ah" means, and quickly.'

'It means that the Norwegian police have uploaded all the computer-based evidence from Asrael, and also from Learsa. There's many terabytes of data, but I've got virtual bots crawling over it, looking for any connection between Asrael/Learsa and MI6. And they've found one.'

'What is it?' Bex said, feeling her heart growing heavier within her chest.

'The identity of the person who hired Asrael to kill us was obscured by a secondary false persona, but Hekla and her sisters, being the thorough kids they are, managed to track it down. They have a name.' He paused. 'Avalon Richardson.'

It took Bex a moment, but she got there. A mousy girl, with brown shoulder-length hair and large glasses. Wore a cardigan over a white cotton blouse. Always wore a skirt. Sensible shoes.

'Are they – are you – sure?'

'Sure as sure can be. Avalon Richardson hired Asrael to kill us.'

'But why?'

'Sadly,' Bradley said, 'that information has not been recorded in Asrael's files.'

Bex gazed across the table at him, and judging by the way he flinched, she knew that her expression was very, very dangerous.

'Then,' she said, 'we take the battle to her. Avalon Richardson is our next mission.'

Bradley glanced sideways, at Kieron. 'What about him and Sam?'

Bex closed her eyes for a moment, and nodded. 'If we're going after a target within MI6, we'll have no support and no help. We'll need a team.' She hated herself for saying it, but she said it anyway. 'And the only team we have is Kieron and Sam.' She smiled. 'They're still on the books.'

Look out for more spy action from A·W·⊕·L·

This time the stakes are higher than ever
Can Kieron, Sam and Bex save the world . . .
and make it out alive?

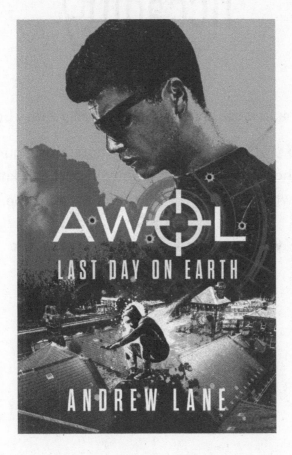

Coming in June 2019

Thank you for choosing a Piccadilly Press book.

If you would like to know more about our authors, our books or if you'd just like to know what we're up to, you can find us online.

www.piccadillypress.co.uk

And you can also find us on:

We hope to see you soon!